Weddings and Funerals

Debbie Williams

Prologue

"Ok, now you can look in the mirror," Jan Burke's best friend and maid of honor, Kim, told her. As she turned and looked in the full-length mirror before her, Jan was completely speechless. Never in her wildest dreams did she think that she would ever look this beautiful. The dress was all she imagined it would be. The lace covered bodice hugged her perfectly in all the right places. The bottom of the dress fell into several layers of pick up and tulle. Kim had applied her make-up to perfection. Her honey chestnut brown hair was curled across her shoulders and from there it fell down her back. The top of her hair was woven into the tiara, from which the long lacey veil trailed all the way to the floor.

"Could this really be me?" she wondered.

"We need to keep moving," Kim announced. "Where is that photographer?" In her maid of honor efficiency, she glided her large frame over to the door of the dressing room. When she opened it, she was startled to see Jan's fiancée, Derek, pacing in the hallway.

"What are you doing here?" she asked. "If you see Jan before the wedding, it will be very bad luck." Then she saw the look on his face and stopped short. He looked as if he were in agony.

"I need to talk to Jan," he said, in a very serious tone.

A wave of dark premonition fell over Kim. Something deep in her gut told her not to argue. She quickly cleared the room of the bridesmaids; on the guise of an outdoor photo session, telling them them that she would be there with Jan shortly; she needed to make a few adjustments to her veil. After the room had cleared, Kim stepped out into the hall, and Derek stepped in closing the door behind him.

Kim paced in the hallway for several agonizing moments, waiting for one of them to emerge from the room. She prayed that the problem was some sort of glitch with the honeymoon, or their new house, which was in escrow. Jan was the best friend Kim had ever had. This wedding meant as much to her as it did to Jan. Due to her large size, Kim truly believed that this was as close as she would ever come to being a bride. If something went wrong she just didn't know what she would be capable of doing. Less than ten minutes later, Derek emerged. He was stone faced. He looked neither right nor left, as he briskly walked down the hall and around the corner.

Kim went right in, and found Jan on the floor, with her dress sprawled around her, weeping uncontrollably.

She sat down next to her, put her arms around her and held her, without saying anything. Finally, through her sobs, Jan spoke. "He has been trying to get the nerve up for two months to tell me he doesn't want to marry me. Two months, Kim! And he waits until today!"

"Sweetie, your makeup is running all over your veil," Kim told her friend, and then quickly realized the foolishness of that statement.

"Good," Jan answered. "Do you know that he actually asked me to send him the dress? He said he paid for it, and maybe he could sell it on eBay; then he went on to say that he was losing so much money, it might help offset the costs."

"What a bastard!" Kim exclaimed. "What about the ring? Did he ask for that too?"

"He already has it," Jan told her. "He was going to place it on my finger with the wedding band today. In fact, he just came up with that brainstorm last night, and now I see why." She sighed and then looked at her friend. "Kim, what am I going to do? I dropped out of school for him. I have no job, and no money. What am I going to tell Daddy? He hasn't been well since Mom died. This is going to be very hard on him. Who's going to tell the two hundred people headed this way for my wedding?" She then began weeping uncontrollably again.

"Don't you worry sweetie, you won't have to do a thing, but get out of that dress. I will send

Debbie Williams

you to my hotel room in a cab. I'll take care of things here and we'll sort out your life later.

Chapter One

Five years later.

Jan Burke loved quiet summer afternoons in Bellville, Kentucky. This one was particularly cool and less humid than usual for late August. She had decided to take advantage of the weather and spend the day working to prepare her classroom for the inevitable first day of school, now creeping up in less than two weeks. She had the windows of her room open all the way, inviting in the cool breeze left from last night's summer storm. This time next year she would be encased in the new building, which was under construction across town. While its climate-controlled air-conditioning would be welcome on hot humid days, Jan was going to miss the fresh air on days like this.

As she was standing on a chair stapling material to a bulletin board, the school's secretary, Sandy, stepped through her door. "Jan, you have a new student added to your list. *'Kylie Owens'.* Her father wants to talk to you. I told him I would ask you if it's ok."

Jan looked down at her and said, "That's fine, Sandy. Is there a particular reason?"

"Kylie lived with her mother near Louisville, where she was homeschooled. Last year her mother was killed in a car accident. Mark Owens is a funeral director. I understand that he has purchased a local funeral home and has moved here with Kylie. This will be her first year in school." Sandy explained.

"Oh, that's very sad. Send him down," Jan told her. Sandy nodded and headed back to the office as Jan stepped down off the chair and went to her desk. After wiping her hands with sanitizer, she pulled out her class list and added Kylie's name. After waiting several minutes, she began to wonder if she had misunderstood Sandy. Suddenly she realized that she could hear her friend, Casey, laughing in the hallway and a man's voice joining in. She walked over to her door and stepped into the hallway. A few doors down, she could see Casey standing in the doorway of her classroom talking to a very tall lanky man. The man was dressed in a dark business suit. He and Casey were talking and laughing like old friends. Jan wondered if this man was Kylie Owens' father.

Suddenly Casey looked up and saw Jan standing in the hallway. "Oh Jan," she said. "Come here. I want you to meet someone." Jan walked down the hall towards Casey's room. "Jan Burke, this is Mark Owens. He and Jim were college roommates at UK. Mark has just moved to town."

Mark extended his hand to Jan. "You must be the Ms. Burke that is going to be my daughter's teacher." Jan took his hand and looked at Mark Owens' face. He had steel grey eyes. His face was slightly weathered, and he had just the tiniest sprinkle of grey through his dark brown hair.

"Yes," she answered. "I got that message a few minutes ago. Sandy said you wanted to talk to me. I was waiting in my room, and I was beginning to wonder if I misunderstood. Then I heard you two laughing, so I came out in the hall to see what was going on."

"I'm sorry Jan. I saw Mark coming down the hall and we got to talking about the old days," Casey told her.

"Well, please come to my room where we can talk," she said.

"Thank you," he said to Jan, and then to Casey. "It was good to see you. We will have to get our daughters together before school starts."

"Absolutely, she answered. "Are you coming to the roast Friday night?"

"I wouldn't miss it," Mark answered. "I told Kylie what a big deal it is and she's very excited." In Bellville the first high school football scrimmage of the year was always kicked off with a huge hog roast. Local farmers donated hogs for the roasting, and the whole town turned out. High school football was a big deal in this part of the state. Casey's fiancée, Jim, was the head football coach of the local high school team. She and Jim, and apparently Mark, had met at UK in Lexington. Jim and Casey had dated for a while and then drifted apart. Casey ended up marrying another man she had met at that school. Two children and six years later, Casey was divorced and alone. Two years ago, she had gone to a college reunion, where she saw Jim for the first time in years. The two had immediately picked up where they left off. Last year she and the children had moved to Bellville to be with Jim, and they were planning a wedding in November when football season was over. Casey had been hired as a second-grade teacher, and Jan was in her second year of teaching third grade. They had become fast friends. Jan had accompanied Casey and her kids to all the games, both home and away. They were looking forward to another fun season.

As Jan led Mark into her room, she asked, "So did you play football with Jim?"

Mark smiled. "I was a wide receiver right up until the day I blew my knee out our junior year."

"That's too bad," Jan said.

"Not a total loss," he answered. "It was a great experience, I made great friends and most of my education was paid for."

"Well I guess that was a good deal," she said. "Tell me about your daughter."

"I'll tell you what I can," he said. "We are still getting to know each other." He sighed and then continued. "After I graduated from UK, I quickly learned that employers weren't beating the path for gradates with 'liberal arts degrees'. I ended up in Louisville working for a funeral home. I became fascinated with the profession, so I decided to attend a school of mortuary science. While I was deciding what school to attend and how to finance it, I was dating Tammy, Kylie's mother. It wasn't ever very serious. When I decided to go to school in Pennsylvania, we amicably parted ways. I found out later that she knew she was pregnant when I left, but she didn't think at that time that it concerned me. Tammy was one of those free spirits. She was raising Kylie in her own spiritualistic way, until she got into money trouble about two years ago. Then she decided that it was time to come after me for support. To say I was stunned was an understatement. Anyway, I was living in Houston at the time. I began paying support and I had visited my daughter exactly twice when I got the call that Tammy had been killed in a car accident. I decided to come back to Kentucky and raise my daughter. I had saved some money and was ready to purchase my own funeral home, and I happened to learn from Jim that there was a funeral home and business that was for sale here in Bellville, so here we are. I am sorry for making this such a long story, but I wanted you to understand that Kylie is still in a grieving process. She misses her mother terribly."

"I'm sure she does," Jan answered.

"Also, I am not sure about this home-schooling business. The program Tammy used is supposed to have a good reputation, and Kylie's records indicate good scores. She has never been in school, so I am not sure about how it will go socially for her. I just want you to know that I want to be involved and if she has problems or falls behind, I want to do whatever necessary to help her."

"Absolutely," Jan responded. She took a piece of paper off her desk and wrote her school email on it. He in turn handed her piece of paper with his name and information. It also had the name of a women and her information on it.

"I rented the house across the street from my business for us to live in. Pearl is my landlord. She is a very grandmotherly type who lives next door. She has taken a real shine to Kylie and has offered to babysit for me, so I included her number just in case."

"I understand," Jan answered, making a note on the paper.

"I would like to bring Kylie by here to meet you and see the school, if that's possible," Mark told her.

"I think that's an excellent idea," Jan said. "When would you like to do that?"

"Well, I need to get back to the funeral home right now," he said, looking at his watch. "What about tomorrow?"

"Casey and I are taking her kids to the water park down in Eddyville tomorrow, but I could meet you here before we go; around 9:00?" she asked.

"That would work, but I don't want to mess up your plans," he said.

"Not a problem," she said. "We weren't going to leave until around ten."

"We'll see you then," he said with a smile, extending his hand again. Kate shook his hand and watched him leave. She had mixed emotions. The man had had a large responsibility placed on him without warning, but he seemed to accept it without question. There was another fact about him that stirred up uncomfortable emotions in Jan. He was a funeral director. Memories threatened to wash over her. Jan decided that it was time to go home before her emotions overcame her. She packed her bag and headed down the hall, stopping in Casey's room on her way out. Thankfully, there was another teacher in her room, Casey told her that she would call her later, to finalize plans for the next day.

Kate's townhouse was not far from the school, so she had elected to walk earlier that day. During the walk home, she allowed herself a small amount of reflecting. After the horror of her wedding day, Kim had come through like a trooper. Jan could smile now about the stories of what had happened after she left. Kim had organized the bride's maids like an army of vengeance. Apparently, they had attacked Derek, demanding that he open the trunk of the car, where their luggage was packed for the honeymoon. The girls had opened the luggage, placed everything that appeared to be Jan's in one suitcase and scattered everything else in the trunk of the car. Somehow a sign appeared on the door of the church, and the reception hall, announcing the cancellation of the wedding. Kim dealt with the florist, the caterer, the minister, and the photographer, referring all bills to Derek. The next day, Kim packed the dress in a garbage bag and dumped it on his parents' front porch. They then headed back to Kim's apartment in Louisville where she allowed Kate exactly two weeks to mope and cry, and then she drove her to the University of Louisville, where she forced Jan to enroll in their education program. Jan's father, who lived just outside of Louisville, seemed to be wasting away. He died quietly in his sleep, two months to the day after the disastrous wedding day, and she went through another difficult emotional time, but Kim was there to push her through. Jan threw herself into her studies. Just when she was beginning to recover from that loss, tragedy struck again. On a dark rainy night, six months after the death of her father, Kim's car slid off the wet icy road, and rolled over a steep embankment. She was killed instantly, and Jan's life came to a grinding halt. She remembered the funeral; the grief of Kim's family, her own feeling of being so alone in the world. Her parents had died, and now she had lost her only friend in the world. Jan fell into a deep despair. She dropped out of school and hid from the world. Falling into a severe depression, she lost nearly twenty-five pounds and became a total hermit. Jan truly believed that she would have died of pure sadness, except for the fact that one morning, she woke up to the sound of Kim's voice saying, "Get off your ass." She had sat up with a start and looked around. She wasn't sure if she dreamed Kim's voice, but she suddenly felt very close to her. From that day forward, she slowly began to pull herself up out of the hole she had fallen into. She managed to get back into school and earn her degree. Finding the job in Bellville and moving here had been a huge step in her recovery. After arriving, she allowed herself the emotional luxury of making a few friends, but for her own protection she had three adamant rules she lived by; she never went to weddings, she never attended funerals, and she never ever dated.

The first rule was looming large right now, because of Casey and Jim's upcoming wedding. Casey knew her entire history, and all about her rules. She understood that participating in the wedding would be way too much to ask of Jan, but she hadn't given up on convincing her to be a guest, even if it was only to the ceremony. It hadn't been discussed between the two of them lately, but it was, without a doubt, the elephant in the middle of the room.

The next morning, Jan was in her room at nine o'clock. She had walked over, and Casey was picking her up there. Mark and his daughter arrived about ten minutes after she had arrived. Kylie was a small child who must have looked like her mother, because she didn't appear to resemble her father at all. She was petite for her age, and she had thin blonde hair, which was pulled back by a head band. Her eyes were a deep shade of blue. The child was strikingly beautiful, but there was a sadness about her. She stayed close to her father for the first few minutes, politely answering Jan's questions about her likes and dislikes. Then suddenly she noticed the bookshelf and was drawn to it like a magnet. Jan was surprised and pleased that she was drawn to the higher-level chapter books. "Pearl has taken her to the library a couple of times," Mark told her. "She pours over books." Jan smiled at him. Today he was not wearing a suit like yesterday, but khakis and a dark polo. It made him seem less like a funeral director and more like a little girl's dad.

Suddenly Casey and her kids burst into the room. Although she was small in height, Casey was a strikingly beautiful woman, who never seemed to run out of energy. She wore her chestnut brown hair in a short, but stylish crop. Her small body was perfectly proportioned. Her daughter, Lisa, who would also be entering third grade, but in another class, was a miniature version of her mother. Her son, Ty, would be entering would starting first grade. He was a quiet child, whose looks favored more of his father. He stood quietly near his mother, but Lisa sailed right over to Kylie and introduced herself and began a non-stop monologue about the school and all her friends. Kylie seemed to be completely wrapped up in the attention and information she was being given.

The adults watched this for a moment, and then fell into a conversation about the upcoming football season and the chances of making it to the state play-offs this year. After a few minutes, Lisa approached her mother and asked if she could show Kylie the cafeteria and the playground.

With Mark's nod of approval, Casey gave her permission. She gave her daughter her wristwatch instructing her to return by 9:50. Ty couldn't resist the temptation and followed his sister and her new friend out into the hallway. Jan and Casey gave Mark a quick tour of the building and told him about the new building which would be opening in the next school year. When they returned to Jan's room, the children were there waiting with a question. "Mommy," Lisa began, "can Kylie come to the water park with us?"

This request took all the adults back a little. Casey answered first. "Well, I don't see why not. Kylie, do you have a bathing suit?"

The child answered quietly. "I think so, but it's old and I don't know if it still fits."

Casey looked the child over. "I think maybe Lisa has some suits that she has outgrown. I am sure we could find you one. That is if you would like to go."

Kylie looked at her father hopefully. Mark looked at Casey. "Are you sure about this?"

"Oh absolutely," she answered. "What's one more? We'll just swing by our house, find a suit and grab some extra towels. She'll have a great time. There are several slides, a lazy river, and a wave pool. We'll be back around six. My kids' father is picking them up for the weekend. Will that be all right?"

"That's fine," he answered, reaching for his wallet.

"Oh no," Casey told him with a laugh. "We have some free passes, and I fully intend on dumping one or both of mine on you in the very near future, so be prepared. That's how it works in the parent game."

Mark laughed and put away his wallet. Within the hour, Casey and Jan and the three kids were headed down the road in Casey's Expedition with three kids in tow. They had a great time, going from slide to slide, and then relaxing down the lazy river on inner tubes. Finally, the two women had a chance to relax on lounge chairs, while they watched the kids jumping around in the wave pool."

"So, what do you think of Mark?" Casey asked her.

"He seems nice, for a funeral director." Jan answered her. "I'm sure it isn't easy being an instant father."

Casey thought for a moment as she lathered more sunscreen on her legs. Then she asked a question. "What do you mean, 'nice for a funeral director'?"

"It wasn't an insult," Jan said. "I just never knew one outside of the business side. It kind of brought back memories of funerals."

Casey resisted the urge to sigh loudly, but instead sighed inwardly. After lathering her arms, she asked. "Have you thought anymore about coming to our wedding?"

Jan opened her mouth to speak, but she was interrupted by the ringing of Casey's cell phone. While watching her friend reach into her pool bag to retrieve her phone, Jan thought about how she would answer the question she was just asked, but she soon couldn't help but become intrigued by the one side of the conversation she was hearing.

"Why?" Casey asked the caller.

She listened and sighed before she answered. "No, you can't trade for next weekend. We have plans that the kids won't want to miss, and I won't make them. It's wouldn't be fair."

After listening a little longer Jan could tell that Casey was trying to control her agitation. "No Rich it isn't that they don't want to come, it's just that they say they are bored, because you spend the whole weekend on the phone and computer or watching sports on TV."

Casey rolled her eyes while listening to the next part. "It doesn't take money to spend time with them, that's all they want. Can't you get them tomorrow morning?"

"Well that's your choice, then. This is your weekend. If you don't want to have them then you lose it. I'm sorry."

Shortly after that Casey closed her phone up. "Did he hang up on you?" Jan asked her.

Casey nodded as the children came up to them at that time, clamoring for a snack. Jan felt bad for Casey, always having to deal with that situation; but at least it distracted her from her previous question.

The following week passed quickly for Jan, with all the school preparations, meetings and professional development in-services. On Friday evening she walked through the gate of the local high school stadium. A huge crowd was already milling around the concession area. There was an air of excitement buzzing through the crowd, and the smell of roasted pork hung in the air. The sound of the high school marching band tuning up could be heard in the distance.

She soon spotted Casey well into the long line at the food booth. Casey made a motion to her that Jan knew meant she would get the food and Jan should go find them some seats. Just as she settled herself in a seat, she was joined by Lisa, who sat with her chattering away about all her friends and the upcoming school year. Suddenly the child jumped up and began to wave. Jan looked down and saw the object of her furious waving. Mark Owens and his daughter were settling themselves about six rows down, and off to the right. As Lisa began to shout, both Mark and Kylie looked up. Mark smiled and waved at

Jan, who smiled and waved back. About that time, Casey was coming up the aisle, with Ty. She was carrying a tray of drinks and a bag of food, and Ty was carrying another bag. She stopped when she reached Mark and began to talk with him. Jan saw her motion up toward where she and Lisa were sitting.

"Oh no, don't," Jan thought. Something about that man unnerved her, but she didn't know why. Mark nodded and stood, but he didn't head up towards their seats. Instead he started down the aisle. Kylie followed Casey and Ty. When they reached Jan, the two girls hugged excitedly as eight-year-old girls do. They settled themselves in the next row down, and Casey and Ty sat by Jan. "Mark is going to get some food," Casey said, as she began to distribute food and drinks. Jan did not reply. She realized that Jim, Casey and Mark were all old friends and she was going to have to deal with the fact that she would be thrown into social situations with him. She valued Casey's friendship greatly, and she didn't want to offend her by being rude to her friend.

Mark soon returned with food for himself and his daughter. He sat on the other side of Casey and Ty. The two old friends were soon engaged in a heavy conversation about "the old days at UK". Fortunately, one of the other third grade teachers and her husband sat on the other side of Jan, and they began a conversation about the school year about to begin.

The rest of the evening passed uneventfully. Scrimmage football games as a rule were not very exciting. As always Jan enjoyed watching the halftime time show. They always brought back memories of her days on the flag team of her own high school. She remembered the pride she felt knowing her father sat watching in her in the stands, never missing one of her moves. Fortunately, her mother never attended any of the games, saving Jan the embarrassment of her mother's drunken behavior.

This dance team seemed to have some talent, but Jan had the feeling they needed to be pulled together. The team coach was a middle-aged woman who appeared to be bored with the whole situation. When one of the younger members stumbled and dropped her flag, the coach looked quite annoyed. After the performance was over and the team had been dismissed to be free for the third quarter, Jan spotted the coach talking to the young girl. The coach's back was to Jan, but by the motions of the woman's hands and the tearful look on the young girl's face, it was obvious that the woman was very angry with the poor girl. After the coach stomped off, a few of the other girls came to comfort her. A few minutes later, Jan spotted a man and a woman talking to the coach. They did not appear to be happy. Jan assumed these were the parents of the young girl. "Good for them," she thought. "It's not a coach's job to berate team members over mistakes, but to help them not to make them again." The conversation did not last long, but Jan had the feeling that was not the end of that.

When the game was over, Jan, along with Casey and her kids, met up with Jim and some of the other coaches and their families at a local restaurant, and of course Casey insisted that Mark and Kylie join them. This whole situation was going to become a problem. Jan just knew it. The season opener was next week in a town about forty miles away, and she and Casey had planned to drive to the game next week. Lisa and Ty would be with their dad, so it was going to be just the two of them, but Jan knew what was coming. She also knew that she was being ridiculous and selfish, and she felt bad about it. After trying to give herself a mental attitude adjustment, she settled herself in a seat at a large table and attempted to join in the fun. It happened to be one of the coach's birthday, so a cake soon appeared and there was a rousing chorus of "Happy Birthday". The time in the restaurant did turn out to be fun and passed quickly.

    Later that night Jan laid in bed unable to become sleepy. Her mind was tossing and turning as much as her body was. Part of her felt bad about her negative feelings toward Casey for trying to bring her old friend into her new life. From what Jan could tell Mark was drawn right into Jim's round of coaching friends at the diner. It was not a problem being around him in a large crowd, it was just being near him, and why? Jan wasn't sure. She just knew he made her uncomfortable. It was wrong to resent him for what he did for a living. Being a funeral director was a perfectly acceptable profession.

    Then her mind wandered to that poor girl who had dropped her flag. Jan's heart went out to her. She remembered dropping her flag during her very first performance. She had been unbelievably mortified. When she came off the field, she couldn't even look at the coach. However, the coach had come to her, placed her arm on her shoulder, and simply said, "It happens." The women had had the wisdom to know that no one could make Jan feel any worse than she already did. After that Jan relaxed and began to enjoy performances and she never dropped a flag again. If she had been berated like that poor girl was, she probably would have quit, and her high school years would have not had any escape from trying to keep the embarrassment of her mother's drunken behavior a secret from the few friends that she had.

    Jan spent the rest of the weekend quietly at home working on last minute projects for her classroom. By Sunday evening all her reading folders were assembled, her seating charts were finished, and her lesson plans were complete. All these items were tucked safely in her bag, which had already been placed next to the door. She took a long hot shower and tried to push all of those nagging little last-minute ideas and thoughts out of her head. As she surfed through her TV channels, finding nothing to entice her, her mind again wandered to that young girl on the team. Jan knew that she shouldn't let it worry her, but she couldn't help it. The thought even crossed her mind to go to the next practice and offer herself as a volunteer. She told herself that that was a ridiculous idea and she would do nothing but upset herself and possibly irritate the coach even more.

The next day she was up early and in her classroom an hour before the students were due. The building and the classrooms looked clean and fresh. All the teachers and staff were dressed in their new and fresh looking first day of school outfits. In the air, there was a mixture of nervousness and excitement. At 8:40, Jan took one last look around her room and decided everything was in order. She adjusted a sign on her wall and posted herself at the door of her room, ready to greet her new students, and any parents who accompanied them down the hall. This was the only day of the year when parents were permitted to accompany their children past the lobby area. Just as the 8:45 bell rang, Casey and Jan exchanged thumbs up signs, wishing each other good luck. Jan spent the next ten minutes smiling, greeting student and parents, and having her picture taken with students. One of the last students to arrive was Kylie. Mark walked her down the hall, wearing dress pants and a shirt and tie. Jan wondered if there was a funeral today. She shuddered a little inwardly but greeted them with a smile. Kylie looked as if she were terrified and Mark looked nervous for her. Jan showed Kylie to her seat and introduced her to the little girl next to her. Mark followed as if he wasn't sure what to do. At this point Jan did feel a little sympathetic for him. As Kylie began to put away her folders and supplies, she looked at Mark and quietly said, "I will email you this afternoon and let you know how she is doing." He smiled and mouthed, "Thank you." After leaning down and giving his daughter a quick hug, he was gone. Kylie still looked terrified, but Jan sensed that she had decided to be brave. Ten minutes later all the parents had cleared out, and Jan's day and her school year had begun.

The morning went very well. Jan had planned interesting activities that made the time go very quickly. When she announced that it was time to line up for lunch, her students looked surprised. Kylie had relaxed somewhat, but now looked a little nervous again. Jan made a point of asking Sue Ann, the girl who sat next to her, to be Kylie's lunch partner and show her where everything was. When lunch and recess were over, the afternoon went more quickly than the morning. After Jan left her class with the art teacher, she took the time to send Mark a quick email to let him know that all was well. He answered almost immediately thanking her and letting her know that he had a funeral that afternoon, and that Pearl would be picking Kylie up as she would most days.

    Later that afternoon, as Jan was preparing her class for dismissal, Kylie came up to her and handed her a beautiful picture of a bouquet of daisies that she had drawn in her art class. At the bottom she had written, "Thank you for being my teacher. I like you." Jan looked at her and saw the hopeful look on the child's face. Taking the picture to the bulletin board behind her desk, she pinned it to a place of prominence. She turned and saw Kylie's beaming face, as the child turned to take her place in the line of students being picked up. Later, when all was finally quiet in the room, Jan looked at the picture. On an impulse, she pulled out her phone and took a picture of the drawing. She then emailed the photo to Mark, somehow knowing that he would understand that Kylie had

had a good day. He didn't answer right away, but Jan knew he was probably busy with the funeral.

Just before she shut her computer down, she checked her email one more time. There was nothing from Mark, but there was a group email sent to all staff announcing a new job posting in the district; flag team coach. The email seemed to leap off the page. It seemed to be directed specifically to her. Without even thinking, she picked up her phone and dialed the board office.

Chapter Two

"Let's get those flags snapping in the wind!" Jan called out as the cool September breeze picked up into an actual wind which was perfect for flag performances. She watched her team as they danced to the recorded band music playing from her iPod speakers.

It had been three weeks since Jan had taken over as flag coach, and she was beginning to feel as if she was earning the girls' trust, and that they were beginning to have fun. She had had a long talk with all of them when she had first taken over. Apparently, several of them were on the verge of quitting. Although the superintendent told her that the former coach had resigned for personal reasons, she learned from the girls that some of their parents had visited the superintendent over her treatment of the team members and had demanded some action. Shortly after that the coach had turned in her resignation. Jan was the only person who expressed an interest in the position and was quickly hired. She had asked the girls to give her a chance, and not quit the team just yet. They all agreed and after the first home performance, several parents had come to her and complimented her on the performance. They also expressed their appreciation for the way she was handling the team. They reported that their daughters now looked forward to practices and performances.

As Jan was watching, one of the older girls stumbled on a hole in the practice field and fell, knocking down the girl in front of her, starting a domino effect. Eventually four girls ended up in a pile on the ground. Jan turned off the music. The field became very quiet. The four girls on the ground looked at Jan somewhat fearfully, along with the rest of team. She stared at them for a moment and then said, "If I had only thought to record that with my phone. It would have gone viral." Then she began to laugh and was soon joined by the girls.

"Let's take a break," she told them. A few minutes later, they were all sitting on the ground in front of Jan. "Tomorrow night is predicted to be downright cold," she told them. "I think we will perform in our warmup suits. There is no sense in you freezing to death in your short outfits."

"Thank you," one of the older girls said. "Coach Collins always told us to suck it up, no matter how cold it was. She said we weren't allowed to perform in our warm up suits because of some school rule."

"That's ridiculous," Jan told them. "You paid for them and you will wear them. Now let's run through it one more time, before we head home."

Thirty minutes later, as the last of the flags were being put up in the music room, one of the older girls approached Jan.

"Coach," she began. "I need to talk to you."

"Yes, Penny?" she answered.

"I don't have a warm up suit," she told Jan.

"Why not?" she asked. "Wasn't one ordered for everyone last spring?"

"Yes," she answered. "I worked all summer babysitting and saved the money to pay for it. I hid it in my room, but it disappeared. I wanted to make payments on it, but Coach Collins told me that it was just too bad. If I didn't have all the money, I couldn't have it. She said that if we wore the warm up suits, I would just have to look ridiculous, and maybe I would learn a lesson in responsibility." The girl's eyes began to fill with tears.

Jan stared at the girl trying to comprehend the words she had just heard. She then turned and headed for the storage room. There on the bottom shelf, she found one warm up suit in a plastic bag with Penny Taylor name marked on it. She took it back to where Penny waited.

"Are you sure the money disappeared?" she asked her. "Have you searched everywhere?"

Penny nodded. "You have to hide money in our house. It isn't safe to keep lying around. I guess I didn't hide it well enough. I should have known better. I have saved another fifty dollars since then. Can I pay on it?"

Jan nodded, and then asked, "What do you mean, it isn't safe to leave money lying around your house?"

Penny's face reddened. "My mother isn't good with money. She … well she spends a lot of it."

Something in the girl's words rang familiar with Jan, and she decided to not to question her any further at that point. Penny reached in her pocket and pulled out a hand full of cash and handed it to Jan. "I'll pay the rest as soon as I can," she said.

Jan handed Penny the plastic package containing the suit. She took it nodding gratefully and hurried out of the building. Jan went to the desk of the music room and wrote out a receipt marked "paid in full". On her way home, she stopped at the ATM and withdrew enough cash out of her account to pay the balance owed on Penny's suit. She placed all the money in an envelope to deliver to the board office with the receipt the next day.

The following night was even colder than predicted. After the performance the girls quickly put their coats on. After texting Casey, Jan bought two cups of coffee and went and sat with her friend in the stands. She was sitting there with her two kids and Kylie, who were all sipping on hot chocolate.

"Mark was here, but he got a call to pick up a body," she said. "Some woman was found dead in her house, so I think a sleepover is in order."

Jan shuddered. She would never understand why someone would want to do that for a living.

"Hopefully it will warm up before the corn festival next weekend," Casey said to Jan.

"I certainly hope so," Jan answered. "If it's this cold I certainly won't be staying very late. After the parade I will head to my nice warm home. I am not exactly an outdoor winter girl."

Casey laughed. "Wimp!"

Jan laughed back. "I'll own that."

The following Sunday afternoon, Casey called Jan. "You will never believe who the woman found dead in her house was."

"Who?" Jan asked.

"Marsha Collins!" was her response.

"Marsha Collins?" Jan replied. "Why do I know that name? I can't seem to place it."

"She was the flag coach before you," Casey reminded her.

Jan gasped. "Dear God! What happened?"

"No one knows. I guess her husband came in and found her lying dead on the couch with the TV on. She had apparently been dead for a few hours. They will probably do an autopsy."

"That's terrible," Jan replied. "I was not a fan of the woman, but I certainly hate to hear of her death."

The following week Marsha Collins' surprising death was the talk of Bellville. Jan heard every possible speculation imaginable; everything from suicide to her husband poisoning her. She was concerned about what the girls on her flag team would have to say about the death of their former coach. As it turned out there were several days of severely heavy rain that week. The football game scheduled for the Friday night of that week, was an away game in the southwestern part of the state. Neither the band or flag team were approved to make the long trip. The gym was unavailable to use, so Jan cancelled all practices for that week. It was still rainy and cool on Friday, so Casey and Jan spent the evening with a pizza and some pay per view movies. Jan enjoyed the evening thoroughly. It was the first "girls' night," the two of them had spent in a while.

The following day the sun did shine, and the temperature rose a little. The parade was in the late afternoon. Once her girls had finished the parade route, Jan wandered into the vending area of the festival. Jim and Casey were selling sausage sandwiches at the athletic boosters' booth. There was quite a line at that booth, so Jan waved and moved on. She would get her fill of the sausage smell when she worked her turn tomorrow afternoon.

She finally decided on a corndog and a cup of coffee. After she placed her order, she reached into her pocket and suddenly realized she had forgotten her money. Just as she was about to embarrassingly ask the woman at the stand to cancel her order, she heard a familiar voice behind her.

"Jan!"

She turned to see Cindy Spicer, one of her fellow third grade teachers, standing with her husband, Tom, just off to her right.

"We're heading over to the diner to get some lasagna," she called out. "Do you want to join us?"

Jan smiled. She cancelled her order and walked over to her friend. "I would love to," she told her. "This is embarrassing, but I just realized that I left home with no money."

Cindy laughed. "No worries," she told her. "We've got you covered. Come on."

"All right," Jan answered, "but I'll pay you back Monday."

"We have that in-service meeting on Friday," Cindy said. "I'll let you buy my lunch."

"Deal," Jan told her and then followed the two of them down the street.

Twenty minutes later, Jan took a bite of lasagna and sighed. The diner was famous for making this homemade dish. She was having a great time, except for one distraction. There was a great deal of loud laughter coming from a booth located diagonally across from them. The sound and scene were all too familiar to Jan. Looking over at the booth, she saw a large red-faced woman, who was the source of the laughter, sitting on one side of the booth. On the other side of the booth was an embarrassed looking man and young girl who was presumably his daughter. The young girl looked up at Jan and made eye contact with her one time and then quickly looked away in embarrassment. Jan's heart went out to Penny. Now their conversation about the missing money made sense. The child was living the same nightmare that she had lived during high school. Her attention was drawn back to her friends as Cindy asked her a question.

"Guess who Shelly is going after now?"

"Who?" Jan asked rolling her eyes. Shelly was a fifth-grade teacher who made a habit of shamelessly going after single parents in the school.

"The father of your new little girl, Kylie," she answered.

Jan stopped her fork in mid-air. "Mark?" she asked. "Where did you hear that?"

"I saw her talking to him just a few minutes ago," she answered. "It was very obvious."

Jan had a funny feeling in the pit of her stomach. After a moment, she recovered and shrugged. "Are you surprised?" she asked.

"No," Cindy answered. "I saw Casey in the bathroom a little while ago. She saw it too, and she is irate, but Jim told her that Mark is a big boy, and she is to stay out of it."

"Exactly," Cindy's husband, Tom, added to the conversation, "and that is exactly what you are going to do. He'll figure it out all by himself."

Jan and Cindy exchanged a look that could have been interpreted as "gag me".

Changing the conversation, Cindy asked Jan a different question. "Are you coming by yourself to the wedding?" Then before Jan could respond, she continued. "You are welcome to sit with us."

Jan knew that Cindy was aware that she had a broken engagement, but she did not know all the details. She had a feeling that this offer had been made through Cindy's speculation that Jan might be leery of going to the wedding.

Weddings and Funerals

Before she realized it, she heard herself thanking Cindy and accepting the offer. Then before the conversation could continue, their attention was again drawn back to Penny's mother. She was now loudly berating her husband and telling him that he would *not* be telling her how to live her life. The whole dining room became quiet as everyone stared at the woman.

She looked around and realized that she was being stared at and then yelled, "See what you've done. How embarrassing!" Then she stood and marched out of the diner.

Penny's father took some bills out of his wallet and dropped them on the table. Then he and Penny both quietly left the restaurant; both looking down, making eye contact with no one.

Cindy and Jan exchanged a sad look. "That poor child," Cindy said. "She was in my third-grade class. Her mother usually showed up for events, but she almost always had the smell of liquor on her. I see it has gotten worse. Penny is such a sweet child. It is a shame that she has to be humiliated like this."

"Yes, it is," Jan answered with more hurt in her heart than Cindy realized.

The following week on Thursday afternoon, Jan sat watching her flag team practice. The homecoming game was the following night. She frowned as she watched Penny miss a cue for the third time. After turning off the music, she quietly asked Penny to come over to her. When the girl was seated next to her, she turned the music back on. The two of them watched the team for a few minutes, before Jan turned to Penny and spoke.

"You seemed distracted. What's the problem?" she asked.

Tears appeared to well up in her eyes, and then she said, "I'm sorry. I'll try to do better."

Jan sighed. "Penny, I'm not upset with you. If something's bothering you, I would like to help. Is there a problem with one of the other girls?"

Penny shook her head, and quietly said, "No."

Jan waited a moment and the decided to go straight to the lightning round. "Is this about your mother?"

Penny looked up, and then quickly hung her head and looked down.

Jan put her arm around the girl and spoke softly. "I know it's none of my business, but I know exactly what you are going through." She waited for a moment and received no response.

"Do you know why I know?" she asked.

The girl shook her head without looking up and Jan could see tears dripping down from her face to the grass below.

"If I tell you something about myself, will you keep it in confidence from the other girls?" she asked.

Penny looked up in surprise and nodded.

"My mother was a raging alcoholic. She was an embarrassment to me, especially during my teenage years. By the time I was in high school, she very rarely went out in public, unless it was to a bar or restaurant. Being on the flag team was my escape."

She paused for a moment and then asked, "I have lived your life, haven't I?"

By this time, Penny's eyes had grown very large. She nodded silently.

"So, what is going on this week?" Jan asked.

Penny looked down again, but she did answer. "Tomorrow is Mom's birthday," she began. "She is inviting some friends from out of town in for the weekend. They may even come to the game. Dad is worried about it. They had a big fight over it last night. She doesn't pay any attention to him anymore, because she is drunk most of the time. She just blows him right off. This weekend is going to be a fiasco, and I just can't deal with it anymore. Dad used to take me away for the weekend when this happened, but he told me that he needed to stay around this time in case someone needed to call 911. He said that I should see if I could find a friend to stay with until Monday."

"Were you able to do that?" Jan asked.

She shook her head and said, "I don't have that many good friends, and they are all going to the dance Saturday night anyway."

"I see," Jan said. She thought for a moment and then continued. "Penny?"

"What?"

"You are welcome to spend the weekend with me. I have nothing special planned."

The girl looked up with a look of total shock on her face. "Are you serious?" she asked in a voice that sounded almost hopeful.

"I am totally serious," she said, "but I need to talk to your father to make sure that it's all right with him."

"I'm sure that he will be relieved for me to be away from the chaos, but I will have him call you," she said, now smiling.

"All right," Jan smiled back just as the music ended. "Now would you get your rear back out on the field?"

She watched as Penny grabbed her flag and took her place on the field, then she stood up and yelled out, "If this next time is flawless, we will go home. If it's not, we will do it two more times. Let's go!" Then with a smile, she switched on the music and watched her team.

The homecoming game turned out to be a fun evening. Penny's mother and her friends decided to stay home, so her father quietly slipped her the keys to her mother's Camry. She drove it to the school and planned to follow Jan home after the game.

The flag team was one member short that night as one of their own was crowned

Homecoming Queen. Jan couldn't have been prouder.

After the game, Penny's father, Joe Taylor, stopped to tell his daughter goodnight and thank Jan again for inviting her to spend the weekend.

Penny went to put her flag away in the band room, leaving Jan alone with her father.

"I can't thank you enough for taking her in for the weekend," he said.

"Did Penny tell you what I told her about my childhood?" she asked.

He nodded. "She did. I am sorry that happened to you," he said, "but I am happy to know that she has someone in her life that understands what she is going through." He hesitated, then continued. "I don't know what to do. Things are really getting out of hand. I have thought about taking Penny and leaving, but I am afraid of what would happen to Sue. She could hurt herself or someone else." He looked at her for a moment and then asked, "What happened to your mother? Did she ever stop drinking?"

Jan shook her head. "She basically drank herself to death. I think the cause of death was listed as cardiac arrest, but it was brought on by years of drinking."

Joe was about to respond when Penny approached them, and for whatever reason, he decided not to speak.

Penny and her father exchanged a good night hug, and then as he was leaving, he gave Jan another grateful look and walked off toward his car. Her heart went out to the man; what a heavy burden he was carrying. Jan decided that he would have been a good-looking man if he wasn't showing the years of stress brought on by his unfortunate family life.

Thirty minutes later, Jan and Penny were sitting on the couch in the living room of her townhouse, drinking hot chocolate. They talked about all the events of the evening. Penny became quiet for a moment and then said, "Miss Burke, can I ask you something?"

"Sure," she said, expecting the same question that her father had asked earlier about her mother's fate.

"I was wondering about something," she began. "You said you were free all weekend, so…."

"So, what?" Jan asked.

"I guess you don't have a boyfriend?"

Jan laughed at her own surprise at the question. "No, Penny. I don't have a boyfriend."

"Why not?"

Jan shrugged. "I just don't have one. Do you have a boyfriend?"

"No, I don't."

"Why not?"

Penny looked at her. "I did for a while last year, but he just up and dumped me for no reason, and I was really hurt. It kind of made me leery of having a boyfriend."

Jan stared at her and smiled. "Wow. Our lives are parallel."

"Did you get dumped too?" Penny asked.

Jan nodded.

"Were you together long?"

Jan nodded again. "Three years."

"Jeez," Penny answered. "That's cold. I got dumped with a text message. Did you at least get dumped face to face?"

"Oh, it was face to face, all right," Jan said, then she hesitated for a moment before she continued. "He chose to break off our engagement about two hours before we were supposed to walk down the aisle. He just walked into my bridal room and told me that he just couldn't do it, and could he have the wedding dress back? He had paid for it and maybe he could sell it on eBay."

Penny's face showed shock.

"What did you do?"

"He didn't give me a chance to do anything, really. He just made his speech and walked out." she answered. "I was too stunned to speak anyway."

"I mean what did you do about the wedding?" Penny wanted to know. "Did you have to stand up in front of your guests and tell them to go home?"

Jan laughed. "You watch a lot of movies, don't you?" she said. "No, I didn't have to stand up in the church. "My maid of honor, Kim, who was also my best friend, took care of everything. She put me in a cab and sent me to her hotel room. Then she and the other bridesmaids took care of everything." She giggled. "The next day, we put the wedding dress in a trash bag and dumped it on his parent's porch."

Penny burst out laughing. "That's great. I love it."

"Kim was awesome," Jan continued. "She let me mope for a short time and then ordered me to get back into college, which I did, and I eventually earned my teaching degree."

"You were lucky to have such a good friend," Penny told her. "Where is she now?"

Penny watched the expression on Jan's face change dramatically.

After a moment Jan spoke. "My mother died just before I met Derek," she said quietly. "My father died about a month after my 'wedding day'. Then six months later, Kim was killed in a car accident."

Penny's face showed a look of unbelievability, but she said nothing.

Jan sighed before she smiled and said, "It was devastating, but I pulled myself together, finished school and then moved here and started a new life." She decided that it was better not to share the part about the deep hole she fell in after Kim's death.

"How long have you been here?" Penny wanted to know.

"Just about two years," Jan told her.

"You and Ms. Pointer are good friends, aren't you?" Penny asked her.

Jan nodded.

Weddings and Funerals

"Isn't she going to marry Coach Craven?"

Jan nodded. "Next month."

"Are you going to be in the wedding?" Penny asked almost excitedly.

Jan shook her head. "No, it's going to be a small wedding. Casey's sister and Jim's brother are going to be the only ones that stand up with them. Even if she was having more people in the wedding, she wouldn't have asked me."

"Why not?" Penny asked.

"Casey knows what I have gone through," she began. "I haven't been to a wedding in the last five years. I wasn't sure if I could even attend the wedding at all, without falling apart, but Mrs. Spicer and her husband offered to let me sit with them."

"Mrs. Spicer was my third-grade teacher. She was really nice," Penny said with a smile. Then after pause, she asked an unexpected question. "Were you relieved that you didn't have worry about your mother embarrassing you at your wedding?"

Jan thought for a moment. "I never thought about it that way. By the time I was making wedding plans, my mother had been gone for more than three years, and I had put my unhappy memories of her away." She stared at Penny for a moment.

"Is that something you worry about?" Jan asked.

Penny nodded. "I told my Dad that if I ever got married, I was going to elope. He will be welcome to come along, but my mother won't know."

Jan smiled. "What did he say about that?"

Penny sighed. "He told me that I wouldn't be getting married for a long time, and that I shouldn't spend time worrying about that. After that he was quiet for a moment and then he told me that at the rate she was going she probably wouldn't be around by then anyway."

Jan didn't answer, but she couldn't help but think how sad it was that the child seemed almost hopeful.

Chapter Three

※

The rest of the weekend passed quietly and pleasantly for Jan and Penny. They slept late on Saturday morning, then after lunch they drove to a mall near Lexington and spent several hours browsing leisurely through the stores. Back in Bellville, most of the restaurants were overflowing with students dressed for homecoming, so the two of them decided to order pizza and watch movies.

Jan watched Penny carefully for signs of anxiety either over what was happening at her home, or the fact that she was not at the homecoming dance, but the girl seemed to be thoroughly enjoying herself.

On Sunday afternoon, Jan helped Penny study for a chemistry test, and Penny returned the favor by helping Jan grade papers and prepare folders for a new Social Studies unit that she was planning. After dinner, Jan invited a couple of other flag team members over and the four of them spent the evening choreographing some dances that might work for basketball season. It was a fun end to the weekend. When the others had gone, and the two of them were preparing to turn in, Penny looked at Jan with tears in her eyes.

Jan was immediately concerned. "Is something wrong?" she asked. "Did you talk to your father?"

"Yes, I talked to him" Penny said. "Everything's fine at home. Mom's friends left early. I guess they have finally started to outgrow drinking. They were a little turned off by her antics. Dad and I kind of got a kick out of that. It was kind of relief actually."

"Then why are you crying?"

"It's just that..."

"What?"

"This was such a wonderful weekend," she said softly. "I don't know when I have felt so light hearted and happy, and now...I have to go back...to my life."

Jan studied her for a moment. Then she took her hand and raised Penny's chin up, so they could make eye contact.

"This won't last forever, believe me," she told her. "Eventually you will be able to lead your own life the way you want." She thought for a moment more, before she continued. "In the meantime, you are always welcome here. My door is open to you anytime day or night. All you have to do is call."

Penny smiled and then hugged Jan tightly before she turned and headed down the hall. There was a bittersweet feeling in the pit of Jan's stomach, as she hoped things worked out simpler for Penny than it did for her.

On Wednesday of the following week, Jan stayed after school for a while to finish some paperwork. She was so absorbed in her work that she was startled when she heard a male voice speak her name.

She looked up to see Mark Owens standing in the doorway of her room. He was dressed in blue jeans and a navy sweater. She wondered if it was his day off, and then asked herself, "Did funeral directors take days off?"

"Hi," she said. "I'm sorry. I was so absorbed in my lesson plans that I didn't hear you come in."

"No problem," he told her. "I won't bother you for long. I signed this paper about working at the class booth for the fall carnival next weekend, but I forgot to give it back to Kylie." He walked across the room and handed her the paper.

As he neared the desk, Jan got a whiff of some sort of very subtle cologne or aftershave. It reminded her of something that she couldn't place. Whatever memory that it was associated with was a pleasant one. She shook her head ever so slightly to clear the thoughts away as she looked at the paper.

She raised her eyebrows as she looked at the paper.

"I marked all three hours," he told her. "I can work any or all those times. I can't always volunteer, but I will make this night work."

Jan thought for a moment before she responded. "I really appreciate that," she answered. "I haven't had a very good response so far. Usually I would just work the whole shift, but this year I have my flag team working a face painting table, so I will need to work back and forth. I asked the coordinator to put the two activities close together, but it's crowded this year and the table activities are out in the hall."

"No problem," he said. "I will just plan to work the whole night. By the way what kind of game is it?"

She smiled. "It is the pop toss, so be prepared to do a lot of bending over and picking up rings from the floor."

Mark returned her smile and was about to speak again when Casey sailed into the room. When she saw Mark, she stopped short. Then something happened that Jan had never seen happen before. Casey was at a loss for words. She looked confused for a moment and then finally spoke.

"Hi Mark. I'm sorry for interrupting. I'll come back later." Then she was gone as quickly as she had come in.

Mark stared after with a surprised look on his face. Then he shrugged and began to speak again.

"Jan, I wanted to ask you another question," he began. "Do any of your flag team girls babysit? I need a sitter Saturday night and Pearl is so good through the week, I hate to invade her weekend. I thought that it might be a good idea to have a high school girl or two on call."

Just as she opened her mouth to answer him, she noticed Shelly casually stroll by her door and innocently glance in. Fortunately, she did not stop, but strolled right on by. The woman was not one of her favorite colleagues. Jan redirected her focus to answering Mark's question.

"Yes, I can think of one girl that I know babysits," she told him. "I can check with her and see if she is available and then get back to you."

"That would be perfect," he said. "Thank you so much." He then turned and walked toward the door. "Have a good evening," he said as he walked out the door.

Jan spent a moment turning over the last five minutes in her mind. Just as she was telling herself that his reason for needing a sitter on Saturday night was none of her business, Casey appeared in her room again, and this time she was not speechless. She went on for about five minutes about men and how they could be so stupid. Couldn't they see when they were being played? Then she came up with several colorful words that could be used to describe Shelly. She finished her monolog with "but *I'm* supposed to stay out of it!"

As Jan tried to suppress a smile, Casey asked her a question in a sarcastic tone. "So, what did he want? Shelly's phone number?"

Jan laughed. "No, he dropped off the festival volunteer letter."

"Oh," Casey said. "He probably already has her number. She has him cornered in the lobby right now." Now Jan understood what had set Casey off.

She sighed and then spoke. "Well brace yourself. He is looking for a sitter for Saturday night. He asked me if any of my flag girls do any babysitting."

Now Casey sighed. Then after a moment of thought, she said. "So, do any of them babysit?"

Jan nodded. "Penny does."

Casey's eyebrows raised. "Good. Make that hookup. Then we will know what's going on."

Jan looked at her friend. "Aren't you supposed to stay out of this?"

Casey gave her a look of disgust. "I can't just stand by and let this happen. What Jim doesn't know won't hurt him."

Before Jan could answer, Lisa appeared at the door, with her brother.

"Mommy, we're tired and hungry," she said. "Can we go home now?"

Casey glanced at the clock on the wall and raised her eyebrows in surprise. "Oh, it is getting late. All right. Let's go." She moved toward the door. "Let me know how that works out," she called over her shoulder.

Two days and a few phone calls later, the arrangements were made for Penny to babysit for Kylie on Saturday evening. On Friday after the football game, the girls were putting away the flags in the band room. Jan noticed Penny talking on her cell phone with a distressed look on her face. As she watched, Penny walked over toward her.

The girl looked around to see if any other girls were within earshot. She waited until she felt it was safe before she spoke.

"Things are not good at home," she began. "Could I stay with you again this weekend?"

"Is that your father on the phone?" Jan asked. Penny nodded.

Jan motioned for the phone. Penny handed it to her.

"Mr. Taylor?"

"Yes. Hello Ms. Burke."

"I told Penny she was welcome to stay with me anytime that she needed a place to stay. If she needs or wants to stay this weekend, it is fine."

"Thank you, Ms. Burke. I really appreciate this. Things are spinning out of control here. I have some family members coming in tomorrow and we are going to try to do some sort of intervention and get Sue some help. I really don't want Penny around for that. It will probably get ugly. She had such a wonderful time with you. I guess you should know that she practically worships the ground you walk on. She has had very little happy time in her childhood, so her time with you is so valuable to her. Thank you very much."

"You are most welcome, Mr. Taylor. It is my pleasure." She returned the phone with a smile to Penny.

"Do you have your mom's car?" she asked. Penny nodded.

"All right. I'll see you at my house in a few minutes."

Penny lit up like a Christmas tree as she went to finish putting away her flags.

The next morning Penny went home early to pack a few items before her mother got out of bed. She didn't mention anything about the pending intervention, so Jan did not bring the subject up. She had the feeling that Penny was unaware of that plan.

At 6:30 that evening, Penny left for her babysitting job. As Jan was wondering what to do with herself for the evening, her cell phone rang. It was Casey.

"Is Penny gone?" she asked.

"She just left," Jan told her.

"Hmm. I wonder what time she will be back."

"I have no clue," Jan said. "I'm not concerned about it. She knows the code to my front door pad."

"What are you going to do tonight?"

"I'm not sure. Why?"

"We were going to go get something to eat and maybe have a drink. Do you want to come with us?"

Jan thought for a moment. She started to say no, and then she told herself that she needed to try to get out more. She finally decided to accept the offer and agreed to let them pick her up in half of an hour.

The evening turned out to be more fun than Jan thought it would be. They had dinner at Applebee's and then stopped in at a bar that had a local country band playing. It happened that there were quite a few people that they knew who were there enjoying the music, including her friend Cindy and her husband, Tom.

Jan noticed that Casey seemed somewhat preoccupied. They had a clear view of the door from their table and it seemed that every time the door opened, Casey looked up expectantly. Jan soon realized that Jim had noticed Casey's monitoring of the door too, and he seemed amused by it. Then a realization came to Jan. Casey was looking up to see if Mark was going to come in, with or without Shelly. The next time the door opened, and Casey looked up, Jan looked at Jim and the two of them exchanged a small laugh.

"What?" Casey asked.

Jim just looked at her and shook his head. "Give it up, babe. It's none of our business."

Weddings and Funerals

Around eleven Jim and Casey brought Jan home. Penny's car was in the driveway. Jan could see Casey suppress a smile because she knew that Mark had not been out late.

Inside the house, Jan found Penny in the kitchen munching on some cookies they had made earlier that day.

"Hi," Jan said. "How did it go?"

"Great," Penny said. "Kylie is adorable, but I guess you already know that."

Jan smiled. "Yes, I do know that. Mark didn't stay out too late."

"No, he didn't," Penny answered. "I think it was the first time he had left her with a sitter other than Pearl and he might have been a little nervous. He was glad to know that everything went well. He said he might call me again sometime. I hope so. He paid really well."

Jan tried to resist the temptation to be as nosy as Casey, but her efforts failed.

"So, did he have a date?" she finally asked.

"I'm not sure," Penny answered. "He didn't say. I guess he could have. He was dressed nice and he sure did smell good."

Jan had a flash of remembrance of that fragrance she had smelled the other day.

"What about you?" Penny asked. "Did you have a date tonight?"

Jan laughed. "Hardly. I went to dinner with Jim and Casey and then we went and listened to a band at Tabors."

"That sounds like fun," Penny answered.

"It was," Jan told her, "but now I'm tired and I'm going to bed."

"I'm going to stay up a while and watch TV if that's ok," Penny said.

"Sure, just make sure to turn off the TV and the lights before you go to bed."

"No problem," Penny answered and then continued. "Ms. Burke?"

"Yes?" Jan asked as she turned back toward Penny.

"Mark is not a bad looking guy," she said. "I wouldn't say he's hot, but not bad. If I were you, I would give him some serious consideration."

Jan was stunned. That was the last thing she expected to hear. She decided not to react.

"Good night, Penny."

The only response that Jan heard as she walked away was a giggle.

The following afternoon, Jan received a text from Penny's father. He asked her to call him out of Penny's earshot.

When she did, he told her that Penny's mother had agreed the night before to enter a rehab facility. However, when he woke this morning, she was gone. After checking their credit card statement online, he learned that she had purchased a flight to Fort Lauderdale, Florida, where her sister lived. He was planning to follow her later that evening, if Jan was willing to help him, by keeping Penny for an extended amount of time. When she agreed, he asked her to send Penny home, so he could explain the situation to her and give her some emergency medical guardianship papers that he had printed from the internet. Jan agreed to let Penny stay as long she needed to. Joe Taylor thanked her repeatedly and told her that he hoped that between Sue's sister and himself that they could get Sue safely settled into rehab. As soon as that happened he would return to Bellville.

Jan did as he asked and sent Penny home to see her father. She was surprised that the girl did not question why she was being sent home. After Penny left, Jan took the opportunity to run to the grocery store. While she was waiting in line at the deli counter, she looked up to see the school secretary waiting behind her. She smiled at her.

"Hi, Sandy."

"Hi Jan," she answered. "Did you hear about Carol Fisher's husband?" Carol was the vocal music teacher at the high school.

"No," Jan answered.

"He died in his sleep last night," she answered.

Jan was shocked. The man couldn't have been more than forty. "That's terrible," Jan said. "Has he been ill?"

"I guess he has had a bad cold," Sandy answered, "but other than that he was the picture of health."

"That's a shame," she answered. "Poor Carol."

"Number 36," called the deli clerk breaking into the conversation, and Jan turned around to give the woman her order.

Back at home, Jan shifted her worries from her teacher friend to Penny. As she was putting away her groceries, she wondered what Penny's reaction to her father's news would be. Trying to place herself in the situation, she thought that her feelings would be a mixture of relief and worry. In Penny's case, however, she seemed to have no concerns as long as she herself did not have to deal with the situation personally. Then remembering all the hurt of her own childhood, she thought that was how the child was surviving emotionally.

A few minutes later, Jan heard the front door open and then she heard Penny calling out to her.

Jan walked into the living room and saw Penny standing by the door with a larger suitcase than she had brought the day before.

She smiled at Jan somewhat nervously as she spoke. "I guess I'm going to be here longer than I thought."

Jan smiled back. "Your father told me all about it. You're welcome here, of course."

Penny's face seemed to show a sense of relief and then she headed back to the spare bedroom.

Jan stood and watched her for a moment and considered following her to her room, but her phone began to ring.

It was Casey, who had just heard the news about Carol's husband. They chatted for a few moments and then Jan walked to Penny's room and found her sound asleep on the bed. She looked at her for a moment and decided to let her sleep until dinner.

During the rest of the evening, Penny seemed to be in a happy mood, so Jan thought it was best not to rock the boat for the time being.

The next week at school, all the talk was about "poor Carol's" husband. The word soon circulated that the cause of death was "natural causes".

"Isn't that the same thing that they said about Marsha Collins?" Casey asked Jan, on Wednesday afternoon as they stood on the playground monitoring their students.

Jan thought for a moment. "I think so," she told her.

"What does that mean?" Casey wanted to know.

"I'm not sure," Jan answered.

"Mark would know," Casey said. "Why don't you ask him."

Jan laughed. "Why don't *you* ask him?"

"Isn't he working at your booth Saturday night?" Casey asked.

"Yes, but I will be spending most of my time with my flag team while they paint faces."

"I see," Casey said.

"See what?" Jan asked.

"Nothing," the only answer that Casey offered.

A few hours later, the two women were coming back into the building after the bus loading. As they neared the lobby, they both spotted Mark standing a few feet from the door, holding Kylie's hand. The child was pulling on her father's hand as if she were ready to leave, but he wasn't moving because he was involved in a conversation with Shelly. As they neared them, Jan was pretty sure that she heard Casey sigh. Then she tried not to laugh as Casey walked right up to the two and interrupted the conversation.

"Mark, Jan and I were wondering about something this afternoon and we thought you might have the answer."

"What's that?" Mark asked, turning from Shelly to Casey. Jan glanced at Shelly and caught her giving Casey a glare of total annoyance.

"What does it mean when someone dies of natural causes?" she asked.

Mark looked surprised at her question and then said, "It just means that death was not caused by an outside force. Something inside of the body malfunctioned or ceased to function causing death."

"You mean like a heart attack or a stroke?" Casey asked. "Maybe an undiagnosed disease?"

"Something like that," Mark answered.

Shelly looked at Casey with disgust. "Why would you two even be thinking about something like that?"

Before anyone else could speak, the intercom system beeped, and the secretary's voice asked Shelly to report to the office immediately. Then Mark's cell phone began to ring. "I have to take this," he announced as he looked at it and waved at all of them as he moved toward the door with Kylie happily following him.

Shelly walked away, looking disappointed and Jan looked at Casey, laughed and began walking back toward her room.

When she arrived home a little while later, Jan found Penny in the kitchen, fixing dinner. She smiled and said, "Something smells good."

"Spaghetti and meatballs," Penny replied. "The salad's ready. Let's eat that while the spaghetti is cooking."

"That works for me," Jan said. "I'm hungry."

The two of them ate a quietly for a few minutes, before Jan asked, "Have you talked to your father?"

Penny shook her head. "On Monday morning when I woke up, there was a text from him saying he had arrived safely, and that he loved me. Oh, and he told me to behave myself."

She was quiet for a moment and then said, "I tried to call him this afternoon, but he didn't answer. If I don't hear from him in a few days, I'll call go over to the house and find Aunt Barb's number and call her."

Sarah nodded, but didn't speak. For some unknown reason she suddenly had an uneasy feeling about the situation. She shrugged it off for the time being and focused on enjoying her dinner.

On Saturday night the school was full of people and bustling with activity. The gym was lined with makeshift wooden booths along with two hallways of games and activities.

     Jan arrived early and was pleased to see that the setup crew had all the pop bottles arranged and the game was ready to go. About five minutes later, Mark arrived with Kylie. He was dressed in dark blue jeans, and a dark green polo shirt. She smiled thinking that he had the foresight to realize that even though it was cool outside tonight, it would be warm inside the building with so many people milling around. As he walked up to the booth, she again got a whiff of whatever cologne or aftershave that she had smelled before. She wished that she could remember what it reminded her of.

     She gave Mark the game instructions and the short list of volunteers that would hopefully be showing up. He then assured her that he had everything under control and told her to feel free to go help her girls set up the painting table. She thanked him again and started to walk across the gym. As she neared the door, she noticed Shelly setting up the cake walk on the stage. She had only two students helping her. Jan smiled thinking that Casey would love the idea of Shelly being short-handed, leaving her too busy to flirt with Mark.

The next few hours flew by very quickly. The line at the face painting was long all evening, but her girls did a good job to keep things moving. She checked on her pop booth several times, but everything was well there also. Jan saw a side of Mark that she had not seen before. He was laughing and playing with the kids and seemed to be having a great time.

When the time for the games to close finally arrived, Jan made her way back to the pop booth, where she found Mark, Kylie, Jim, Casey and her two kids. She looked at the booth and was surprised to see that most of the pop was gone. She looked up at Mark and laughed. "I've always had a lot more left than that."

"I gave a few throwing lessons," he said.

"I see," Jan answered.

"Do we need to tear the booths down?" Mark asked.

"No," Jim told him. "There is a cleanup crew coming in the morning. Turning to Jan, he continued. "We're all going to Morelli's to get some pizza, do you want to come?"

Before she could answer, Casey suddenly spoke up. "Let's just call it in. We can pick it up and take it to our house. Then the kids can watch a movie or something and we can play some cards." Jan suppressed a grin, because she caught Casey very subtly taking a quick glance toward the stage. She knew what Casey was thinking. Shelly could follow them to Morelli's but not to her house.

"All right," Mark said. "I'll pick it up. It'll be on me."

"Great," Casey said, as she pulled out her phone. "Let's go gang. Kylie you can come with us if you want."

"Yay," Kylie said. "Is it ok, Daddy?"

"Sure," Mark said. "Go ahead." Then suddenly Jim, Casey and the kids were gone, and Jan was left alone with Mark.

He looked at her and said, "I noticed that no one waited for you to say if you wanted to go. Is it all right?"

She smiled before she answered. "Thank you for noticing. Yes, I'll go over for a while. I am kind of hungry. Besides if I don't show up Casey will just come and get me. She doesn't usually take no for answer. I just need to get my car if I'm going all the way out to their house."

Mark looked confused. "How did you get here?"

"I walked," she answered. "I only live a few streets over from here."

"What street?" he asked.

"I live in a townhouse on Elm," she told him. "I knew parking was going to be a problem, so I walked, thinking I could get a ride home with Jim and Casey."

Mark laughed. "We're practically neighbors. My house is on the corner of Vine and Oak. Kylie and I walked too, so we're both stranded. Come on, we can walk to my house and get my truck. I'll bring you home later. It's not like it's out of my way."

She laughed again. "If I know Casey, she ordered the cinnamon twists. We can eat some on the way, before the kids and Casey get at them."

"Oh yes," he said. "She had that sweet tooth back in college. I don't know how that woman eats so much sugar and stays as tiny as she does."

"Amazing isn't it?" she asked. Jan leaned over to pick up her jacket that had fallen off a chair and onto the floor. As she stood back up, she could see Shelly standing on the other side of the gym clearly watching her and Mark. She shrugged and thought that it was none of her concern.

As they walked outside, the cool, almost cold air was refreshing after the warm stuffiness of the gym. They walked at a leisurely pace. Mark told her about the antics of some of the kids who came to the pop toss booth. She laughed as she recognized some of the kids by his description.

It didn't take long to reach his house. It was white stucco, with an oversized friendly looking front porch. Jan liked the look of the house. It had a friendly feel to it. She deliberately avoided looking across the street at the funeral home. Mark walked to the garage door and punched a code into it, causing the door to rise almost immediately.

"I want to run in and check my answering machine, if you don't mind?" he asked.

"Go ahead," she answered. "I'll just wait in the truck, if that's all right."

He nodded. "I'll only be a minute."

It wasn't long at all before he reappeared. "No messages," he said.

This made a Jan a little curious. "Business messages?" For some reason part of her hoped so.

He nodded as he began to back out of the garage. "The funeral home phone rings into the house, so I am less likely to miss the calls." He let out a small half laugh. "It's a strange business. It's nice if nobody dies, but I do have to pay the bills."

"I guess I never thought of it that way," Jan said.

"Most people don't," he said. "You would be surprised the number of people who say things to me like, 'how you can do a thing like that for a living?' I just laugh to myself and think that they will appreciate me when they need me."

Weddings and Funerals

Not wanting to admit that she probably fell into that category, Jan said, "That is very true."

A few minutes later, as they pulled away from the restaurant, Jan dug through the bag and found that Casey did not disappoint them. She pulled out a cinnamon twist and handed one to Mark and took another for herself.

About fifteen minutes later as Casey was laying out the food on her kitchen table, she looked at the bag of cinnamon twists and then looked up at Mark and Jan.

"I don't want to know which of you two vultures got into these, but you don't get anymore."

It turned out to be a fun evening. The kids took their cheese pizza and quickly disappeared. Jim and Casey were a fun couple. There never seemed to be a dull moment around the two of them. Jim could have a serious coaching personality, but at the same time, he had a sarcastic whit about him that matched Casey vivaciousness. Soon after meeting the two of them, Jan realized that Jim was about the only person that could slow Casey's sometimes overactive antics. The four of them played cards for about two hours. It was the second time in the last month that Jan had spent a relaxing evening with good friends. As she was leaving with Mark, the thought crossed Jan's that mind that maybe, just maybe, the hurt in her heart was beginning to heal.

Mark dropped her off at her house around 12:30. She walked into the quiet house, not turning on any lights. She glanced down the hall toward Penny's room. Smiling she thought that the house seemed quiet without her, but she was happy that Penny had agreed to join the other girls for the slumber party they had planned at one of the other girl's house. The girl badly needed to be a teenager.

The next afternoon Penny was in a good mood, still excited about the good time she had had the night before, so she volunteered to do the grocery shopping. She returned an hour and a half later, and Jan noticed that she had a bag that she must have brought from her house. That explained why she had been gone so long.

After Jan finished putting away the groceries, she went back to the living room and found Penny on the couch and her demeanor had completely changed.

"Did I hear you talking on the phone?" Jan asked. "Was that your father?"

Penny shook her head. "That was Aunt Barb" She looked up at Jan. "My father never called her. She didn't know he was coming, and she hasn't heard from my mother. She has no idea where either of them are."

Chapter Four

Jan stared at Penny, not sure how to respond to what she had just heard. The ominous feeling that she had felt earlier returned.

"I know this sounds really strange," Penny said, "but I think I know what is going on." Again, Jan could not respond, but only stare.

"This has happened before," she began. "Not for this length of time, but they have gone off together like this." She sighed and continued. "See, Dad keeps thinking he can fix this. I don't know why, but he has this crazy idea that he can reason with Mom if he can just get her attention. They have this pattern. She runs off. He follows her. He wears her down and then she does better...for a while. I am guessing that it is taking him longer this time, because he is trying to convince her to get some help. I know this all sounds very dysfunctional, and it is, but this is my family. It happens all the time."

Jan finally found some words. "Do you find it strange that your father didn't call your aunt?"

"Yes and no," Penny answered. "I would have thought he would have, but I think I know why he didn't. He wanted to find mom and deal with her without Aunt Barb getting involved."

"Why didn't he want her involved?" Jan wanted to know.

Penny sighed. "Aunt Barb can be a little...controlling, I guess you could say. She has a lot of money; more than she really knows what to do with, I think. She is very generous with her money, but she sometimes thinks that it gives her the right to tell people how to run their lives. She means well, but it irritates my father. I am sure his thought was to find mom, convince her to agree to go to rehab and get her out Florida without listening to ultimatums from Aunt Barb."

Penny was quiet for a moment, and then she continued. "Aunt Barb would like to talk to you. I gave her your number. She is going to call you around six if that's all right with you."

Jan nodded. "I think I would like to talk to her."

Suddenly Penny looked concerned. "Ms. Burke, if you don't want to be involved in my family's craziness, I understand. Aunt Barb said I could come and stay with her. I would hate to leave school and my friends, but maybe it would be for the best." Tears of hurt and disappointment then filled her eyes and Jan's heart went out to her. She held her arms out and said, "Penny, come here."

The girl stood and went right to Jan who held her tightly and quietly for a few minutes, before she spoke softly. "I told you that you were welcome here and I meant it. Let's not make any rash decisions. Your parents may turn up in the next few days and then you would have to turn around and come right back. So why don't we just sit tight for a few days, all right?"

Penny's only response was to whisper hoarsely, "Thank you."

"There is one more thing," Jan said, a minute later.

"What's that?" Penny looking up, with a slight look of concern on her face.

Jan smiled. "Don't you think that it's time you dropped the 'Ms. Burke'? When we are alone, I think it would be all right if you called me Jan."

Penny's face brightened. "I was thinking about that, but I wasn't sure."

"I think it will be fine, except at flag practice and games and around the other girls," Jan told her.

Promptly at 6:00, Jan's phone rang. She answered the unfamiliar number almost immediately.

"Hello."

"Hello is this Jan Burke?"

"Yes, it is." Jan stood from her seat in the kitchen and went to the living room. Out of the corner of her eye, she saw Penny go down the hall to her room.

"My name is Barbara Summers. I am Penny's aunt."

"Yes, Ms. Summers. Penny told me that you would be calling."

"Please call me Barb. Ms..."

"Jan."

"Thank you. First, I would like to express my appreciation for all you have done for Penny. She speaks very highly of you."

"That's nice. I enjoy having her around. She is well-behaved and actually very helpful. I don't know if she told you, but I lived in a similar situation when I was a child. My mother was also an alcoholic. I can relate to what she is going through."

"Yes, Penny did mention that to me. I am so sorry."

"Thank you. Penny seems to feel that her parents' disappearance is part of an ongoing pattern. Would you agree with that?"

"I partly agree, but there is something that disturbs me."

"What's that?"

"Joe has always been a good parent to Penny; which is more than I can say for my sister. I am surprised that he hasn't called to check on her or returned her calls. Now his phone seems to have gone dead. I didn't express that concern to Penny. I told her to let me attempt to contact him from now on. She accepted that, because that is how she deals with this insane life she is forced to lead; out of sight, out of mind."

"I've noticed that too, but I can relate to her feeling that way. We did have a talk earlier. She offered to take me out of the situation, by coming to stay with you. I told her that wasn't necessary, because her parents could turn up soon, so we shouldn't make any rash decisions. She has her school and her friends. I think for now it is best for her to keep her in a familiar routine."

"I think you are right. I have some medical conditions that make it impossible for me to travel, so I can't come to her. Regardless, I think I should stay here in case either Joe or Sue turn up."

"I agree. Then Penny stays with me for the time being. Joe did sign a temporary medical guardianship paper before he left. I was looking at it earlier. I didn't realize it, but it is good for six months."

"Good. Now I would like to send you a check to help cover her expenses."

"That is not necessary. She doesn't eat that much."

"Still, she may need some things."

"Why don't you send a check to Penny? Then she can have money in case she needs anything."

"That's an excellent idea. I will put a check in the mail in the morning, if you will text me your address?"

"Certainly. Another thought has crossed my mind, though. What about the house? I wonder if they are gone much longer, will there be bills that will need to be paid?"

Now Barb let out a small laugh. "I have that covered. I have been paying more and more of their bills, unbeknownst to Joe. I have access to all their accounts. Don't worry. Is Penny driving the Camry?"

"Yes, it is here."

"Good. I've paid for a good deal of it. I'm glad she is getting use of it."

"Do you have a plan of what to do if they don't turn up soon?"

There was a pause, and then; "I'm afraid so. I am going to wait until Friday and if I haven't heard from either of them I am going to report them missing."

"I think that is probably wise, but let's pray that it doesn't come to that."

"Yes, let's do. Please let me know if Penny needs anything. I will be happy to take care of it."

"I will. Thank you." Jan told her, but what she was thinking was, "Money can't buy what this girl needs."

The next few days passed quietly. There was no news from either of Penny's parents or her aunt. The last football game of the year was on Friday night. The team lost the game which eliminated them from any possibility of going to the playoffs. Jan knew that Casey had mixed emotions about the loss. While, she felt bad for Jim, she was secretly glad for the season to be over, because their wedding was coming up in two short weeks.

Saturday was Halloween. Mark hired Penny to sit at their house and pass out candy while he took Kylie around the neighborhood to trick or treat. When they came to her door, Jan couldn't help but smile. Earlier in the week, when the class was discussing their costumes, Kylie had reported that her father wanted to buy her a costume, but she had insisted on making one for herself. Jan had to admire the child's spirit. She had turned herself into a living scarecrow. The costume was comprised of some bib overalls that she had borrowed from Lisa, and Pearl's gardening hat. Penny had helped her paint her face with her make-up, and her pockets were stuffed with straw that Mark had begged off a local pet store. When

Jan complimented her on the creativity of her costume, the child glowed.

When the trick or treating time was over, Jan closed her door, leaving the front light on for Penny. Shortly after that, her phone rang. Looking at it, she realized that it was Barb. Her stomach clenched, and she took a deep breath before she answered.

"Hello Barb."

"Hello Jan."

"Do you have any news?"

"Yes, I do. I have some news. I'm not sure if it's good or bad."

"Oh?"

"I haven't heard from them, but I decided to check the credit card statement before I called the police."

"That was good thinking. Were there any recent charges?"

"Yes, there were." There was a sigh and a pause. "Apparently they rented a boat right after they arrived. At least Joe did. I can only assume

Sue is with him. It was a large boat and he rented it with the option of keeping it for a month."

"Oh my. Would they know how to handle a large boat like that?"

"Yes. Joe was a boat captain down here years ago and Sue worked as a server on a yacht. That's how they met. I think that Joe may be trying to bring back good memories of the past to convince Sue to straighten out her life."

"So, did you contact the authorities?"

"I did. I talked to a detective friend of mine. He told me that since they went on the boat of their own free will there is nothing we can do unless the rental company reports the boat missing, and they won't do that until the month is up and the money runs out."

"But why hasn't he called?"

"I can only assume that they are out of cell phone range. I don't think he planned to be gone this long. I know this is hard for you to understand, but they have a very strange and complicated relationship. Sue has a very strong hold over him, and she uses it to her advantage." There was another pause. "I'm sorry, but I am afraid we have no choice but to sit tight until we learn more. Again, you can always send Penny to me. Is she all right? "

"She is fine. Right now, she is out on a babysitting job. I still feel that it is best for her stay here until we hear further news. She is doing fine, and she is no problem to me."

"I think you are right. Let's keep her life as normal as possible for now. Thank you so much Jan."

"It's my pleasure. Let's continue to keep a good thought that this could all still work out."

"Yes, let's pray for that."

Penny's reaction to the latest news was simply a shaking of her head. "It figures," she said. "They are off sunning themselves on a boat vacation without a concern to anyone else." Then she walked off without another word. Jan sincerely hoped that it was that simple.

On the afternoon of Jim and Casey's wedding, Jan took her new dress out of the closet and laid it across the bed. She took her new shoes and placed them on the floor below the dress. She stood staring at the outfit for a moment until she realized that Penny was standing in the doorway. She smiled at her and said, "I think it will work."

Penny laughed. "I told you that when we picked it out last week. It's a good thing I'm here. You would have gone in something five years old." Jan just rolled her eyes. "Can I fix your hair and make-up?" Penny asked excitedly.

Jan narrowed her eyes. "What exactly did you have in mind?"

"I just wanted to curl your hair a little and do a basic face," Penny said, a little too sweetly.

"All right," Jan answered, "but don't go overboard. I want people to be able recognize me."

Now Penny rolled her eyes. "Oh Jan," she said. "Why don't you go ahead and get showered. I have to be at Mark's house at 4:45."

Jan was pleasantly surprised that the wedding ceremony caused her very little anxiety. The wedding was held in a small local church. The ceremony was simple, but tastefully done. The only negative moment that Jan had was when she turned around and saw Mark sitting with Shelly.

Her heart sank a little. Then she told herself that it was none of her concern. It wasn't like she was interested in him, but on the other hand, he was a nice man and he deserved better than a woman like Shelly.

Immediately after the ceremony, Jan, Cindy and Tom worked their way through the receiving line and then got in Tom's car and headed toward the reception, which was being held at a converted barn, just a couple of miles outside of town. The three of them entered the barn and were immediately struck by the tables which were covered with white tablecloths and wine-colored overlays. The centerpieces were colorful arrangements of fresh fall flowers. Each table was already set with beautiful china. At one end of the room the caterers were busy setting up the buffet. On the other end, there was a table of appetizers already set up. In another corner a DJ was setting up his system. Tom headed for the bar to get some cocktails for the three of them. Jan and Cindy went to the appetizer table and filled a couple of plates with a variety of the delicious offerings. On their way back to their table, they noticed Shelly walking toward the restroom. They both subtly looked around and didn't see Mark.

They exchanged a look that could've been interpreted as "interesting". Maybe he was in the men's room was Jan's thought.

As they sat back down and began eating, Jan forgot about Mark and Shelly. They were soon joined by some other teachers and the evening took a fun turn. The last person to join them was a high school math teacher named Gary Baker. Jan had seen him at school functions but had never actually met him. He ended up sitting next to her and he immediately struck up a conversation with her. She found him to be quite likeable. As the evening wore on, Jan found herself to be having a good time. Gary asked her to dance a few times and she enjoyed it more than she thought she might. Once while they were dancing she looked over Gary's shoulder and she noticed Mark and Shelly dancing. He was facing toward her and the two of them briefly made eye contact. He smiled at her and she smiled back. Then Gary suddenly turned her away and he was no longer in her line of vision.

The evening was winding down and Jan did have some anxiety about the possibility of being thrown in the middle of the throwing of the bouquet. Fortunately, she was saved from that because Tom and Cindy realized what time it was and announced that they had a young babysitter and she needed to be home early. Jan was relieved and prepared to leave with them. Just before they left Gary asked her if she would like to go out sometime. Surprisingly, she didn't panic, and then she actually heard herself agree. The two of them quickly exchanged numbers and she said her good-byes along with Tom and Cindy.

    Back in her house, she went straight to her bedroom and then to the closet, where she kicked off her pumps. She sat on the bed for a few minutes, rubbing her aching feet, while reflecting on the evening. It had turned out to be way more enjoyable than she imagined it would be. Yawning she gave a few moments thought to Gary. She could always make an excuse if he called, or maybe she could go out with him. It could be a friend thing. Maybe he wouldn't even call at all. Yawning, she realized that she could think about that tomorrow. Fifteen minutes later she was sound asleep. She didn't even hear Penny come in.

    The next week at school all the chatter was about the wedding. Casey only took two days off. She and Jim planned to take a cruise between

Christmas and New Year's while her children were spending time with their father and his family.

Jan and Casey didn't get a chance to talk alone until Wednesday after school in Jan's room.

"I am so happy you came to the wedding," Casey told her. "It seemed as if you really had a good time."

"I did," Jan said. "I really enjoyed myself."

Casey paused and then said, "I hear you made a new friend."

Jan smiled. "Gary?"

"Yeah, I saw the two of you dancing a few times," Casey said.

Jan shrugged. "We sat at the same table and we were both there alone. It was no big deal."

"Did he ask you out?" Casey wanted to know.

Jan was beginning to get a slightly uncomfortable feeling. "We exchanged numbers, but he was probably only being polite."

Casey was thoughtful for a moment. "If he asks you out, are you going to go?" she asked surprisingly unenthusiastically.

Now Jan was definitely beginning to feel uncomfortable. For the first time since she had known Casey she was able to see a flaw in her character. There seemed to be some control issues.

"Is there some reason that I am unaware of that I shouldn't?" she wanted to know.

Then Casey got a strange look on her face. "No," she said, almost too carefully. "I just didn't think he was your type."

"Like Shelly was not Mark's type," Jan thought, but she didn't say it out loud. Casey had harped at her almost since the day they had met to move on in her life, and now that the opportunity had presented itself, she seemed to not be happy about it; maybe because it was not her idea?

Jan decided to change the subject, before she said something she might regret.

"I haven't heard from him," she said. "He probably won't call at all." She stepped over to her desk and picked up her bag and began placing papers in it. "I really need to get home. I've got some things I need to get done."

Casey stood quietly for a moment and then said, "Sure, I understand. I'll see you tomorrow." Then she turned and walked out of the room. Jan watched her leave and realized that she was suddenly seeing the world differently.

The next two days passed quietly and uneventfully. There was no news from Penny's parents or her aunt. Jan also heard nothing from Gary Baker, so she assumed that matter was laid to rest. While things outwardly seemed the same between Jan and Casey, there seemed to a coolness between them and their conversations seemed to be rather superficial.

The following week was a two-day work week due to the Thanksgiving holiday. On Tuesday afternoon she was having a discussion with her class about their Thanksgiving plans. She was interested to learn that Kylie was excited that her grandparents had already arrived from Knoxville to spend the holiday with her and her father. She reported that her father had told her about what wonderful holiday meals his mother had made when he was growing up. Jan felt a warmth inside of her. This little girl had suffered great sadness in the past year, but now she was glowing with excitement. Suddenly Jan felt a new respect for Mark. He was doing a wonderful job for a novice parent.

"Miss Burke?" Sue Ann said, with her hand raised.

"Yes?" Jan responded.

"Where are going to have your Thanksgiving Dinner?" she asked.

The question took Jan back a little, even though she should have expected it. She didn't want to admit that she and Penny were spending Thanksgiving alone, because neither of them had any family, at least nearby. Last year she had spent the day with Casey and Jim, but this year her children were spending the day with their father and his parents, so she and Jim were going to Bowling Green to Jim's parents' home.

"I am going to spend the day with some good friends," she told her.

"Don't you have any family?" Kylie asked, looking concerned.

"My family all lives far away from here," she told Kylie with a smile. Then, before more questions could be asked that would force her to reveal that she had no family, she changed the subject. "Oh my, look at the time. We need to get ready to go home."

After school, as she walked in from the bus line, she saw Kylie standing with a woman who must have been her grandmother. She was an attractive woman with Mark's dark hair and grey eyes. When she spotted Jan, the child began waving at her furiously. Jan walked over and allowed Kylie to introduce her to her grandmother, Linda Owens.

"Kylie insisted that we couldn't leave until you walked by," Linda told her. "She wanted me to meet you."

Jan smiled at her student. "I am so glad you waited," Jan said. "Just a few minutes ago, Kylie was telling me how excited she was about her Thanksgiving."

"We all are," Linda answered, with her grey eyes twinkling. "This is going to the best holiday season we have had in quite some time."

Jan's heart swelled, happy for the Owens family. "I'm sure it will be. I will see you on Monday, Kylie and you can tell me all about it."

"All right," Kylie said. Then she impulsively gave Jan a hug before she turned and walked off with her grandmother, hand in hand.

Jan stood and watched the two of them for a moment, feeling a sense of happiness, realizing that sometimes when bad things happen to people the world had a way of righting itself.

As it turned out, Jan and Penny did have a wonderful holiday. They spent Wednesday baking more sweets than they knew what to do with. Then on Thursday, they put a small turkey in the oven around noon. When it was finished they enjoyed a simple meal with all the traditional foods of the holiday. After a very short clean up, they agreed that was nice to spend a stress-free holiday. On Friday there was a holiday parade in which the band and flag team participated. The weather was very cold with a hint of snow in the air. Jan and Penny were happy to return right home after the parade.

Jan had left her phone at the house, so when they came in, she immediately picked it up and saw a missed call. It was from Gary Baker. Jan had a funny feeling in her stomach. She didn't know if it was a feeling of dread or one of excitement. She quickly checked to see if there were any voice mails or texts. There were neither. Now she had a debate with herself. Should she return the call? If she didn't would he think that she deliberately didn't answer the call? Then he would not call back. Did she want him to call back? After a moment of thought, she decided to not call him, and leave the matter in the hand of fate.

Three hours later, the hand of fate made its move. Just as she and Penny were finishing a round of leftovers, Gary called back. A few minutes into their conversation, Jan relaxed. He seemed so easy to talk to. He asked about her holiday. She gave him an explanation that was similar to what she had told her students; she had no family nearby. As for Penny, she simply explained that her parents were out of town, and she was staying with Jan. He then told her that he was familiar with Penny because she had been in his math class last year. "Of course," Jan thought. "He would know her." Then a thought occurred to her. "I wonder if he is aware of her family problems?"

Gary's voice then broke into her thoughts. "Some friends of mine are going to go to a winery near Lexington tomorrow night. I know this is late notice, but if you aren't busy would you like to go? I hear the food is excellent."

Before she hesitated and talked herself out of it, Jan accepted the invitation. "That's sound like fun. Yes, I would love to go."

"Great," he said. "How about I pick you up around 6?"

"That would be fine," she said and then told him her address. They talked for a few more minutes before they hung up. Jan then walked into the kitchen, where Penny was.

"What was that all about?" Penny asked. Then her face turned red and she said, "I'm sorry I guess that is none of my business."

Jan laughed. "That's all right. What are you doing tomorrow night?"

"I am babysitting for Kylie," she said. "Why?"

A funny feeling went through Jan for some reason, but she quickly shook it off. Then with a grin, she said, "I have a date."

Now Penny smiled. "Whoa," Penny answered. "Anyone I know?"

"As a matter of fact, yes you do," Jan said. "I am going out with Mr. Baker."

Now the look on Penny's face changed. "Mr. Baker, the math teacher?"

"Yes, that would be the one," she said. "Why do you look so surprised?"

"Oh," she began. "That's just …not what I thought you were going to say."

Jan laughed. "What did you think I was going to say?"

At that point Penny seemed to recover from whatever her initial thoughts were. "Oh, I don't know. Never mind. This is cool. Can I do your hair and make-up again?" she asked with a smile.

Jan studied her for a moment and then said, "Sure."

Gary arrived the next evening right on time and the two of them quickly left and then went to pick up his two friends. They were a married couple that Jan had never met before, by the name of Cam and Jenny Tucker. The drive to the winery passed quickly. The conversation was light and pleasant.

The winery was located inside a charming, rustic, older building. The group was seated at a quiet corner table. The waiter came to the table and inquired about their drink order. Gary immediately ordered a bottle of wine, which was brought promptly by the waiter. Jan tried not to let this bother her. Wine had always been her mother's choice of drink and the sight of wine bottles always conjured up bad memories for her. She ordered herself to shake the feeling off. These people were her new friends and they were responsible adults; not her mother. She drank one glass of the wine. She didn't particularly care for it, but she didn't say anything, she just asked for a glass of water. The others all requested one too. No one seemed to notice that she wasn't drinking any more of the wine. It was an hour before the group ordered any food. Jan had become quite hungry, but the others didn't seem to be concerned about dinner. By the time their food arrived, the third bottle of wine was nearly gone. The dinner was delicious. Jan enjoyed a strip steak and au gratin potatoes. After dinner, Gary ordered them all Irish coffees. Jan was not a fan of whiskey and she was very full of her dinner, but she did not want to be rude, so she forced herself to appear to enjoy the drink.

On the way home, Jan suddenly felt very tired. She hoped there would not be any discussion of any other stops. There wasn't because Jenny suddenly stated that she had a headache. After Gary dropped the Tuckers off, he drove directly to Jan's house. He walked her to the door. She thanked him for dinner. He made no attempt to kiss her but told her would call sometime in the next week.

Penny was not home, so Jan went straight to her room and undressed. Curling up on her bed, she mentally took stock of her evening. It had been mostly pleasant, but she did not enjoy herself as much as she did when she spent time with Jim and Casey or Cindy and Tom. Her mind wandered back to the evening she had spent playing cards at Jim and Casey's. That had been a relaxing fun evening. She tried to compare tonight to that night. She immediately thought of the wine. Jim and Mark had both had a couple of beers on that earlier night and she had not given it a thought. She finally decided that she was putting too much thought into the wine, because her of her mother. The woman had been gone more than eight years and she was still messing with her life. Jan sighed and decided that she had been unfair in her judgement. If Gary called her again, she would give him another chance.

Jan drifted into a dreamless sleep. She was awoken abruptly by the sound of her phone ringing. She rolled over and looked at her bedside clock. It was 8:00 in the morning. She picked up her phone and looked at the name: Barb.

For some unknown reason, Jan's blood ran cold. She picked it up and answered.

"Hello? Barb?"

"Yes, Jan it's me." Her voice sounded strange.

Jan took a deep breath and asked, "Do you have news?"

"I'm afraid so," she continued in that strange hoarse voice. "The boat has been located."

"The boat? Weren't they on it?"

There was a pause. "Yes, they were on it, but... I'm afraid...they..."

Chapter Five

Mark Owens sat in his office contemplating the memorial service that he had arranged for Penny Taylor's parents. This was a strange situation. How do two people take off on a boat and both die quietly in their bunks and then drift miles off course without being spotted? Since there were no phones, wallets, or identification on the boats, the authorities believed that the boat was boarded by unknown persons who discovered the bodies and then took all the valuables and moved on. Joe and Sue Taylor both appeared to have died peacefully, and the autopsy showed their deaths were brought about by natural causes. When Mark spoke with the funeral director that had handled the cremation in Florida, he learned that the investigators were likely to rule the cause of death as a double suicide, probably by some sort of ingestion.

His thoughts then wandered to Jan Burke. She had an admirable spirit to stay loyal to this poor young girl. A lot of people would have immediately shipped the child to her aunt in Florida, but Jan elected to allow her to stay in her home for the time being. The aunt, who seemed to be very wealthy, had a very sharp attorney who quickly arranged for an emergency hearing to appoint Jan as a temporary guardian. When school was out for Christmas break, Jan and Penny were flying to Florida to spend the holidays with Penny's aunt. While they were there, they planned to spread the ashes of her parents into the ocean.

Mark thought that it was generous of Jan to give up spending the holidays with her family. He mentioned this to Casey and she explained to him that Jan had no family. Then she went on to explain to him some of Jan's family history and Mark suddenly began to understand the connection between Jan and Penny, and his admiration of the woman grew.

    The turnout for the memorial service that had been had earlier that day had been quite respectful. He had worked with both Jan and Penny to plan the short service. Penny seemed to have few opinions about the situation. Mark found it interesting that Jan strongly felt that the service should be held somewhere other than the funeral home. She didn't seem to care where, but just that it should be held elsewhere. This was not a difficult problem and the service took place at a small church. Penny was calm and quiet the entire time. Since she had been babysitting for Kylie, Mark had gotten to know Penny, and found her to be a well-mannered, respectable teenager. His heart went out to her and he wished there was something he could do for her. He expressed this sentiment to Jan after the service. She smiled a genuine smile at him, thanked him and told him she would let him know. After thinking about the unfortunate situation for a moment more, he stood and stretched. He had learned that the warning signs of becoming too involved with his clients. After locking up, he started across the street and decided to take Kylie to Pizza Hut for dinner.

Three weeks later, Jan was in her room zipping up her suitcase. She glanced around to make sure that she had not forgotten anything. As she did, she saw Penny standing in her doorway.

She smiled at her and asked, "Are you all set?"

Penny nodded. "Jan?" she asked.

"You and Aunt Barb are going to make some decisions about me, right?"

Penny looked directly at her and said, "I told you that we are going to meet with her lawyer."

"I know, but I was just...."

Jan just stared at her and waited for her to continue.

Then suddenly she just blurted out, "I don't want to live in Florida. I want to stay here, in

Bellville. This is my home. If I have to go, I will, but..."

"Penny, I know that and so does your Aunt Barb," she told her. "We just have to make sure your rights are protected and that we are within the bounds of the law. By the way, I have been meaning to ask you something. Barb has mentioned to me a couple of times that she has medical conditions that make it unable for her to travel. What does she mean by that?"

Penny took a moment before she answered. "She suffers from a mental condition. You know the one where she is afraid to leave her home.... uh, what is it?"

Jan thought for a moment and then asked, "Agoraphobia?"

"That's it," Penny said. "She never leaves her property."

"Never?"

"Never," Penny repeated. "She has everything delivered or brings people in; chefs, lawyers, doctors, you name it."

"Doctors?" Jan laughed. "I thought doctors only made house calls on TV, not in real life."

Now Penny laughed. "They do if you pay them enough."

Jan started to respond, but she stopped because the doorbell rang. "That must be Casey. Get your bag. We need to get going."

Penny walked toward her room and Jan went to the front door. When she opened it, she was surprised to see Mark and Kylie Owens standing there.

"Hi," he said with a smile. "We are your substitute airport transportation."

"Oh. What happened to Casey?" Jan asked.

"Ty was climbing on the kitchen counter to get something from the cabinets and fell off and hurt his arm," he said "She thinks he's all right, but they decided to take him to get it x-rayed just to be sure. Jim called me and asked me to fill in, so here we are."

"Poor Ty," Penny said, walking up behind Jan, "but it's nice of you to fill in."

"Yes, it is very nice of you," Jan told him. "I think we are ready."

"All right then," Mark answered. "I'll get your bag, Jan, and you can lock up."

Forty-five minutes later, Mark pulled his truck up in the drop off lane of the terminal. All four of them exited the vehicle. Mark pulled both of their bags out of the back of his truck.

"Daddy, I need to go to the bathroom," Kylie suddenly blurted out.

Penny laughed. "I'll take her. I think there's one right inside of the door." She grabbed Kylie's hand and they were off. Mark and Jan looked at each other and smiled. He grabbed Penny's bag and Jan grabbed her own. The two of them walked inside together.

While they stood and waited, Mark spoke. "Jan there is something I have been meaning to tell you. I really admire you for helping Penny." He paused for a moment and then continued. "If you don't mind me asking, is she going to continue to stay with you?"

"I think so," Jan answered. "She desperately wants to stay, and I would like her to. Her Aunt Barb is the only family she has, and she's probably not the best fit to be her guardian. We are going to meet with Barb's attorney while we are down there. He is trying to set up an arrangement where I become the physical custodial parent and Barb will be the financial custodial parent, or something like that. The lawyer says that he is confident that it will work out."

"I am totally impressed that you are willing to take that on. It's a big responsibility," he said.

Jan sighed. "It is, but Penny is a really good kid, and I have grown very fond of her. If she were like twelve or younger, I would think differently, but she is about to turn seventeen. It will only be about a year and a half and she will be out of school and a legal adult."

"Yes, she is a good kid," he told her. "She has been wonderful with Kylie. I trust her completely."

Just at that moment, Penny and Kylie returned. "Daddy, Penny is going to bring me a bag of shells, and we are going to make jewelry from it when she gets back. Isn't that cool?"

"It certainly is," her father told her. "Well you better say your good-byes. Miss Burke and Penny need to get checked in for their flight."

Kylie hugged both Penny and Jan and then after another round of good-byes Mark and Kylie headed back to their car, and the other two started toward the escalator.

A mere three and one-half hours later, the two of them were sitting inside of a rented Buick Regal that had been arranged and paid for by Barb. After programming the address into the GPS, they began the thirty-mile journey to Barb's home, which was in a gated community very near the beach. After identifying themselves at the gate, they were immediately allowed to proceed. Penny had been to visit her aunt several times, so she was easily able to direct Jan to the house. After pulling into the driveway and putting the car into gear, she switched off the engine and stared at the house. Tropically beautiful was the only way to describe it. The one-story tan stucco home was trimmed in a light orange with hints of green, and the landscaping was a perfect nod to southern Florida. There were just enough palm trees to sway in the lazy breeze. Jan was surprised because it was not what she expected at all. After all her conversations with Barb, and Penny's talk of all her money, she thought the home would be a large mansion, but this was an upscale beach home. She had another surprise when Barb stepped out the door. The woman was barely average height, and her build rather petite.

As the two of them emerged from the car, her face lit up with a beautiful smile. Her dark eyes sparkled and matched her equally dark hair which was cut into a smart short style.

The next thing Jan noticed was the warm sunshine shining through the green trees. At the airport, they had been shuttled straight from the terminal to the rental garage, so this was the first taste she had of the warm winter weather of south Florida.

Penny jumped out of her side of the car and ran to give her aunt a hug, which was well received. Jan stood and watched the two of them until they released each other and turned to Jan. After Penny performed the introductions, she extended her hand, but Barb ignored that and gave her a generous welcoming hug. When she released her she said, "Let's get you inside and settled. Then we can have a nice visit on the patio."

Barb then led them through what appeared to be a semi-formal living room and down a long hallway. Jan immediately realized that the house was larger than it appeared to be from the front. Barb directed each of them to a nicely decorated room with a private bath. She then told them that she would have lunch ready on the patio in about twenty minutes.

When Jan stepped outside on the patio, she took a breath. The scene was like something out of a magazine. The patio was made of beautiful stone and was partially covered. There was a comfortable looking table and chairs under the covered area. A few feet out from the cover, the patio gave away to a wooden deck, which led to a beautiful kidney shaped pool, where a flowing waterfall fell from a large rock formation. Beyond the pool, was a stunning view of the Atlantic. The entire area was beautifully decorated with potted tropical plants and the fence beyond the pool was lined with brightly colored oleander bushes. Jan was so mesmerized, that she did not realize that Barb had walked out and was standing beside her.

"Please have a seat," Barb said, as she walked to the table and set down a tray of small sandwiches and another tray of veggies and fruit. Five minutes later she was back carrying a tray with fresh lemonade and three tall glasses of ice.

Penny arrived on the patio at that time and the three of them sat down and enjoyed the food and the balmy weather.

"Was it cold when you left this morning?" Barb asked.

Jan nodded. "The temperature was about thirty-five and it was only going up to about forty-two. I think it is supposed to snow a little later in the week."

"Well, just put those thoughts out of your mind, and enjoy the weather here. Now, I want both of you to make yourselves completely at home. Help yourselves to the pool whenever you feel like it. Jan, the little gate over there leads to the beach access. It's a lovely beach for walking."

"Thank you," Jan told her. "I love the beach. I am looking forward to taking some nice walks."

Barb was quiet for a moment and then she turned to Penny. "Have you thought about when you would like to spread the ashes?"

"Yes," Penny answered. "I have." She paused for a moment and then continued. "I would like to do it this evening and be done with it."

Barb and Jan both nodded. Then Penny spoke again. "There is one more thing," she said.

"What's that dear?" Barb asked.

"I would like to do this by myself," she said. "I want to say good-bye in my own way."

Without hesitating, Barb answered her. "Absolutely, if that's what you want, that's what you should do. I have the ashes in the den. Would you like them now?"

Penny shook her head and said, "I'll get them when I am ready."

Barb was thoughtful for a moment and then spoke to Penny again. "I understand that you want to do this alone, but you aren't planning to go down to the beach alone after dark are you?" In looking at Barb's face, Jan realized that there was some underlying anxiety that was unspoken.

Penny evidently picked up on the same thing, because she gave her aunt a reassuring smile. "Of course not, Aunt Barb. I was planning to do it around sunset, and it won't take long."

Barb's face seemed to relax. "That seems like a good plan. Would you like to have dinner before or after you go down to the beach?"

Penny thought for a moment before she replied. "I think after would be fine, since we are having a late lunch."

"All right, dinner after sunset it is," Barb said with a smile.

Penny then then said, "Jan, let's go for a swim."

"Let's do it," Jan told her.

A few minutes later as Jan was leaving her room, dressed for the pool, Penny's door opened. Jan motioned her back to her room and closed the door.

"Can I ask you something?"

"Sure," Penny answered. "Did something happen to Barb to cause her anxiety issues?"

Suddenly Penny's face changed to a sort of unhappy expression. "Yes, it's really sad." She sat down on the bed and Jan sat beside her and waited for her to continue.

"I'll tell you the story that my dad told me. When Aunt Barb was very young, she became a child bride of a very wealthy man who was a lot older than she was. I'm not sure exactly where his wealth came from, but I know he was really loaded. Anyway, he died about five years after they were married. He had no children, so he left everything to her. She lived in a penthouse apartment in downtown Miami. As I understand it, she was very active in the community and had a lot of friends. Evidently, her husband had a couple of nephews who were very upset about him leaving everything to her, so one night they got drunk and broke into her apartment and...I guess they brutally raped her several times. Eventually, they passed out, and she was able to get out and call for help. They went to jail of course, but you can imagine how it affected her. She has built herself a home where she can be comfortable but protected from the world."

Tears began to roll down Jan's face at the horror of the story. "Isn't she afraid to live here alone?"

Penny smiled. "This place has a very sophisticated alarm system, and she has a married couple who live right next door that are paid very well to take care of her. Frank takes care of her maintenance, the pool, and the gardening. Myra helps with the house and runs errands for her."

"She doesn't go anywhere? Not even down to the beach?" Jan asked.

"She does go down to the beach sometimes, if someone is with her, but never alone," Penny told her. "The only time that she has left this property in the last few years, that I know of, was during hurricane evacuations."

"Where did she go?" Jan wanted to know.

Penny laughed. "Having money makes suffering from agoraphobia much simpler. She owns a small house quite a few miles inland from here. If a hurricane comes up she, Frank, and Myra pack up and go stay in that house until it's safe to come back."

Jan nodded and said, "She has built herself a world to hide in."

"Exactly," Penny answered.

"She is so different than I imagined that she would be," Jan said.

"She really is very sweet," Penny told her. "I may have painted a picture of her as a controlling old biddie, but she actually only has control issues where my mother was concerned. Evidently, she was supporting us more than Dad, or I knew, and I think she was getting tired of it. You see, I am pretty sure that Mom and Aunt Barb grew up in a very poor and dysfunctional home of some sort. Mom dealt with it by drinking and Aunt Barb went out and found someone who could take care of her."

Jan nodded again. The dynamics of Penny's family were beginning to make some sense now. "So, even if you wanted to live here, it probably wouldn't be a good idea, because she would worry about you all the time, causing her anxiety to rise?"

"Exactly," Penny said.

"So, we need to be careful while we are here not to put ourselves in any situations that could cause her to worry?" Jan asked.

"Yes," Penny said, "but how about right now we put ourselves in the middle of the pool?"

The rest of the afternoon was relaxing and enjoyable. The two of them enjoyed the refreshing water for a while, then they relaxed in the comfy recliners. Barb did not join them in the water, but she sat on the poolside swing and read a book. With the warm sun bearing down on her, Jan began to feel drowsy, so she excused herself to finish her nap in her room. She felt so warm and relaxed, that she soon drifted off to a pleasant sleep. When she woke she was surprised to see that it was after five o'clock. She quickly dressed and went in search of the Barb and Penny.

She found Barb in the kitchen, putting the crust on the top of a pie. She looked up at smiled at Jan. "Did you have a nice nap?" she asked.

"I did," she asked. "Where is Penny?"

"She just left for the beach," Barb told her. Then she had a slight look of concern. "I hope she will be able to handle this alone. She did tell me that the counselor at school had given her some good advice about how to handle the situation and that she had a plan."

"We do have a wonderful counselor working for our school system," Jan told her. "I have talked with her a few times about Penny, and while she couldn't discuss specifics with me, she did tell me that Penny is very emotionally mature for her age and that she was handling things very well, considering." She watched Barb place the pie in the oven and then asked, "Is there anything I could do to help?"

Barb looked around and then said, "You could cut up vegetables for the salad. I need to mix the spices to make the rub for the salmon. Just help yourselves to whatever vegetables you can find in the fridge."

The two women then spent the next hour in the pleasant kitchen preparing dinner. Jan told Barb all about her life in Bellville and about her students, and her flag team. Barb was very easy to talk to and Jan soon found herself telling her all about her mother and even about her broken engagement with Derek, and the tragedies in her life that followed. Maybe it was easy to talk to Barb, because Jan now knew that this woman had been through much worse heartache in her life.

About an hour after she left, Penny appeared in the kitchen, dripping wet. The two women stared at her, until Jan finally spoke.

"Did you go swimming in the ocean?" she asked.

Penny let out a small laugh. "No, it's pouring down rain outside. Didn't you notice?"

Now the other two women laughed, and Barb spoke up. "No, I guess we didn't. Let me get you a towel, honey." She disappeared into the utility room off the kitchen and reappeared with a towel, which she handed to Penny.

While she dried herself off, she said to them, "I'm fine really. What I just did was, very…therapeutic. I am going to change and then I would like to tell you about it."

She left the kitchen and returned in dry clothes, and with her wet hair in a pony tail. She poured herself a cup of coffee from the pot that Barb had just made. The other two women did the same and they all sat at the table together.

Penny sighed and then began. "I spread the ashes just a few at a time, and I talked to them the whole time, about my feelings. I didn't spare anything. I yelled and screamed at my mother, telling her how she ruined my childhood. Then I let my dad have it for not taking me from away from her and at both of them for going off and dying and leaving me alone. After a good twenty minutes of that, I started to feel the anger going away and I began to feel sorry for them. They had sad pathetic lives. I told them that I was sorry that their lives ended up that way and vowed that I would not let that happen to me. Then I told them that I loved them and just as it started to rain, and I felt like I wanted to come in, I told them good-bye, and I felt a kind of release. Now I just feel tired and relieved."

Jan was stunned. "Did Ms. Benson tell you to do that?" she wanted to know.

"We kind of came up with that plan together," she said. "She has been very helpful. When we get back, I am going to keep seeing her. She told me that I will have good days and bad days, but she keeps reminding that I need to accept whatever emotion I am feeling. It is all right to feel angry or sad, and that I should not feel guilty for feeling happy."

"That sounds like a wise woman," Barb said. "Let's have some dinner and talk about how we want to spend the holidays."

The next few days were spent peacefully and quietly. The three of them fell into a routine; almost every morning, the three of them took a walk on the beach. Penny told Jan that she was pleasantly surprised at how far her aunt was willing to go from the house. After lunch, they would usually spend some time in the pool, or Jan and Penny would go into town and do some Christmas shopping. On Monday, just three days before Christmas, at Barb's request, they came home with a small artificial Christmas tree. The three of them spent a wonderful evening decorating the tree.

Christmas Eve, was spent watching Christmas movies and munching on their favorite junk foods. The next morning, they rose early and exchanged gifts. Jan and Penny each received beautiful silver pendants from Barb. They laughed when she opened her gift from the two of them. It was a silver necklace and bracelet, similar in style to the ones she had given them.

Later in the day, they enjoyed a traditional Christmas dinner with ham and all the trimmings. They topped the day off with a sunset walk on the beach. Before turning in, they agreed that it had been a very special holiday.

The next day they were all sitting outside in the sun, when Jan's cell phone rang. Penny was sitting on the edge of the pool dangling her feet in the water, trying to decide whether it was warm enough to swim. She could hear Jan talking to someone, and she soon became curious as to who she was talking to.

"Hello,"

"Oh hi. How are you?"

"Good thanks. How was your holiday?"

"That's sounds nice."

"Yes, the weather has been fantastic. It's about seventy-three right now. We are sitting out in the sun by the pool."

"Oh no. I'm afraid not. We are flying back on the 2nd, so we will be spending New Year's Eve here."

"I'm sorry that I won't be able to make it, but thanks for asking."

"It was good talking to you too. Bye."

Right after Jan hung up, Penny immediately moved from her spot on the edge of the pool to a chair next to Jan and asked. "Who was that?" This time she didn't bother to apologize for involving herself in Jan's business.

Jan looked at her gave her a small smile. "That was Gary."

"Oh," Penny answered, seeming almost disappointed.

"You don't like him very much, do you?" Jan asked her.

Penny shrugged. "I don't know. When he was my math teacher, I always thought that he was kind of...full of himself."

Jan thought for a moment and then said, "Who other than Gary did you think would be calling to ask me out for New Year's Eve?"

Penny was quiet for a moment and Jan could tell that her wheels were turning in her head. Then she shrugged again and said, "Maybe Mark?"

"Mark?" Jan said, a little surprised. "He wouldn't ask me out."

"Why not?" Penny wanted to know. "It seems to me that he kind of likes you."

That statement took Jan back a little, so it took her a moment to compose an answer, which caused Penny to smile. "He wouldn't ask me out," Jan said, "for the same reason that I would turn him down if he did ask me to go out."

"And that reason would be?"

"His daughter is my class," she answered. "It wouldn't be appropriate for me to date the parent of one of my students."

Penny studied on that for a moment. "I could see how that might be a problem," she said.

"Thank you," Jan told her.

"However," Penny continued with a grin, "You are only going to be Kylie's teacher for a few more months and then the problem is solved."

Jan didn't even respond to that remark but picked up the book that she had been reading, completely ignoring Penny, who was looking at her aunt and giggling.

A few hours later, as they were in the kitchen heating up leftovers from the day before, Jan's phone rang again. As luck would have it, Penny was closer to it than Jan, and she grabbed it off the table.

"Well, what do you know?" Penny said with a giggle.

"What?" Jan asked.

Penny walked over to Jan with a sly smile and handed her the phone. "It's Mark," she said. "Isn't that interesting?"

Jan looked down at the phone and saw that Penny was telling the truth. She glared at her and shook her head, as she walked away with the ringing phone. She answered it just as she entered the hall.

"Hello,"

"Hi, Jan. How are you?"

"I'm good. How about you? Did you and Kylie have a good Christmas?"

"Yes, we did. We went to Knoxville for Christmas Eve and Christmas Day with Mom and Dad. We just got back a little while ago. For our first Christmas together, we did pretty well. How about you and Penny? Was Christmas rough for her?"

"No, she has done very well, considering the situation. She has had a few bad moments here and there, but I guess that's too be expected."

"I'm glad to hear that she is all right. She's quite a girl. Tell her I said hi, and that I may have plenty of work for her when she gets back."

"Oh really, why is that?"

"Pearl dropped a bombshell on me. She has decided that she can't stand another cold winter and she is going to Florida next week to spend the next few months with her sister. Mom has agreed to try to come up every other week, so between her and Penny I can probably get by. I think she is almost old enough to stay at the house by herself if I am right across the road for a little while, but not at night."

"Oh, I agree. Mark, I could probably help you out some days after school. I could always take her to flag practice; she would probably like that."

"I am sure that she would love that. She is always talking about how she is going to be on your flag team when she gets into high school."

Jan laughed. "That's the first I've heard of that. That is very flattering."

"Yes, it is. Have you met with the lawyer yet?"

"No, that is scheduled for Monday morning."

"When are you coming back?"

"We are flying home on the 2nd."

"Then you are going to miss Jim and Casey's New Year's Eve party."

"Oh, I hadn't heard about that. That's too bad."

"Yes, it is. We'll miss you."

"Maybe they'll have another one next year."

"Maybe. I've got to go. Kylie wants me to watch a movie with her. It was good talking to you, Jan. Give Penny my best."

"And mine to Kylie. Good night Mark."

"Good night Jan."

Jan sat on her bed for few minutes contemplating her conversation. Was there something to Penny's silly teasing? Maybe and maybe not. One thing was for sure. She couldn't ever remember two men calling her in one day and asking her about her New Year's Eve Plans.

Chapter Six

On Monday morning, Barb's lawyer arrived at her home, promptly at 10:00. Jan thought that Martin Benson's appearance and demeanor was very lawyer like. He was a tall man with grey hair, and he wore what Jan thought was a very expensive looking dark blue suit. Shortly after he arrived he sat at the dining room table, pulled his glasses out of his suit pocket, put them on, and then began pulling papers out of his briefcase. After distributing the papers to he correct persons, he began to explain the legal procedure that he had planned. When he had finished, he asked each of them separately if they understood what he had just explained, and if they had any questions. All three of them agreed that they understood. At that point, he then had Barb and Jan sign several papers. When they finished he notarized each one of them and placed them back into his briefcase. He then explained that the papers would be filed with the court in Kentucky, and they would receive final copies from there. In the meantime, Jan would continue to be Penny's temporary guardian. He told them that he foresaw no problems with the procedure. Then he wished them all a good day and he left.

The three of them sat quietly for a few moments, and then Penny began to cry softly.

"Oh, Penny, it all just became real didn't it?" Barb asked.

Penny looked at her aunt. "Maybe it's a little bit of that, but mostly I'm just relieved that nothing happened at the last minute to mess everything up. I love you, Aunt Barb, but I think it is best for both of us for me to stay in Bellville."

"I think you are right," Barb told her, "and believe me, sweetheart, my feelings are not hurt over this. I am just so grateful that Jan came into your life."

Penny looked at Jan with a tearful face full of love, and said, "So am I." She hesitated for a moment and then said. "I promise that I will never give you any cause to regret taking me in."

Jan smiled and said, "I am sure you won't, honey. We will get through the next few years together. I am sure there will be some adjustment, and we will have some ups and downs, but we will make it work."

Barb looked at her niece and her new friend, and suddenly a small spark was lit within her, and she decided that the time had come for her to make things work too. It was going to take time, but now she had a reason to create a new life for herself.

The next few days passed all too quickly, and then New Year's Eve was upon them. There was a lighted boat parade at a marina not far from them, and Penny was eager to go, and Jan agreed to take her. As they were preparing to leave, Barb asked a question.

"Do you think you will be staying in the car?" Jan and Penny both looked at her expectantly.

"I was thinking of going with you...if I could watch from the car," she told them.

Jan was the first to recover from her surprise. "Oh course. That's a wonderful idea. Let's get going so we can get a good spot."

Barb smiled. "I'm ready. Let's go."

It turned out to be a wonderful evening. They found a small parking area a few miles from the crowded marina, where they would still have a good view of the boats. At the last minute, Jan had thrown some lawn chairs into the trunk of the car, and Barb stunned them further by getting out of the car and enjoying the parade from the outside of the car. If she suffered from any anxiety during the outing, she hid it well. On the way home they got milkshakes from the drive- thru of the Dairy Queen. Jan could not remember when she had enjoyed New Year's Eve more.

Weddings and Funerals

When the ball dropped at midnight, Jan was the only one of the three, still awake. Barb had gone to bed an hour earlier, obliviously tired from the outing. Penny fell asleep on the couch around eleven thirty. Jan watched the festivities on TV for about twenty minutes, then she roused Penny off to bed, before retiring to her own room. Just as she was pulling back the covers, her phoned pinged. She frowned, wondering who was texting her at this time of night, and hoping that nothing was wrong.

When she looked at the message, she smiled, and her heart warmed a little. It was from Mark.

"Happy New Year Jan"

She continued smiling as she typed her reply.

"Happy New Year Mark"

There was no reply, so she slid and the covers and drifted into a peaceful dreamless sleep.

Their plane landed at 4:45 on Saturday afternoon. Penny slept for the last hour of the flight, but Jan stayed awake, leaning back in the seat, reflecting on the past couple of weeks and the future. The time they had spent in Florida had turned out to be a very special time. She felt even closer to Penny, and she was more determined than ever to help her maneuver through the next few years of her life. Another unexpected gift from the trip was finding a new friend in Barb. She and Jan had taken a few early morning walks down the beach by themselves, while Penny slept in. They shared stories of their lives, and Barb had told Jan about some of the unfortunate events of her life, not alluding to specifics. Jan noticed that she used the word "assaulted" instead of raped. She supposed that was an easier word for her to say. Regardless, Jan was happy that Barb had trusted her enough to share some of her pain with her. She also shared that she had a new therapist that she really liked, and she had made more progress recently with her than she had in years with her old therapist. Jan was happy for her and hoped that the progress continued. Before they left, it was agreed that Penny would return for spring break. Jan said that she would think about joining her.

When the wheels of the plane touched the ground with a screech, Penny woke up with a start. As the plane taxied to the terminal, Jan turned her phone back on and found a text from Casey, letting her know that she and the children were waiting for them in the baggage claim area. Jan quickly texted a reply that they had landed and would see them shortly.

As they were coming down the escalator, Penny spotted Casey and her two kids, and Kylie waving at them. She smiled, happy to see her friend. Casey was smiling up at her and Jan truly hoped that whatever strangeness had been between the two of them had passed.

When the two of them reached the bottom, there were lots of hugs all around. Casey gave Jan an especially big one, and it warmed Jan's heart.

A few minutes later, they all piled into Casey's Expedition and they were on their way.

"Mark had a big funeral this afternoon," Casey told her, "so I volunteered to keep Kylie who was thrilled to get to come with us."

Jan looked back at the child and smiled. "I'm sure she was." After a few minutes, she asked. "So, who was the big funeral for? Anyone we know?"

Casey shook her head. "An older couple died in their sleep. I guess they were both in poor health; the man had cancer. At first, they thought it might have been a double suicide, but then they found a small leak in their gas line that might have been enough to kill two elderly people that were in poor health."

Jan suddenly had a cold chill. She looked back at Penny who was sitting in the third-row seat. She was tickling Ty and all three of the kids were squealing loudly.

She looked back at Casey and spoke quietly. "That would have been strange to have two couples in the same town do that in such a short period of time."

"Yes, I heard Jim and Mark talking about that," she said, "and Mark told Jim that sometimes things like that can be contagious."

"You mean that this old couple could have got the idea from Penny's parents?" Jan asked.

"Right," Casey said, "but apparently it didn't happen that way anyway, because the coroner ruled the cause of death as the gas leak."

Jan was quiet for a moment before she responded. "Barb doesn't think that Joe and Sue committed suicide."

Casey took her eyes off the road briefly and gave Jan a strange look. "Really?"

Jan took another look in the back before she replied. "She doesn't think that Joe would have done that to Penny. She thinks that Sue may have poisoned him and then herself." She was quiet for a moment and then she continued. "I'm not sure that I don't agree with her."

"Does Penny know about this theory?" Casey asked.

Jan shook her head. "No, she has been through enough. The coroner ruled it a double homicide and she seems to have accepted that, so we decided to keep that idea to ourselves."

"Did they find poison in their systems?" Casey wanted to know.

Jan shrugged. "All I know is that they were badly decomposed from the heat and they floated through some nasty storms, so they were bashed by a lot of waves, so I think it was a quick assumption and a quick autopsy, followed by immediate cremation."

Jan could see Casey visibly shudder at her description of how Penny's parents met their fate. She knew that feeling. She had it every time she thought about that boat floating around freely carrying the bodies of Joe and Sue Taylor.

The next day Jan and Penny went to her former home and collected everything she wanted to keep. It was a very small load to return with. She insisted that wanted nothing of her parents' personal items. This concerned Jan. She felt that there must be at least photos or sentimental items that Penny might regret losing later in her life. Later that night, after Penny had gone to bed, she phoned Barb, and talked to her about the situation. They agreed that the reason that Penny didn't want anything of a personal nature was that the hurt was still too raw. After discussing the situation, they came up with a plan. Her lawyer was in the process of hiring a company to come into the house and prepare it and all the items in it for auction. Barb was going to ask for an itemized list of everything in the home. She was then going to select a few items, such as photos and jewelry and have them sent to her. She would store them away until a time that she thought Penny might be more prepared to enjoy having them.

Jan felt better after their conversation, and she was then able to settle into a restful sleep, anticipating all she had to do the next day, when she returned to school.

The next few days were very busy at school. She was starting several new units and most of her free time was spent running papers and stuffing folders, so she saw very little of Casey. On Monday and Tuesday right after school, she had flag team practice. During basketball season they were more of a dance team since the flags were a little large for half-time shows in the gym.

On Wednesday and Thursday Casey left right after school, to take her kids to various activities, so the two women saw little of each other that week. She did not see Mark all week either. He must have been busy, because his mother had picked Kylie up every day. She was looking forward to seeing him. The thought of his New Year's Eve text still warmed her heart when she thought of it. She had not heard from Gary either. That was a kind of a blessing, because she had all but decided not to go out with him again.

On Thursday after school, she stopped in the staff mail area on her way back from the buses. The only other person in there was Shelly, so she felt obligated to speak to her.

"Hi, Shelly," she said, "How was your Christmas?"

"It was fine," she answered with a sigh. "Like every year, I drove my aunt to Mom and Dad's house in Georgia. We had a pretty good time, though. My whole family made it this year. It would have been so bad, except Aunt Edith always insists on bringing those stupid Oleander flowers back."

"Why?" Jan asked.

Shelly shrugged. "I don't know. She dries them out and decorates the whole house with them or something," She laughed. "Aunt Edith is a little...shall we say eccentric? Anyway, I try to avoid going in her house." She had been looking through her mail while she spoke, but now she looked right at Jan.

"So how was your Christmas?" she asked. "You certainly got a great tan."

"Thank you," Jan answered. "I spent Christmas in Florida and the weather was fantastic."

"I know," Shelly said, with a smile. "Mark told me all about that. I think it is awesome how you took that poor girl in. She is lucky to have you. Well, I need to get my things together and get out of here. See you later." Then before Jan could reply she was gone. Jan stood alone for a moment contemplating what Shelly had just said. She finally decided that if the woman intended to take the wind out of her sails; then mission accomplished. She walked back to her room and packed up her things.

At home, she warmed up some leftover lasagna. Penny was at a friend's house studying, so she was alone. She ate half of what was on her plate and threw the rest out.

Then she told herself that she was being ridiculous. She had let herself get way too emotional over a simple little gesture of kindness. It was fortunate that she didn't run into Mark this week, because she might have made a fool of herself.

The following night there was a home basketball game and her girls performed at half-time. Right before the performance, she felt her phone vibrate. She pulled it out of her pocket and saw that it was Gary. She didn't answer it because it was way too noisy in the gym, and she didn't have time to talk.

She waited until she was home to return his call. Penny was excited when she returned home. She had spent the second half of the game talking to a boy she knew from her history class, and she was very hopeful that he was going to ask her out the next week. Once Penny finally settled down and floated off to her room, Jan returned Gary's call.

It took him a few minutes to answer, and Jan was beginning to wonder if he had gone to bed. When he did, she realized that was not the case, because she could hear a lot of noise in the background. Then it began to fade away, so she assumed that he had turned the television down.

"Hi, Jan. I was wondering if you were going to call me back." Was it her imagination or did he sound slightly annoyed?

She explained about the basketball game and her team's performance. "I'm sorry. It was really noisy in the gym."

"Oh, that's right you do that dance thing," he said, and then dismissing that completely, he continued. "Would you like to go out to dinner tomorrow night?"

Jan considered her long lonely week, and then decided to accept his offer. "Sure," she told him. "That sounds great."

"All right," he said. "I'll pick you up around 6."

"That would be fine," she answered.

"I'm getting another call," he told her. "I'll see you tomorrow."

"Bye," Jan said, and he was gone. She had a couple of thoughts as she put her phone down. "Did the TV get louder just before he hung up?" Then it occurred that he never seemed to call until the last minute. She shrugged and told herself that she was overthinking the situation.

She felt tired then, so she decided to go to bed. She tossed and turned for unknown reasons. Eventually she got up and watched mindless television until she became sleepy enough to go to bed.

Her date with Gary was more enjoyable than the first. This time it was just the two of them. They went to a small restaurant just outside of Lexington. The food was good; not outstanding, but good.

He asked her about her trip to Florida. She told him about it, but she sensed that he didn't want to hear about Penny, just about Florida. Then the conversation to turned to school. Jan picked up on some dissatisfaction with the district, but she wasn't sure exactly why.

On the way home, he told her that he had managed to get some tickets to a concert of a popular country singer for the following Saturday night. Jan hesitated to accept another date from him, but she thought the concert sounded like fun, so she decided to give it one more try.

When they arrived at her house, he walked her to her door. This time, he did kiss her good night. While he was kissing her, all Jan could think of was that she was tasting his dinner, and it wasn't particularly pleasant.

The next morning, after a somewhat restless night, she came to a decision. She realized that there weren't any sparks between her and Gary, so after the concert the next weekend, she was going to break it off with him.

The next week at school, she wasn't as busy as the week before. On Wednesday, she found herself eating lunch with Casey in the teacher's lounge. For the first few minutes, they had to listen to Shelly complaining to another 5th grade teacher about being in a college friend's wedding the next weekend, and what a bore it was going to be. Interestingly, Jan heard her make no mention of Mark this time.

After she and the other fifth-grade teacher left, Jan and Casey found themselves alone.

"How was your weekend?" Casey asked.

"All right, I guess," Jan answered. "I went out with Gary."

"Did you have a good time?" Casey seemed to be straining to ask.

"It was all right," Jan answered. "He has tickets for a concert next Saturday night, but I don't think I'm going to go out with him anymore after that. He's nice, but there's …just no spark there. Do you know what I mean?"

Casey nodded and then laughed. "I do, and I admire you for going to the concert before you dump him."

"You're awful," she said and then laughed herself. "I got the impression that he went to some trouble to get the tickets and I agreed to go before I decided to…dump him." She thought for a moment and then let a little giggle. "You know what else?"

"What?" Casey asked.

"He's a lousy kisser." This brought a round of giggles from both of them.

She saw Mark picking up Kylie a couple of times, but she just waved on her way to the buses. He always seemed to be gone by the time she came back through. Jan did her best to push thoughts of him out of her mind. She began to look forward to the concert on Saturday night. She loved country music.

Weddings and Funerals

Gary was about fifteen minutes late picking her up. The concert didn't start until eight, but they planned to stop for some dinner beforehand.

As they pulled away from her house, Gary made a sudden announcement. "We've had a change of plans," he told her.

Jan looked at him and for some reason, her stomach suddenly clenched. She didn't say anything but waited for him to continue.

"Cam got some VIP passes to a new club in Lexington," he told her. "They are only good for tonight. The passes will get us fifty dollars' worth of drinks and the best seating in the house. It's going to be awesome."

Now Jen's heart sunk to the bottom of her stomach. Clubs were at the very top of the list of things that she hated. She remembered the few that Derek had dragged her to. They were full of things that she had a hard time dealing with crowds, extremely loud music, spinning lights, cigarette smoke, and lots of highly intoxicated people.

When she finally found her voice, she asked, "What about the concert tickets?"

He actually laughed and said. "Those were freebies I won in a raffle off some insurance salesman at school a couple of weeks ago. I sold them to my neighbor for a hundred bucks. Worked out quite nicely. Now I have more drink money."

At that point Jan became annoyed with him. The least he could have done was let her know about the change in their plans. She looked over at him. He was so excited about going to this club that he didn't even notice that she was upset. Penny was right. The man was totally into himself.

When they arrived at Cam and Jenny's house, she found them to be as equally delighted with the situation. Jan seriously considered bailing out that point with a headache or something, but before she could find a break in their excited chatter, they were on their way again. She prayed that maybe since this club was new that it might be nicer than the ones that she had been in several years ago.

As it turned out, the club did have one advantage over some of the older ones. There didn't seem to be any smoking in the building, however the music seemed to be louder and the spinning lights were brighter. Without even consulting with her, Mark ordered a round of shots. The other three did their shots and then looked at Jan's shot still sitting on the table. At this point, she was quite annoyed with him and was about to explain why, when another voice interrupted them.

"Gary?"

They all turned to see a beautiful well-built blonde, standing there smiling at Gary.

"Abby?" Gary almost squealed. Then he jumped up and the two of them exchanged a very long and healthy hug.

When they separated, she spoke in an equally ecstatic voice. "I am here to celebrate my birthday. I can't believe you are here."

"That is right," he said. "Today is your birthday. I was thinking about that this morning."

"Like hell you were," Jan thought with a smirk; "What a tool."

Gary then flagged down the waiter and ordered another round of drinks and shots. Suddenly the music seemed to get louder and the lights began to spin faster, and for the first time in a long time, Jan felt the onset of a panic attack.

Feeling the need to move, she excused herself to the ladies' room.

Fortunately, there wasn't anyone else in there when she went in. She stood in front of the mirror, breathing slowly. About the time she began to feel normal again, the door opened, and Jenny entered. She looked at Jan with sympathy.

"I honestly didn't know that was going to happen," she said. "How awkward."

"What do you mean?" Jan asked.

"Abby showing up like that," she answered.

Jan was confused as to what Jenny was trying to tell her. "Oh, you didn't know? Ah jeez." She sighed. "Abby and Gary were engaged. They lived together for about a year."

Now Jan laughed. Jenny thought she was upset the girl showing up. She decided to explain. "I don't care about that. I was going to break it off with Gary after the concert tonight. The noise and lights in places like this make me ill. If he had bothered to tell me about the change in plans, I would have saved him the trouble of bringing me. Now, when you go back out there, please tell him that I am not feeling well, and I have called a friend to come and pick me up." She walked to the door, opened it, and turned back to a somewhat stunned Jenny and said, "You have a good night." Then she walked out of the restroom and right out the front door of the club, ignoring the attendant offering to stamp her hand. She tore her VIP bracelet off her wrist and threw in a trash can by the door.

After taking a moment to enjoy the crisp sharp air, she looked around and spotted a diner across the road. Thank goodness they were having a warm spell, so that she only had to wear a down vest that night. Ten minutes later, she was seated in a booth drinking some delicious hot coffee. The diner was blissfully quiet, and the steady brightness of the fluorescent lights was welcome. Reaching into her pocket, she pulled out her phone, and her credit card, which she had brought in case she wanted to buy a t-shirt at the concert. Her plan was to call an Uber to take her home. It would be costly, but worth every penny. As she stared at her card, she suddenly froze in horror. A few days ago, she had received a new card in the mail. She had called to activate the new one. She had placed them both on her dresser, planning to shred the old one and put the new one in her wallet. She had never gotten around to doing either, and she must have picked up the old one earlier tonight when she was getting ready. This one was no good. It was expired.

She reached into her other pocket and pulled out exactly two dollars and thirty-two cents. Pushing down her newly rising panic, she picked up her phone. As much as she hated to do it, she was going to have to call someone to come and get her. Scrolling down her list of recent calls, she quickly began crossing possibilities off her list.

Penny: she was out on a double date with her friend, Chrissy and then they were going to spend the night at Chrissy's house. She wouldn't want Penny driving to Lexington at night anyway.

Jim and Casey: It was a three-day weekend and they had taken their kids and a couple of their little friends to a lodge in Cincinnati with an indoor waterpark.

Cindy and Tom: Also gone for the weekend.

Suddenly, she stopped scrolling. Mark? She could call him, but he would have to bring Kylie, and ...no Kylie was the friend that Lisa had chosen to take to the waterpark. He would be free unless...he was with Shelly at the wedding. She smiled a little at how it would piss Shelly off if she called Mark tonight. After another moment of thought, she decided to call Mark, embarrassing as it was. She also knew that he was a nice guy and if he couldn't come and get her, he would find someone who could. The only problem would be if he didn't answer. If that happened she would just have to call Penny.

She took a breath and made the call. He answered after only two rings.

"Jan?"

"Hi, Mark."

"Hi. What's up? Is everything all right?" he sounded a little concerned.

"Are you busy right now? I kind of need a favor."

"I am sitting at home, with my feet up, watching basketball. What's going on?"

Jan sighed. "I am kind of stranded. I need someone to come and get me."

"Sure, I can come and get you. Are you having car trouble?"

"No," she sighed as embarrassment washed over her. "I was out with this guy, and he changed the plans at the last minute and brought me to a club, which I never would have agreed to, had I known. Anyway, after he appeared to hook up with an old girlfriend and ordered the second round of shots in fifteen minutes time, I became very uncomfortable with the situation, so I just walked out."

"Sounds like a good decision," he said. "Where are you right now?"

In another embarrassing moment, she had to ask the waitress for the address of the diner. She texted it to him, and he promised he was on his way out the door.

After two more cups of coffee, and a muffin brought to her by the waitress, who must have felt sorry for her, Mark suddenly appeared and slid in the booth across from her.

She smiled at him and tried not to cry with relief. "Thank you so much. I am so embarrassed."

"Don't be embarrassed," he told her. "I'm glad you felt that you could call me. That's what friends are for."

"Everyone else is out of town," she said. "Penny is spending the night with a friend, but I really didn't want her driving to the city at night anyway. That would have been my last resort."

"Well, fortunately you didn't have to do that." Looking around he said, "Something smells good in here. Have you had dinner?"

"No," she said and then told him about her unfortunate credit card problem.

He laughed and said, "Jeez Jan, you are having a bad day. Let me buy you some dinner."

"That's the best offer I've had all day," she said. "Thank you."

After ordering two of the diner's signature burgers, Mark asked her about Penny and how she was doing. Jan told him about how she had bravely spread the ashes alone and used the time to vent her emotions, because of a plan that she and the counselor had devised. He nodded and told her how helpful the woman had been in helping Kylie deal with her grief. The food arrived, and it was the best burger Jan could ever remember having. They came with a side of golden brown sweet potato fries, coated with brown sugar. For a few minutes, they were both totally absorbed in the delicious food. Jan was starving since she had planned to eat with Gary before the concert.

Thirty minutes later, they left the diner and started toward home. On the way home they discussed Penny some more and she explained the arrangement between Barb and herself. Jan was her legal guardian, responsible for providing her with safe shelter, food and clothes. She had legal authority in all matters involving Penny. Barb was responsible for her financially. She was paying a very generous monthly support to Jan. It was not part of the agreement, but she was also sending Penny a very healthy monthly allowance. She told Jan that she did not want Penny to feel the need to work at this point in her life. The child had missed out on so much of her childhood, that Barb wanted her to enjoy her last year and a half of high school. The car that Penny was driving was deeded over to Barb, so that she could pay for the license and insurance. The rest of the Taylor's property was being sold at an auction and the money would be put into a trust for Penny.

As they pulled into her driveway, Jan let out a sigh of relief. Without thinking she spoke her thoughts out loud. "I guess it worked out that you didn't go to the wedding with Shelly."

"What?" he asked, looking at her with a somewhat confused look on his face.

"I heard Shelly talking about the wedding she was in this weekend. I thought you might have gone with her."

He looked at her again as he put the truck into park, even more confused. "I have no idea what in the hell you are talking about."

Chapter Seven

Mark and Jan stared at each other for a moment before Jan finally spoke. "Maybe I'm the one who is confused?"

"I think maybe you are," he answered.

"You are not dating Shelly Patterson, the teacher?" she asked quietly.

"No, I am not," he said.

"But didn't you take her out once or twice last fall?" she asked

"No, I didn't," he answered.

Jan frowned. "Didn't you take her to Jim and Casey's wedding?"

Mark sighed and rolled his eyes. "Didn't Casey explain that to you?"

"Explain what?" she asked.

"I came to the wedding alone and Shelly just showed up and sat by me. Then she followed me to the reception, and then she... for lack of a better word, leeched on to me. I tried to be nice, especially since it was Jim and Casey's wedding, but looking back now, I should have been more direct. It really messed up the whole evening for me."

Jan thought for a moment and then asked him a question. "Did you have a conversation with her about my trip to Florida?"

Mark shook his head. "I have tried to limit my conversations with her since the wedding. I think that girl has some issues. Why do you ask?"

"Last week, she complemented me on my tan," Jan told him, "and when I mentioned having gone to Florida, she said, 'I know. Mark told me about that.' So, I just assumed ... you know."

Mark shook his head. "Never happened."

"Wow," she said. "I guess she really wants the world to believe that you two are dating."

"Kind of creepy, isn't it?" he asked.

"It sure is," she told him, "but I'm glad you aren't dating her, Mark. You are a nice guy and you can do a lot better than that."

He smiled. "I've been thinking the same thing about you lately," he said.

"That was my first dating venture since I had a broken engagement about five years ago." She sighed and then continued. "Maybe I need to go back to my 'I don't date' safe zone."

Mark smiled at her. "Don't do that. There's still a few of us nice guys floating around out there."

She smiled back at him. "You're right, and I think I would be open to going out with a *nice* guy.

I just wish someone would point me in the right direction."

"Well, ..." he began, but he was interrupted by the ringing of his cell phone. He answered it and then listened for a moment. "All right," he said. "I will be there in just a few minutes."

He hung up and looked at her. "Business calls. I have to go to a nursing home." He thought for a moment, and then said, "What do you think about next weekend, we get together with Jim and Casey and play cards like we did last fall? That was a lot of fun."

"Yes, it was," she answered. "There is a home basketball game Friday night, and my team is performing, but Saturday night would work."

"Perfect," he said. "I'll talk to Jim and you talk to Casey and we'll get it worked out."

"All right," she said. "Thanks again for rescuing me."

"Any time," he smiled. She opened the door and stepped out of the truck. After walking to the door, she punched her code into the lock and turned and waved at him. He waved back and then backed out of the driveway. After watching him drive off, she went into the house and dropped onto the couch. What a night. There were an array of emotions running through her.

First there was sheer relief that the whole Gary episode was over. She had not been comfortable with the situation from the start, and she was glad it was over. Then there had been the anxiety of being stranded and the relief of Mark coming to get her. There was something else, though. In her mind she replayed the conversation she and Mark had in the truck. Just before his cell phone rang, he was about to respond to her remark about being pointed in the right direction. Was he about to ask her out? Was the suggestion of getting together with Jim and Casey a date, or was it a friend thing? Suppose he did ask her out, did she want to go? There was no doubt about that now. She absolutely would like to go out with him. The only question was if he was planning to ask her and what about Kylie? Should they wait until after the school year was over? After a few more moments of thought, she realized something. That just didn't seem like such a big deal anymore.

Then as she yawned, she realized just how tired she was. These questions did not all have to be answered tonight, she decided. The thing to do was go to bed and let time work everything out.

In the middle of the next morning, Penny came bounding in, all excited from her date the night, before. She poured herself a cup of coffee and sat down at the kitchen table. Jan stopped unloading the dishwasher, refilled her own cup and sat down to listen to Penny. Her heart warmed to see the child finally enjoying being a teenager.

After a few minutes of excited chatter, she suddenly stopped and asked, "So how was your night? Was the concert good?"

"I'll never know," Jan told her. "He sold the concert tickets and we went to this lousy noisy club, which is exactly the kind of thing I hate. The whole night was a disaster."

"That's too bad," Penny said. "I know you were looking forward to the concert. Does this mean that you won't being going out with him anymore?"

"That is exactly what that means," Jan told her, as she stood up and went back to unloading the dishwasher.

"Good," Penny said. "You did tell him, didn't you? He isn't going to call in a few days and then you will decide to give him one more chance?"

"Not a chance," Jan told her. "I think he is pretty clear on my feelings, and I don't he think is interested in me anymore anyway, so the Gary Baker episode of my life is over."

"Glad to hear it," Penny answered, standing up. "I have studying and laundry to do. Do you have any clothes that you want me to throw in?"

"No thanks. I finished mine yesterday," Jan said, smiling as she watched her walk away.

The next morning Casey called her around nine.

"Hey," she said. "I hear you had quite an interesting evening Saturday."

"Yes, I did," Jan answered. "Where did you hear that so quick?"

"Mark came out to pick up Kylie last night after we got home," Casey explained. "Then he mentioned that the two of you talked about getting together next weekend. Naturally we were curious as to how it worked out that the two of you came to be making plans for next weekend."

"So, Mark told you about what happened?" she asked.

"Well, he said that things didn't work out on your date and you needed a ride home," Casey told her. "He didn't say much more than that."

Jan laughed. "Then it was all you could do to wait until this morning to call me to get all the details. Right?"

"Jan, you know me." Casey said almost apologetically. "It's not that I am nosey; well, yes I am, but you are my best friend, and… are you going to tell me or not?"

"Of course, I was planning to tell you," Jan answered her. It's too good a story not to, but it's kind of a long one."

"I'm about ready to leave to go to the grocery, but I thought I would stop by your place for a cup of coffee first. Will that work?"

Jan smiled. "I will be here and I'm about to put on a fresh pot."

Twenty minutes later, the two women were seated at the kitchen table. Casey's eyes got bigger and bigger as Jan told her every detail of her disastrous date. From time to time, she interjected a few phrases, such as: "Are you serious?" "No Way!" and "What an ass!"

When the story shifted to the part about Mark coming to get her the phrases changed to a more positive nature: "Oh really?" followed by "That was nice."

Just as she finished her story, Jan looked up and realized that Penny was standing in the doorway, with a big grin on her face.

"When you told me the story, you left out the part about Mark coming to get you," Penny said. "That was cool."

Jan sighed. "I didn't tell you because I knew you would overreact, like you are about to do. Is eavesdropping your new hobby, or do you have bionic ears?"

"I came out here to see if you would like me to go to the grocery," she answered, "but you were in the middle of telling this great story, and I didn't want to be rude and interrupt."

Jan tried to look at her sternly, but she broke into a laugh instead. "The list is on the refrigerator. See you later."

Penny giggled and looked at Casey. "You can fill me in on the rest of the details later."

"You've got it," Casey said with a laugh.

"Good-bye," Jan said.

"Bye," Penny giggled again, as she grabbed the list and headed for the door.

Jan shook her head and then looked back at Casey.

"Why didn't you tell me about the stunt that Shelly pulled at your wedding?" Jan asked.

"I don't know," Casey began. "There was all the excitement over the wedding, and then I was really upset about you and Gary. Once again Jim was telling me to stay out of it. Then there was the whole mess with Penny's parents and then you went to Florida, and I guess I just forgot about it."

Jan then went on to tell her about Mark texting her on New Year's Eve and how happy it made her. Then she told her how Shelly spoiled it and that is what pushed her to go out with Gary again.

Casey stared at her and then finally said, "I wish you had told me that. I could have straightened the whole thing out in a big hurry."

Jan shrugged. "I'm done with Gary, and I now know that Shelly was just messing with my head."

Casey smiled. "Good," she said. "Now you can focus on Mark, right?"

Jan frowned. "I guess, but I'm a kind of confused about something."

"What is that?" Casey asked.

"I'm not sure if he is interested in me, or if he's just being nice."

Casey's mouth dropped open, and then she said. "Oh, my lord, Jan. Let me clear that right up for you."

Jan stared at her friend in confusion.

"He is most definitely interested in you," Casey told her.

"Really?" Jan asked. "Did he tell you that?"

"No, of course not," Casey said. "He told Jim, quite some time ago. Jim told him that you were very vulnerable, so he was thinking it over and then along comes dumbass Gary, so he backed off. He was really hoping that you would be back here by New Years, but you weren't."

"That's why he called and then texted me?"

Casey nodded her head. "When he was at our house last night, talking about going and getting you, I could tell that he was really happy that you were done with Gary. He's got it bad for you Jan, but if Jim ever finds out that I told you about this, he will be really upset with me, so please keep this to yourself."

Jan smiled. "Don't worry. I've got your back, but I am glad you told me."

Later that afternoon, Jan realized that she was out of her prescription allergy pills. After driving to her regular drugstore, she was a little frustrated because it had closed early due to the holiday, so she had to go to another store to get her script filled.

Inside the drugstore, Jan wandered around picking up some essentials, while she waited on her medication to be refilled. After her named was called, she went to the counter to pick up her order. While she was waiting for the clerk to ring up all her items, she noticed an elderly woman, who was working back in the prep area. She looked somewhat familiar, but Jan couldn't quite place where she knew her from. The woman had been looking intently at her until she realized that Jan was looking at her. Then she looked away and began focusing on the work she was doing. The woman was standing too far away for Jan to read her name tag, so that was no help. The clerk then finished ringing up her items, and Jan slid her card into the machine. By the time she finished paying, and walked out to her car, she had completely forgotten about the woman.

On her way home, as she went by the funeral home, she noticed there were a lot of cars in the parking lot, and people coming in and out the door, so she assumed that there was a visitation going on. From this, she assumed two things; Mark probably wouldn't call her tonight, and there would be a funeral tomorrow, so he most likely would not being picking Kylie up. There was a strange car in his drive-way, which she assumed belonged to his mother, who was probably staying with Kylie.

The next week passed more slowly than Jan hoped it would. She had plenty of things to keep her busy, but she was really looking forward to the weekend. Mark did not pick up Kylie on any of the days, but he did call her on Wednesday night to confirm their plans for Saturday night. It was decided that they would get together at Mark's house. Casey was going to make barbeque sliders, and mac and cheese. Jan was going to bring a salad and dessert. Mark said he would get his mother to make her famous Accent cheese ball before she left for home on Friday. After that conversation, the two of them talked for over an hour. During that conversation, Mark made no mention of going out after Saturday night. He did mention that he had been planning on going to the game on Friday, but he had remembered that he had a friend in Louisville that was having a bachelor party that night. He wasn't very excited about it, but he had promised to make an appearance.

After they finished talking, Jan thought the situation over. She reviewed the conversation that she and Casey had on Monday. Had Casey exaggerated the situation because of her own desire to see the two of them together? Then she sighed, and once again told herself that she was overthinking the situation.

The days seemed to drag on forever, but Saturday finally rolled around. The plan was to meet a Mark's house at six. About 5:15, he called her.

"Hi," he said. "What are you doing?"

"I just put the salad in the refrigerator," she told him.

"Is there any chance you could come over now?" he asked. "I need some help with something. I can come and get you."

"I can come over now," she told him, "but it's a nice day for January. I'll walk over. I will be there in about ten minutes." After she finished talking to him, she smiled. Finally; this was what she had waited for all week.

Fifteen minutes later, she was in his kitchen, and he was looking in the container that held the cookies.

"Those look really good," he told her.

"Penny made them," she said. "She added cranberries." Looking around, she giggled. "Maybe we should hide a few."

He laughed. "From Casey?

"Yeah," she answered, studying him. He was dressed in blue jeans, and a long-sleeved navy shirt. He had the sleeves pushed up on his forearms, evidently because he was working on mixing up something on his kitchen counter.

Looking at the mixture, she asked him, "What exactly did you need help with?"

He smiled, and his face turned slightly red, before he answered. "Mom was going to make the cheese ball before she left yesterday, but then when she decided to take Kylie with her, I guess she got caught up in getting her things together, because she forgot to make it. She remembered ten minutes after she left, so she called and told how to fix it. I thought I would remember all of it, so I didn't write it down, like she told me to." He stared at his mixture for a minute. "It's missing something."

She looked at him, trying not to laugh. "And you don't want to call your mother, because she will say, 'I told you to write it down.' Right?"

"Exactly," he said. "Would you taste it and see if you can figure it out?"

"Sure," she said, leaning over the bowl and taking the fork he handed her. As she did, she once again smelled that familiar soap, or cologne that he wore. She wished that she could figure out what it reminded her of. After tasting what he had mixed up, she thought for a moment.

"Does this recipe have Accent flavoring in it? She asked.

"Yes," he answered. "I put it in along with the beef, cream cheese, and green onion."

Jan then walked over to the refrigerator and opened it. She looked around for a moment and then pulled out a bottle of Worcestershire sauce. After handing it to him she said, "Add a little of this. I have made a similar recipe. It needs more salt too."

"Be my guest," he told her. She laughed and realized that he was pretty much done with the whole thing. A few minutes later, she had his mixture formed into a neat little ball, with dipping crackers, spread all around it.

Mark was cleaning up the mess he had made, and when he finished, he stepped over to her and looked at the final creation. He smiled at her, and said, "Thanks. This time, you rescued me."

"Well," Jan said, "I guess, but on a slightly smaller scale."

They both laughed and then they shared a moment of eye contact. Jan was almost certain that he was going to kiss her when they heard a knocking on the door, and then the sound of the door opening. She stifled a giggle, when she heard him let out a very small sigh of frustration.

A few seconds later, Casey entered the kitchen carrying a pan and a package of buns. Jim was right behind her with the crockpot which he set on the counter and plugged in.

"Hey kids," Jim said, "What's happening?"

Mark sighed louder this time and said, "Nothing at all."

Jan stifled another giggle and said, "I just finished helping Mark put together his appetizer. I think it's pretty good. Give it a try."

Jim and Casey both picked up a cracker and scooped up some of the beef ball. "That is good." Then he looked at his friend and said, "It's too good. Your mom made it."

"No, she forgot," he told him. "She told me how to do it over the phone, but I forgot one of the ingredients. Jan took one taste of it, walked to the refrigerator and pulled out the Worcestershire sauce, and then it was perfect."

Jim took another bite and said, "Well whoever made it, it's really good."

A few minutes later they sat at the kitchen table and began their first round of cards. About twenty minutes into the game, Jim looked at his wife and said, "Did you see that?"

"What?" she asked.

"He's winking at her."

"Are there rules against winking?" she asked, a little confused.

"There are when you are winking to send bidding signals," he said.

"I wasn't sending her a signal," Mark said, acting almost too indignant.

"Then just what were you doing?" Jim wanted to know.

"I guess I was ...flirting with her?" Mark said.

"Yeah Jim, it's called flirting," Casey said. "Think hard. I'm sure you remember it."

Jim stared at his wife for a moment and then turned to Jan and said, "It's to you. Are you going to bid?"

Jan looked at Casey and laughed. Then she looked at Jim and said, "I'm afraid I have to pass." Then Casey joined her laughter.

"Of course you do," Jim said.

"I pass too," Casey said, trying to not to laugh, and they all looked at Mark.

He paused for affect and then said, "I bid spades...and I'm going alone."

Jim dropped his cards down on the table and stared at his friend.

"Seriously, Jim," Mark said. "I wasn't trying to cheat, but if it bothers you that much, I'll deal the hand over."

Jim thought it over and said, "No, that's ok, but no more winking."

"We could switch partners," Mark said with a grin "I certainly wouldn't wink at you, or your wife. Then I could wink at Jan all I want."

Jim picked up his cards and began rearranging them in his hand. "When did you get to be such a funny man?' he asked.

Mark smiled and said, "I guess I've just decided that life is good."

After that hand was finished, they took a break and ate dinner. Eventually the conversation turned to Gary Baker. Jim got a serious look on his face and then quietly said, "Mr. Baker is skating on thin ice with the school district. I have a feeling that this may be his last year with us," Jim said.

"Really?" Jan's interest was piqued. "Do you mean that his contract is going to be non-renewed?"

"Well, I think he may be encouraged to resign," Jim told her.

"Because of his partying?" Casey asked.

"Not directly," Jim told them. "The administration is not happy with the public image that he presents, but his drinking is beginning to cause problems with his work performance. He has been absent and late quite a few times and lately he has developed the habit of going to the parking lot and sitting in his car during his breaks. When he comes back, his eyes are bloodshot and there have been complaints about his mixing up his classes."

"Jim, there is something I have wondered about," Jan said.

"What's that?" he asked.

"He hardly drank anything at your wedding," she said. "He seemed so nice."

It was quiet in the room for a minute and then Jim continued. "The reason that he went easy on the liquor is that I put the word out that we wanted a nice wedding without having to deal with people who were falling down drunk."

"And they all know that since you are the assistant principal that you will be the next principal, when the superintendent retires, and Bill Walters moves into his spot. Right, honey?"

"I suppose," Jim said and then sat back in his chair. "Jan, I'm going to tell you something, because I would rather you hear it from me, than someone else."

"What?" she asked, a little nervously.

"The story floating around the high school is that he is telling people that he was dating you to improve his image. He thought that if he was seen around town with a 'nice girl' it might take some of the heat off him with the district."

"I see," Jan answered.

"There is one more thing," he continued. "The story of you walking out on him last weekend has circulated around too, probably from him. He tried to put a spin on it that made him look like the victim, but from what I gather most people are applauding you and laughing at him. So, don't feel too bad. You've been through a lot, and I would hate to see this situation keep you from missing out on something good in your life."

Jan was quiet for a moment before she spoke. "You know Jim, maybe going out with him wasn't the smartest thing I ever did but letting an idiot like him keep me away from the good things in life would be even stupider," she said with a smile. Then she looked up to see Mark smiling at her.

After dinner, they continued playing cards with no more discussion of Gary Baker, and no more winking.

Around ten thirty, Jim began to yawn and he told Casey that he was ready to go home. The cards were put away and the Cravens gathered up their leftovers, said their goodbyes and headed home.

Right after the two of them left, Jan excused herself to go to the bathroom. When she came out, she found Mark in the kitchen, cleaning up the dishes. As he closed the dishwasher, he looked up and smiled. He was about to speak, when Jan's phone began to ring. She looked at it and said, "It's Penny"

"Hello."

"Hi, Jan. We are just leaving the party, and I was wondering if Chrissy and Susan could come over and spend the night."

"I don't care as long as it's all right with their parents."

"Yeah, we are pulling into Chrissy's house right now, and Susan lives across the street."

"All right will you be coming home right after you leave their houses?"

"Yes, but we're going to get some pizza on the way home."

"Pizza? Didn't they have food at the party?"

"Just sandwiches and chips, and the boys gobbled them up pretty quick. Are there are any cookies left?"

"There are a few. I'll bring some home."

"Are you still playing cards?"

"No, I think we are done playing cards."

Jan could feel Penny smiling. "Don't hurry home on our account. We'll be fine."

"I'll see you in a little while. Bye Penny."

She put her phone back in her pocket and smiled at him.

"I was just thinking that we are both new at the parenting business," he told her.

"It's a constant learning curve isn't it?" she answered.

"It certainly is," he said and then looked around. "All right, Jim and Casey have gone home. Penny is with her friends, and Kylie is in Knoxville. I think we are alone, at last."

They made eye contact again, and Jan realized that they were right back where they were just before Jim and Casey walked in. This time they were not interrupted. He walked over to her and put his hand to her cheek and slowly leaned down and began to gently kiss her. Jan felt a warmth spread slowly through her. It was a special kind of warmth that came from connecting with someone special. After a minute he pulled away and there was another moment of eye contact. Then he pulled her completely into his arms and they shared a much longer deeper kiss. When the kiss ended, he gathered her back in his arms and held her for a few moments. Neither of them spoke; it was enough just to enjoy the warmth of the closeness. Jan wrapped herself up in the familiar scent that she still couldn't recognize; she only knew that it was like coming home.

Eventually he pulled back and said, "Let's go in the living room and talk." He took her by the hand and led her to the couch where they sat, side by side.

A grin came across his face as he said, "I think I am doing this backwards, but I just couldn't resist myself. I was sure that one of our phones was going to ring or that someone would come to the door or something crazy like that."

"Mark, it's ok," she said with a smile. "I'm not complaining."

"Yeah, I picked up on that," he said. Then after a minute, he continued. "I want to ask you a question."

"What?" she asked.

"When we first met, you didn't really like me, did you?"

"Oh Mark," she began. "It wasn't that I didn't like you. I didn't even know you. The problem was what you represented."

"My line of work?" he asked. He smiled

She nodded. Then she told him about the people she lost in a short amount of time.

"I am sorry those things happened to you," he said, "and I understand your feelings about funeral homes."

She laughed. "My life has changed so much in the last six months. Up until that time, I lived by all these silly rules. "I never went to weddings, I never went to funerals and I never dated. Well, I have broken all my rules and honestly I think I am so much better for it."

He smiled. "As for me, judging by our recent interaction, I gather that you have upgraded your opinion of me."

She giggled. "You are correct about that."

He laughed with her. "Now I am going to come back to where I should have started. Would you like to go out with me?"

"I would love to go out with you, Mark," she said. "I really enjoy the time we spend together. You have been on my mind a lot, especially since you sent me that text on New Year's Eve. That meant a lot to me. I came home hoping that maybe something might develop between us, then...Shelly pulled that stunt, so I decided to give Gary another chance."

"I know Jan. I understand," he told her. "That wasn't your fault. Let's put Shelly and Gary behind us."

She nodded and laughed. "You're right; water under the bridge."

After a moment of thought she continued, "It's seems that we have quite a fan club in our favor; Casey, Penny, and probably by now her two girlfriends."

He nodded. "You can add Jim and Kylie to that list."

"Kylie?"

"Yes, she has begged me to ask you out on a date. 'Daddy. Please make Miss Burke your girlfriend.' I have pretty much ignored her or changed the subject on her up to this point."

"I have a feeling that she and Penny have discussed it."

"You may be right," he said. "I have a busy week coming up. Let me think about next weekend. Are there any home games next weekend?"

She shook her head. "There is one Tuesday, but we only perform on weekends,"

"I'll figure something out," he said. "The problem is that Kylie has been gone the last two weekends, and I kind of miss her. Oh, by the way, Mom will not be here this week, so I may need some help after school."

"That's not a problem," she told him, "but you are aware that there is a major snow storm moving in tomorrow night. We may have some snow days this week, but don't worry between Penny and I, we can keep her."

"I knew it was going to snow, but I thought it was only a couple of inches. Did they upgrade it today?"

She nodded. "Major winter storm warning," she said and then tried to stifle a yawn.

He laughed and said, "All right, come on. I'll walk you home. I'm kind of hungry. Do you think maybe I could scarf a piece or two of pizza off the girls?"

"I think that is a very good possibility," she told him with a smile.

A few minutes later, the two of them walked from his home to hers, completely unaware that across the street, one of the cars parked in the dark, contained a person watching them intently.

Chapter Eight

The storm moved in late Sunday night and continued into Monday, relentlessly dumping huge amounts of snow all over the state of Kentucky and much of southern Ohio. On Tuesday rain mixed with ice fell most of the day. School was called off for three days. By Wednesday night Jan and Casey both agreed by texts that they were happy to be going back to work, after spending the snow days cooped up with bored kids; Casey with her own two, and Jan with Penny and Kylie all three days.

Not long after Jan arrived at school, Casey came breezing into her room with a smile on her face.

"All right," she began. "I have a question I've been dying to ask you, but I wanted to wait until I could do it in person."

"What's that?" Jan asked as she began pulling papers out of her school bag.

"A while back, you told me that Gary was a lousy kisser," she began.

"Yes, I did," Jan answered, starting to smile because she had an idea where this was going.

"Well, I want the report on Mark," she said.

Jan decided to have a little fun with her friend, so she shrugged in a non-committal manner.

"Oh no," Casey answered. "You are not going to stand there and tell me that he has not kissed you yet."

"Well," she began, but stopped as Cindy walked in carrying a stack of papers which she handed to Jan.

"I ran your spelling lists for you," she said. "How was the card game?"

Jan let out a laugh. "We were just talking about that. It was fun. We all had a good time."

"Yes, we did." Casey told her. "Now Jan is trying to tell me that Mark didn't kiss her. From what I saw, I find that hard to believe."

"I didn't say that he didn't kiss me," Jan told her.

"Ok. Then answer my question."

"I didn't say he did either," Jan answered continuing to grin.

Casey sighed in frustration and was about to speak, when they were interrupted by the sound of Lisa's voice. "Mommy, the zipper is stuck on Tyler's bookbag and it almost time for the bell."

Casey had no choice, but to follow her daughter back to her room. Jan and Cindy both laughed.

"Sometimes she is so much fun," Jan said.

"I know," Cindy answered. "You've got to love her."

Mark and Jan's weekend plans changed several times, but in the end, on Saturday night they went to Chunky Cheese for Tyler's birthday party, along with Kylie and Penny, who asked Chrissy to go with her for just a little while, because she understood that Tyler absolutely adored her. When he saw her on Thursday after school, he asked her to please come, and she couldn't say no.

It was a fun evening, and Jan didn't care about being at a children's game place, as long as she was with Mark.

The next weekend was complicated too. Mark had a large visitation at the funeral home on Friday night, and there was a home basketball game on Saturday. It was the final performance of the season for Jan's team. It was also the weekend of Penny's birthday, so she had asked if she could have a slumber party after the game with all the members of the team who were juniors, since the seniors had planned their own party elsewhere. Jan was happy to oblige, because having a slumber party was another rite of passage for teenage girls that Penny had been denied when she lived with her parents. It was a privilege that Jan herself had never been able to enjoy.

The following weekend was Valentines' Day weekend, and Penny volunteered, without being asked, to babysit for Kylie on Saturday night. Jan was grateful, but she also knew that Chrissy had a date, and things had not worked out with the boy that Penny had gone out with a few weeks ago. Jan was proud of her for not sitting at home and moping. She asked Mark if it was all right to take Kylie out to eat at Pizza Hut and to see the newest Disney Movie. Mark not only agreed, but he seemed pleased. Jan thought that he felt less guilty about leaving her with a sitter, although Jan thought Kylie looked up to Penny more like a big sister than a babysitter.

Mark took Jan to a nice restaurant just south of Lexington. He told her that it was undiscovered gem, that had been there even when he was in college. She had to agree with him. The coconut shrimp that she enjoyed was the best she ever remembered having. The two of them shared some delicious cobbler for dessert, which perfectly capped off the dinner.

On the way back to Bellville, Mark was quiet for a moment, and then he said, "I thought about going to a movie, but I'm not really in a mood for that, unless there was something you really want to see."

"No," she said. "I'm not really in a movie mood either. Do you know what I think sounds good?"

"What?" he asked.

She let out a little laugh. "Coffee," she said. "I would really like a good cup of coffee."

"That does sound good, now that you mention it," he told her. "Where would you like to go to get a good cup of coffee?"

Jan thought for a moment and then answered. "I have a coffee pot at home. It seems like life has been so crazy lately, that it would be nice to just enjoy the coffee and some peace and quiet."

"I think that is an excellent idea," he said, just as he took the Bellville exit off the freeway.

Fifteen minutes later Jan was in her kitchen watching the coffee drip into the pot. Mark walked into the kitchen after using her bathroom. He walked up behind her and slid his arms around her waist. She smiled and turned around. Without a word, they began kissing. After a minute, he pulled away from her, but kept his arms tightly around her.

"Do you know what I have been thinking about?" he asked her.

Jan raised her eyebrows. "Judging by the kiss we just shared, I have a pretty good idea what's on your mind."

He smiled. "Well yes," he answered, "but I was thinking that maybe we could go away for a night or a weekend."

Jan stared at him as if she were thinking over what he just said.

"Jan," he said, "You're very special to me. It isn't like you're somebody I just dated once or twice that I'm hoping to get lucky with." She grinned and resisted the temptation to say something smart.

He thought for a moment more. "I want the first time we are together to be special. I want us to spend the night together, not just sneak off and have a quickie and then go home before our girls figure it out. I don't know, maybe I'm not saying this right."

"Mark," she interrupted. "I know exactly what you are trying to say, and I think that is just about the nicest thing anybody has said to me for a long time, and I totally agree with you. Let's see what we can work out."

He leaned down and kissed her again and then said, "I think the coffee's done."

After they poured their coffee, Mark asked her a question, "By the way, did you ever let Casey off the hook, about the kissing thing?"

"She didn't bring it up again until just the other day," Jan said.

"What did you tell her?" he wanted to know.

"The truth," Jan answered.

"The truth?"

"Yep."

"Which is?"

"I told her that you are a hell of a kisser."

He smiled. "You told her that?"

"I sure did," she told him. "Then I told her to eat her heart out and she hasn't mentioned it since."

Fate took a hand in helping them come up with a plan. The following Tuesday afternoon, Casey and Jan walked back from bus duty together. They were discussing some school issues when they reached the doorway of Casey's room. Hearing male voices, they looked in the doorway and were surprised to see both Jim and Mark standing in the room waiting for them.

"Hey Babe," Casey said. "What are you doing here at this time of day?"

A grin spread across Jim's face. "You will never believe who called me today," he said to her.

"Who?" she asked.

"Kevin Stone," he said.

"Really?" she answered. "What's he up to?"

Jim's smile grew, and he looked over at Mark, who was also smiling.

"He put the band back together," he told her.

"Seriously?" she wanted to know. "He's not trying to drag you guys back into it, is he?"

"No, he's going big time," he said. "He's got a new female singer, and a new bass player. I guess they are supposed to be pretty good."

"Is Paul the Doll still on the drums?" she asked.

"Yes, he is," Jim said, "and they are playing at a little club in Cincinnati Saturday night. Do you want to go?"

"Are you kidding?" Casey laughed. "That's a weekend trip." Then she looked at Mark. "Are you in?"

Mark then turned to Jan, who was looking confused. "I guess we should explain. These friends of ours started a band back at UK. There were pretty good. They did a lot of different kinds of music; a little rock, a little country, and few oldies. Anyway, it should be fun. What do you think? Do you want to take a little road trip?"

Then there was this moment of silent communication between the two of them. After a minute, Casey waved her hand between the two of them.

"Hello," she said. "Speak out loud or save it for later."

"We'll have to make arrangements for the girls," Jan said. "I'm not comfortable leaving Penny alone overnight."

"I think I have a plan that will work," Mark said. "We're in."

Jim grinned. "I'll just bet you do."

Casey turned to Jan. "Mark left out an important part of the story about the band," she said.

"Oh Casey," he groaned. "Let it go."

Casey giggled. "Oh no. She needs to know, doesn't she, Jim?"

"I think so," Jim answered.

"What?" Jan asked.

Casey giggled again. "Mark was the original drummer," she told her. "Before Paul the Doll, there was Mark the Spark."

Jan turned and looked at Mark with a whole new appreciation. "Is that a fact?" she asked.

"Yes," Jim answered. "Your boyfriend is a great drummer, which means he has really good rhythm."

At that point Casey went from giggling to outright laughing. "I'm sorry buddy," Jim said. "It had to be said. It was just too easy."

Mark looked at Jan. "He's just jealous, because he has no musical talent, so he was the lowly roadie. We depended on him to move our equipment. I had to protect my hands for drumming and for catching the football, because I am a man of many talents."

"All right," Casey said. "It's starting to get a little deep in here. I need to round up Lisa and get her to gymnastics. Honey, can you go to the gym and send Lisa to me and take Ty home?"

"I can do that," Jim said.

"Honey, can you send Kylie down to Jan's room?" Mark asked mockingly.

Jim turned to Jan and said, "What have you done to him? Suddenly, he has a personality."

Mark took Jan by the hand and pulled her out of the room singing, *"I got the music in me."*

Once in Jan's room, the two of them had a good laugh. Then Jan asked him a question.

"So, what is this plan that you are forming?"

"I am going to talk to Mom," he said. "Maybe she will take both girls back with her on Friday. You would be all right with that wouldn't you?"

Jan thought for a moment. "I would be all right with it, but what about your mother? I don't want to put her out."

"Are you kidding?" he asked. "She lives for this stuff, and she adores both you and Penny, and I think she would do anything to help the cause of keeping you and me together."

She smiled. "I think Penny would feel the same way. Go ahead and check with your mother."

Mark grinned and made a drumming motion on a desk, before he pulled out his phone. Watching him, Jan felt a tug at her heartstrings. The more she got to know this man, the more she felt attached to him. There was no turning back now.

Linda Owens was more than happy to take her granddaughter home with her, along with her babysitter/adopted big sister. Penny seemed excited to go along, so everything was set.

On Friday afternoon, Linda left with the girls right after school. Mark and Jan left about thirty minutes later. Jim had a principal's meeting after school and the kids' father was picking them up later than usual, so they planned to meet the other two the next day for lunch at the hotel.

It took over an hour and a half to reach the hotel, so by the time they had checked in, they were feeling hungry, so they walked down the street to a restaurant that the desk clerk had recommended. It was a good choice. The food was delicious. After dinner, they walked hand in hand back to the hotel. The weather had turned sharply colder, so they moved along quickly. They were both quiet on the way back, so Jan was wondering if Mark was feeling as nervous as she was.

Upstairs in the room, Jan took her coat off and shivered a little. Mark walked over to the heater and adjusted the temperature. She smiled at him and said, "Thanks."

He smiled back, took his own coat off, and walked over to her. Reaching down, he took her hands in his and rubbed them together. "Your hands are cold," he said.

After a minute he stopped, and she looked up at him and put her arms around his neck. They held each for a quiet moment, before she spoke without moving. "Mark, I am so happy to be here with you right now."

He pulled her a little closer to him and said, "I feel the same way, Jan."

A minute later, he let go of her, kicked his shoes off, stretched out on the bed, and then held his hand up to her. She kicked her own shoes off and laid down next to him. He pulled her close and the two of them lay curled up together.

He began stroking her hair and said, "Jan I want you to know that I feel like this could get very serious between us. We haven't been together very long, but I just...I think about you all the time, and I really need to know if you...feel..."

She put her hand up to his cheek and said, "It's ok. Relax. I couldn't have put it better myself. I think about you all the time too." Then she moved closer and began to kiss him gently. He pulled her closer and they both soon discovered a whole new world of lovemaking.

Two hours later, they were still awake, although Jan was yawning. "You are fighting sleep, aren't you?" he asked her.

"Yeah," she murmured.

"Why?" he asked.

"I want to enjoy the moment as long as I can," she told him.

"Sweetheart, we are going to have lots of moments," he said.

"I know," she told him, "but tonight is special." Then as soon as the words were out of her mouth, she yawned again.

"All right," he said. "I'm not talking to you anymore. Good night."

There was no response, and he realized that she had finally given into sleep. He held her tightly and just before he drifted off, he said a prayer that the two of them could have many more "moments".

The next morning when Jan woke, Mark wasn't in the room. When she entered the bathroom, she was immediately hit by the pleasant scent that she always smelled whenever she was close to Mark. She decided that this was an excellent opportunity to investigate the source of the aroma. His shaving bag was on the counter. At first, she felt a little guilty about looking through it, but then curiosity got the better of her. After all she had just spent the night, curled up in the man's arms. She looked in the bag and then was disappointed. The only items in there were a can of Right Guard, a razor, a contact lens case, and solution. Interesting; she had no idea that he wore contacts, but there was nothing to account for the aroma that seemed to follow him. She opened her own bag, pulled out her soap and shampoo. After stepping into the shower, she looked at the shelf ledge, and smiled because the mystery was solved. She picked up the container of "Old Spice" soap and poured some out in her hand and pulled it up near her face. The delicious smell transported her back to her childhood. Her father had used Old Spice. Whenever he took her away on short trips, so they could get a break from her mother, he had smelled like this. She had forgotten until this moment. Now she knew why the aroma that was around Mark was such a pleasant and calming influence on her. She smiled. This had to be a sign.

When she emerged from the bathroom, he had returned and was stretched out on the bed, watching the news and drinking coffee that he had apparently brought into the room.

"Good morning," he smiled.

"Good morning yourself," she answered, sitting down on the bed next to him. He put his arms around her and pulled her close. He kissed her generously before he spoke.

"Your coffee is on the table," he told her.

"Oh good," she said, jumping up off the bed to retrieve her coffee.

After taking a sip, she sighed. "Umm, that is good coffee. Thank you."

"*You* are welcome," he said.

She grinned at him and returned to her spot on the bed. "What time are we meeting them for lunch?"

"Jim texted me a little while ago and said they would be here between 11 and 11:30," he told her. "He said that after lunch we might go downtown to the casino."

"Ooh, that sounds like fun," she said.

He laughed and said, "Am I getting involved with a gambler?"

"I haven't been to a casino in a while," she told him, "but in the past, I have been known to have some very fortunate encounters with some slot machines."

"Really?" he said. "How fortunate?"

She was thoughtful for a moment and then said, "One time I walked out with about $400."

"How much did it cost you to win that?" he asked.

"That was my winnings," she told him, "and another time I believe won $600."

He raised his eyebrows at her as she continued. "I am trying to remember though, I think my biggest winning was $2200."

"You won $2200 in a casino and you aren't sure if it was your biggest winning?"

"It had been several years, but I think another time, I might have won $2300 or was it $2100? Anyway, I won over $2000 at least twice," she said as if she were trying to remember.

Mark stared at her as if he weren't sure whether to believe her. She grinned. "Derek was a gambler. He was always dragging me to the casino, but I kind of liked the slot machines. I was careful though, I only went in with a small amount of cash. I was just lucky I guess."

"You think?" he asked. Then he grinned and pulled her close. "Stay close to me," he told her. "I think you just might be my little good luck charm."

After putting down her coffee, she smiled and said, "I have no problem with staying close to you. There is no doubt in my mind that you are going to be the best thing that ever happened to me."

He reached over her, put down his own coffee down and spoke softly to her. "Good, because I plan to keep you close." Then he began to slowly kiss her, and she melted into his arms.

About two hours later, they walked into the restaurant just off the lobby of their hotel. Jim and Casey had just been seated. They all smiled and greeted each other.

"Sorry that we couldn't make it last night," Jim told them. "Something went down at the high school yesterday and there was an administrative meeting about it."

"What happened?" Jan asked.

Jim sighed before he spoke. "Right after lunch yesterday I saw Gary Baker leave the building headed for the parking lot. I went straight to Bill's office. We both started to head outside, but he was called back to his office for a phone call, so it was about twenty minutes before we made our way outside. We walked up to Gary's car from the rear, just in time to see him take a swig of brown liquid out of large bottle. Bill walked up to car and wrapped on the window. Gary looked up, completely startled. He recovered almost too quickly, because he rolled down the window and smiled at us.

'I know this looks bad,' he told us, 'but I swear it's sweet tea.'

'Is that a fact?' Bill asked. 'Then you won't mind handing it over to me?'

He became quite indignant at that point. 'I don't have to give you my tea. That's an insult to my character.'

Then Bill leaned closer into the car and took a better look. 'What is that I smell?' he asked.

Gary rolled his eyes and sighed in frustration. 'My brother borrowed my car last night. The dumbass is a pothead. You got nothing on me.' That was when I noticed that his words were beginning to slur. Bill then asked him one more time for the bottle and he refused. Then he ordered him to come to the building to his office. Gary got out of his car slammed the door and locked it, with the bottle inside.

Bill left him cooling his heels while he called the superintendent. When Doug got to the school, he was irate. The man was sicker than a dog with a nasty cold. He was on his way to Urgent Care and dealing with Gary Baker was the last thing he wanted to do yesterday."

"So, what happened?" Mark asked.

"Well, it got real ugly real fast," Jim told him. "Gary was given the choice of immediately resigning or running the risk of having charges filed against him and possibly losing his teaching license. He ranted and raved for a few minutes, and then finally gave in. After scrawling out his resignation, he left shouting all the way out the door that Doug Lawrence would be sorry. He would make him pay and they would see him in court and then in hell."

"Wow," Jan said.

"Doug, Bill and I had a meeting after school about how to cover Gary's classes," he told them, and about how to address the situation with the staff on Monday."

"It's sounds like a mess," Mark said.

"To say the least," Jim answered, "but let's not let that ruin our weekend. I'm anxious to get to the casino. Does anybody feel lucky today?"

Mark laughed, looked at Jan and then over at his friend. "You wouldn't believe how lucky I feel," he said, "but not for the reason you might think." Then and he and Jan both broke into laughter.

As it turned out, Casey was one with lady luck smiling down on her. She won $250 at the slots. Jim won $25 playing black jack, and Mark and Jan both broke even for the afternoon.

They arrived at the club that night just about fifteen minutes before the show began. Kevin had arranged for them to have seats in front, and to have foods and drinks on him. It promised to be a fun evening.

The promise was fulfilled. Jim, Casey, and Mark all agreed that the band was better than it had ever been before. Jan enjoyed herself thoroughly. The two hours passed quickly. Just before the band was about to play their last number, Kevin introduced the band members. Then he went on to make another personal comment.

"As some of you may know we started this band years ago back in my college days at UK. Several of our original members have changed. Most of them graduated and have gone on with their lives. However, tonight, ladies and gentlemen, we are honored to have one of those members in the audience. Our original drummer, Mark Owens, is sitting right here in the front. How about a hand for *Mark the Spark*?"

Suddenly there was a spot light on Mark, and the audience was giving him a round of applause. He smiled and waved. Then the light was back on Kevin.

"We have one more number for you tonight," Kevin continued. "It is one of our original numbers, and I thought it would be fun to get Mark up here on stage to do the number for old times' sake. What do you think? Should we get him up here?"

Then the light was back on Mark, and the audience was chanting, *"Mark! Mark!"* He shot a dirty look at Jim, that seemed to say, "I know you are behind this."

Mark had no choice but to go up on the stage, but Jan had a sneaking suspicion that he didn't mind nearly as much as he pretended to. The song was, "Old Time Rock and Roll". Jan was completely amazed. Jim had told her that Mark was a good drummer, but she had no idea how good he was. Once again, she saw another whole side of the man; a side that she absolutely adored.

When the concert was over, Jan and Casey made their way to the ladies' room. While they were washing their hands, Jan looked over at Casey and smiled. "This was really fun."

"Yes, it was," Casey answered. "Jan, I can't tell you how happy I am about you and Mark. I have...uh... been hoping this would happen since last fall. When you started going out with Gary, I thought I was going to be physically ill."

"And I misunderstood that completely," Jan answered. "I'm sorry. I thought that you were just being controlling."

"I think that we should just put all that behind us," Casey said. "Come on. Let's go find our guys."

Out in the lobby, the band was signing autographs for the crowd that was gathered around them. Two very young girls were standing very close to Mark, smiling up at him. Casey looked at Jan and grinned. "Groupies!" she said.

As Jan walked up to Mark, he looked at her, smiled and said, "Hi Honey." Jan then realized that he was a little uncomfortable with these young girls practically hanging on him. He put his arm around her and the two girls backed up a few steps. A warm feeling spread through Jan and suddenly she was happy to not be a young infatuated girl, but a grown woman in a relationship with a man that she ... was in love with. She had to own it. There was no getting around it now. When he looked down at her, she knew in her heart that he was feeling the same thing. She waited for the warning bells to go off, telling her to run away before she got hurt again, but there were none, so she allowed herself to fall completely into the glow of happiness that she was feeling.

Sometime later, she and Mark came back to their room. The mood was much more relaxed than the night before. As soon as the door closed, they began kissing. After a couple of minutes, they stopped, and she looked up at him. "Mark the Spark," she said as she giggled, trying to imitate the young girls from earlier.

He grinned. "You are all his," he told her and then picked her up and carried her over to the bed. Sitting down with her, he pulled her close to him.

"I love you, Jan."

"I love you too. I don't think I've ever felt as warm and happy as I do tonight."

He didn't answer but just began to kiss her and no more words were needed.

The next morning after having breakfast with Jim and Casey, the two of them headed back to Bellville; tired, but happy. Linda and Martin weren't due to arrive with Penny and Kylie until dinner time. Jan planned to have dinner ready for them at Mark's house when they arrived. It almost didn't happen because the two of them fell asleep and slept for almost three hours. Jan woke before Mark and went into the kitchen and quietly began to prepare the roast. Just as she slid the meat into the oven, Mark came into the kitchen. He poured himself a cup of coffee and sat at the table.

"I would like to offer to help," he said, "but..."

She laughed and answered him. "but you wouldn't be much help?"

"That's about right," he told her. "I can do about just about enough to get by and that's all."

"Poor Kylie," she said.

"Yeah, she's been a pretty good sport about all the frozen meals."

Jan frowned at the idea of the frozen meals and then she decided that it was time to bring up a subject that had been mulling around in her head.

"Speaking of Kylie," she began. "How much do you think she needs to know about us, at this point?"

"I've been thinking about that too." Mark said. "At first I thought that we should keep it low key. Then when I thought it over, I realized that I had a problem not being honest with my daughter, and this kind of thing is hard to keep under wraps in a small town. I would hate for to hear it from someone else. My thought is to have a talk with her and tell her that we are dating and that we like each other very much. Then I think we should make sure to spend time with her and Penny."

"Penny is a different story," she told him. "I am planning to have a talk with her, because very little gets by that girl. She is seventeen and I am pretty sure that she has a good idea about what it means when adults go away for the weekend."

"I imagine she does," he smiled. "As far as you being Kylie's teacher, I think we need to make sure that she understands that she shouldn't make a big deal about this at school. We don't want her to lie about it, but we just need to encourage her to not to overly discuss it."

"I agree," Jan said. "That sounds like a good plan."

At that moment, they heard the front door open, and sounds of excited voices floated into the kitchen.

Dinner was a lively affair. Both girls were excited about their weekend and they wanted to hear about the band that the two of them went to see.

Jan grinned and felt a little bit ornery. "Kylie, she began. "Didn't your father tell you what was so special about this band?"

"No," the child answered.

"Well," she continued, "when the band was first starting out, your dad was the drummer."

Kylie's eyes lit up. "Really?" she asked.

"Yes," Jan answered and looked at Mark who was looking at her as if to say, "You really are not going there, are you?"

Deciding that it is was safe to continue her orneriness, she turned back to Kylie. "And guess what happened last night?"

"What?" Kylie asked Jan, now totally intrigued.

"The lead singer of the band asked your father to come up on stage and be the drummer for the last song."

Kylie's eyes got very big, but it was Penny who responded. "Cool," she said. "I wish I had seen that."

Jan sat continuing to smile and wondering how far to push it. Then she picked her phone and brought up the video. She handed it to Penny. Kylie jumped up and ran over to watch it with her.

"You videoed me?" he asked.

"No," she answered. "Casey did. She sent it to me."

He frowned and pretended to be annoyed, but Jan knew that he was enjoying the moment.

When the video was over, both girls giggled with excitement. At that moment her phone began to ring. Jan took it back and looked at it. It was Casey. For some reason, Jan had a feeling that she should answer it. She took it in the other room.

"Hello."

"Jan, I have some terrible news." Those words caused Jan's heart to drop.

"What?"

"Doug Lawrence died in his sleep last night."

Chapter Nine

The following week at school was strange. There was a sense of shock over the sudden death of the district's superintendent. There was also a lot of speculation about the sudden departure of Gary Baker as a district employee. Jim had instructed Casey and Jan not to discuss the details of what had happened with any of the employees, so the two of them had to listen without comment to all the stories floating around; some that were just about on the mark and some that were quite farfetched.

On Wednesday afternoon after school, Casey came into Jan's room and closed the door. She had a look on her face that said that she couldn't wait to tell Jan what was on her mind.

"You are not going to believe what I just learned," she said.

"What did you just learn?" Jan asked while she was rearranging her calendar numbers, because the next day was the first of March.

"I was getting my mail, and Shelly was in the mailroom babbling to Lynn. I wasn't really paying much attention until I realized that they were talking about Gary."

Jan let out a little chuckle. "Who isn't talking about Gary this week?" she said as she continued working on her calendar.

"Did you know that Shelly and Gary are cousins?" Casey asked her.

Jan stopped working and looked at her. "You're kidding."

"She was talking about how the district really screwed him over and how upset the whole family was about it. I guess they were telling him to get a lawyer. I heard her say that of all her cousins, he had always been the favorite grandchild."

Jan shook her head. "I guess he can't sue Doug Lawrence. Do you think he will go after Bill and Jim? Or just the district?"

"Jim said they had a meeting with the district's attorney on Monday, and he told them that they followed protocol and Gary doesn't have a leg to stand on, because he resigned, and because he wouldn't turn over the bottle."

Jan was quiet for a moment and then she said, "I still can't believe that Doug is gone."

"I know," Casey said. "He had a heart attack a couple of years ago, but since then he has really taken care of himself. It's sad that he apparently just died quietly in his sleep. Jim and I are going to his life celebration on Sunday in Charleston. I am not looking forward to it."

"I don't blame you," Jan said. "It sure does seem like a lot of people have died in their sleep lately,"

"I know," Casey answered. "We were talking about that last night."

Their conversation was cut short when the intercom came on requesting that Casey come to the office.

"Oh shoot," Casey said. "I almost forgot about my curriculum committee meeting. I better go. Thanks for taking the kids. I'll pick them up in a little while."

"No problem," Jan told her as she began to pack her bag. "I told Mark that I would take Kylie everyday unless I heard from him, anyway." After Casey left, her mind was on what she and Casey had been discussing; people dying in their sleep. First Marcia Collins, then Carol Fisher's husband, Penny's parents, the old sick couple, and now Doug Lawrence. She shrugged thinking that maybe she was once again overthinking a situation. As she left her room and went toward the gym to collect the three kids, she made a mental note to ask Mark if he thought it was odd. The thought of Mark made her smile and the ominous feeling that had been in her stomach immediately floated away.

Two weeks later, spring break arrived. School was dismissed two hours early on Friday afternoon. Mark picked Kylie up and Jan drove Penny to the airport to catch her flight to Fort Lauderdale. Jan had had a long talk with Barb on the phone the weekend before. She told her about Mark and how they were planning to spend some time with Kylie during the week off. Barb completely understood and said that she was looking forward to spending time with Penny. The personal items from the house had arrived and she hoped that the two of them could go through them together. She told Jan that she wouldn't force her if she wasn't ready, but she wanted Penny to know where they were.

As she drove back toward Bellville, Jan reflected on the time since she and Mark had gone to the concert together. Both Kylie and Penny seemed to accept their relationship without question, as if it had been going on all along. It hadn't been easy to find time to be alone. One weekend they had left Kylie with Penny to go out on a date. They picked up a pizza and took it back to Jan's townhouse, and spent the evening in. The second weekend Kylie was invited to a birthday slumber party, and Penny then conveniently asked to spend the night with Chrissy. Jan found herself growing closer to Mark as each day passed. It wasn't a perfect situation with both of them having jobs and a child depending on them, but Jan was happy to spend whatever time with Mark that she could.

Casey's kids were spending most of spring break with their father, and Jim was going to be busy with administrative meetings to plan the transition of Bill Walters to superintendent and Jim to principal. They also needed to interview candidates for both Jim and Gary Baker's teaching positions. Finding herself with time on her hands, Casey decided to visit her parents in Dayton, so Mark and Jan planned to spend some special time with Kylie during the break. Jan was looking forward to the week off and to spending time with Mark and Kylie.

She parked her car in Mark's driveway and let herself into the house. Inside she found Mark sitting on the couch with his feet on the coffee table, watching college basketball.

He looked up, smiled and said, "Hi,"

"Hi, yourself," she answered sitting next to him, and giving him a kiss. She looked around and asked, "Where's Kylie? In her room?"

"Nope," he told her. "She just left."

"She left?" Jan asked, confused.

"Right after we left school, Sue Ann's mother called and said that at the last minute they planned to go to Indianapolis to visit her husband's parents. She said that they had been planning a trip to the children's museum there and she thought it would be fun to have Sue Ann take a friend with them. Kylie was so excited," he said. "What could I say?"

"When are they coming back?" she asked.

"Sunday night," was his response.

"So, we have the whole weekend to ourselves?" she wanted to know.

"We do," he answered with a grin. "I have no funerals this weekend, so I plan to enjoy every moment of it." He reached over and grabbed her hand, raised it up and kissed it.

Looking back at the TV he saw the game ending. "Damn," he said. "Loyola just took down Miami."

She now looked at the TV too. "Did you have money in a pool on Miami?" she asked him.

"Yes," he groaned. Then he looked at her more closely.

"Jan?"

"What?" she asked staring at the TV.

"Why are you grinning?"

"I didn't realize I was," she told him, still not looking at him.

"Oh, let me guess," he said. "You have money on Loyola?"

Still straining not to smile, she answered him. "I think, maybe I might have."

He stared at her for a moment and then reached over and grabbed her and started to tickle her. "You are a lucky little thing, aren't you?"

She giggled and said, "Yes, I consider myself a very lucky woman."

He looked at her seriously for a moment and then kissed her before he spoke. "I am so glad to hear you say that. Would you like to go out to dinner with me?"

"No," she said.

"No?" he asked, surprised.

She smiled. "You seemed so relaxed and comfy. Let's just stay here. How do you feel about Chinese? They deliver."

"I love Chinese," was his response. Then a grin spread across his face. "You have money on the next game too, don't you?"

She shrugged. "I might. Who's playing?" she asked innocently.

"I believe it's Tennessee and Kansas," he told her, "but I think you already know that don't you?"

"Yes, I remember seeing that advertised earlier. I think I have Tennessee," she told him.

He grinned. "Good, so do I. Let's get some food ordered."

After they ordered food, they curled up together on the couch.

"You look tired," she told him.

"It's been a crazy week," he said. "There are a couple of things I would like to discuss with you, but I have been waiting for a quiet moment."

"I think a quiet moment has arrived," she said. "Go for it."

"Well," he began, "I have had a very interesting business offer. George Elliot of Elliot Funeral Services called me and wanted to meet with me. We had lunch on Wednesday." He paused a moment and then continued. "He asked me if I would like to enter into a partnership with him. He said that he has been doing it alone for almost thirty years and he wants to slow down. George's kids are raised. He told me that it wasn't easy, but he had a wife there to keep things together. He knows that I am a single parent, so he thought that I might be interested in business arrangement that would allow me more free time. I have been thinking that maybe it's not a bad idea. My business is important to me, but Kylie is way more important. Her life should not have to be adjusted to my working schedule. She deserves better than that." He looked down at her. "And so do you."

Jan smiled. "Mark, I am an adult, and I have no problem arranging my time with you around Kylie and your work. She should come first without question."

"I think that if I take George up on his offer, I will be able to have more time for both of you. He has quite a few employees, including a couple of part time certified morticians. He also has a son attending a school of mortuary science. I know this would solve one problem that I have been wrestling with."

"What's that?" she asked.

"I really would like to take Kylie on a nice vacation this summer," he said. "I didn't think that I could get away long enough, but this would make it possible for me to do that."

"I think it's a great idea," she told him. "because you are wearing yourself out, trying to take care of your business and Kylie."

He gave her hand that he was holding a squeeze. "Having you keep her after school has been a huge help," he said. "I have been able to get things done, so I can enjoy the evenings with her."

"It's not a problem," she said. "We have a good time together."

"I know," he answered. "She adores you."

"Was there something else on your mind?" she asked.

"Yes," he said. "Pearl also called me this week."

"She's not coming back, is she?" Jan asked.

"Only long enough to pack up her things and list both houses," he answered. "Apparently the retirement community that her sister lives in really suits her. She did tell me that she would give me the opportunity to buy this house, before she lists it, though."

"Do you want to buy it?" she wanted to know.

Mark sighed and thought for a moment. "No," he said. "I don't. This house has a few issues, that I don't want to deal with as an owner. It has only one real perk."

"Location?" she asked.

He nodded. "But it just so happens that I noticed that there is a beautiful home for sale just down the street."

"The red brick with the big porch?"

He nodded again. "I called about it and I am going to look at it tomorrow afternoon. Do you want to go with me?"

"Are you kidding?" she laughed. "If you don't buy it, I just might."

"I suppose you will use all your gambling winnings that you probably invested in the stock market and made a fortune with."

"Maybe," she said as the doorbell rang announcing the arrival of their dinner.

The next afternoon the two of them toured the brick home with the listing agent. When they finished, the agent left in her car and the two of them proceeded to walk back to Mark's house. They were quiet for a few steps until he finally asked her, "Did you like it?"

"It's a beautiful home," she said.

"It's an expensive home."

She sighed. "I know."

They reached his porch. "It's such a gorgeous day," he said. "Let's sit on the porch."

The two of them sat on the swing and rocked quietly for a few minutes. Eventually, she broke the silence.

"Do you mind if I ask how far over your budget the house is?"

"I could probably swing it," he said. "Things might be tight for a while, unless…"

"Unless what?"

"I have some inheritance that I got from my grandfather," he told her. "My plan was to save it for Kylie's college education, but I think using it to buy into a partnership and purchase a good home for her to live in would also be an investment in her life."

"I think she might be right about that," she said. "Did you like the house?"

"I did," he said. "It was everything I would want in a home. It has an old-world charm, but it is completely remodeled. The rooms are large and bright from the big windows, and there is a lot of oak which I love."

"The woodwork was beautiful, wasn't it?" she asked.

"It certainly was," he told her. "What really surprised me was the finished basement with two bedrooms and a full bath between them."

"I know," she said. "Would you let Kylie have one of those rooms?"

He shook his head. "No, I think she is too young to have her room down there. I actually had another thought for that room."

"What?" she asked.

"Do you really want to know?"

"Well, yes I do."

He was quiet for a moment and then he looked her directly in the eyes. "All right. I'll just put it out there. I was thinking that at some point it would make a great room for Penny."

It took a moment for Jan to realize the full impact of what he was saying. She stared at him for a moment and then tears began to well up in her eyes.

"Honey," he said. "I know you are not ready for this, but I am talking about whenever you are. Penny has another year of school and then college. I assume that she will be home for summers and holidays."

"Mark," she spoke softly through her tears.

"What?"

"I am not crying because I am scared or upset."

"Then why are you crying?"

"I love you so much, I don't hardly know what to do with myself anymore," she told him. "When you said that, it all just became real to me. I had thought all along that if that happened I would be terrified and want to run away, but I didn't, I just felt so warm and loved, my tears are happy ones."

He pulled her closer and they sat in silence for a while. "There is something I was going to tell you about," she said.

"What's that?" he asked.

She sighed. "I got a letter from the corporation that owns my townhouse. My rent is going to increase by one hundred dollars a month on July 1st. I am afraid that I am going to have to move."

He smiled. "Is it a sign?"

"It's possible," she told him.

He stopped the swing and looked at her. "Jan, will you move in with me?"

She looked at him as her heart swelled with love, but she had to be honest with him. "I don't think I should as long as Kylie is in my class," she said. "It just wouldn't be right, but could you please ask me again when school is out?"

"When is the last day of school?" he wanted to know.

"I don't know the date off the top of my head, but I know it is the Friday before Memorial Day," she told him."

"Got it," he said. "Now would you like to go to dinner with me tonight?"

"I would love to go to dinner with you," she said, "as long as we are back in time for the Nevada – Texas game."

He shook his head. "Maybe I should let you buy the house with your winnings and I'll move in with you."

She laughed. "You would be more than welcome."

Spring came early to Kentucky and the weeks passed quickly for Mark and Jan. He bought the house and he and Kylie moved in the middle of April. Mark did not mention his offer of moving in with him again. Jan assumed that he was honoring her request and giving her some space, but she did give notice on her townhouse, but she kept this to herself, knowing that regardless of what happened with Mark, she and Penny would need to move.

The partnership between Mark and George Elliot became official on May 1st. It was decided that both funeral homes would remain open for the time being under the name of Elliot-Owens Funeral Services. There was a plan of possibly building a new larger funeral home in the next few years. All of Georges employees were at Mark's disposal, which gave him a great sense of relief.

George was a family man. On the 2nd weekend in May, he invited Mark and Jan to dinner with him and his wife. Jan found them both to be very welcoming and friendly. Susan Elliot invited Jan to have lunch with her and to attend her women's club meeting the next month. The Elliot's were excited about a trip they had planned to Vermont the next October. They were both highly encouraging of Mark and Jan to take the girls on a vacation during the summer. Jan was relieved to realize that neither of them seemed concerned about the fact that she and Mark were not married or engaged, and very accepting of her situation with Penny.

Mark and Jan discussed the vacation situation later and he confessed to her that the cost did concern him. The move had been more expensive than he thought it would be, as were the legal fees for arranging the partnership. Jan understood his dilemma, but she knew he really wanted Kylie to have a vacation. Then an idea occurred to her. After one phone call it was all arranged. He wasn't sure at first, but then finally relented. They decided to keep it secret from the girls until school was out, that they would be spending the second week of June at Barb's house.

On the Friday of the third week of May, Jan and Casey were talking in Casey's room after school.

The subject of Mark's new house came up. "I thought when he bought the house that you would surely move in with him," Casey said.

Mark had not mentioned the possibility of Jan and Penny moving in with them since he had brought it up on the porch a couple of months ago. She was trying not to become anxious over the situation, and she really didn't want to discuss it with Casey, so Jan decided that it was time to have some fun with her friend. "If I did, it wouldn't be a month before you would be worrying about when we were getting married."

Casey apparently decided to play along. "So, when are you getting married?" she asked.

"July 4th weekend," Jan fired back. "Now I suppose that you want to know when we are going to have our first baby."

"No," Casey answered, "I would just like to know how many you are going to have."

"Three maybe four," was Jan's response. Then she decided to turn the tables. "What about you Casey? When are you going to start popping babies?"

"In December," Casey answered.

"That's nice," Jan answered, "just in time for the holidays. Will it be a little Nick or a little Noel?"

"No really," Casey told her. "I am going to have a baby in December. I really am pregnant."

Jan's eyes opened wide. "Casey that's wonderful. I am so happy for you." Then the two of them were hugging.

"Well if you two are going to have three or four, I thought I better get started."

"Have three or four what?" Jim asked from the doorway.

Casey turned around and before Jan could speak, she answered.

"Mark and Jan are getting married on the 4th of July and then they are going to have at least four babies," she told him.

"Really?" Mark said as he stepped in behind Jim. "I don't know about that."

The room grew quiet and then he said, "I was thinking more of June 30th and maybe six babies."

"Only if you are having two of them," she told him, "but in the meantime you need to congratulate Casey, she already has one on the way."

"I heard about that," he said. "That's why I walked back here." He gave Casey a warm hug and then turned back to Jan and winked.

"Excuse me," Jim said. "I had a little something to do with this."

"I was going to offer to buy your dinner tonight," Mark said, "but I'm not going to hug you."

"Then I will," Jan said walking over to Jim and gave him a hug.

When she let go, Jim said, "If Mark's buying, let's get going. I'm hungry."

"All right," Casey answered. "Let's round up the kids and get them ready. It will take those two longer because she lives in one house with one kid, and he lives in another house with the other kid. It may take them a while to get organized."

Jan turned to Mark and said, "She thinks she is funny."

He grinned. "Well, if that's what she has to do to entertain herself, let's let her have her fun. We have better things to do with our time." Then before she knew it he had grabbed her and dipped her down and kissed her. Then he turned to them and said, "Meet you at Red Lobster at 6:00." As he pulled her by the hand out of the room, Jan looked at Casey and said, "Eat your heart out."

Exactly one week later, the last day of school had arrived. After her kids had been loaded on the buses, Jan walked back to her room. As always when the last day of school was over, her room always seemed extra quiet. It was almost like a ghost town, with only the echoes of her class that would never again form as a group under her charge. This year was extra sad because all her teaching materials were packed away in boxes in one corner of her room, waiting for the movers to arrive on Monday morning.

She walked across the room and went to erase her white board for the last time. Just as she finished, she looked up and realized that Mark was standing in the doorway watching her.

"Hi," she smiled. Then she realized that he was holding some fresh lilies in his hand and what appeared to be a card in another.

He walked over to her and handed the car and flowers to her. "What is this?" she asked.

"Just a little thank you for being so wonderful to Kylie," he answered.

"But she brought me that pretty bag and wrote that really sweet card."

"That was from her," he told her. "This is from me. If you don't want them I could take them down the hall to Casey."

She laughed. "Don't you dare." She set the flowers down and opened the card. The words written on it were not what she expected.

Jan,

I have spent at least an hour trying to think of some nice romantic way to express myself, and I just couldn't come up with any better way than just saying it.

"Jan, I love you. Will you please move in with me?"

She looked up at his eyes full of love and didn't say a word. Instead she just walked over to her desk, and spent a moment digging through the gifts her students had given her earlier. When she found the stationary with her name on it, she pulled a piece of the paper out of the box. She picked up a pen, and spent a few seconds writing on the page. Then she walked back to him and handed him the paper. He took it from her and looked at it.

Mark,

I tried to find the right words, but all I could come up with was,

"I love you. Yes, I will move in with you. Thank you for asking."

He grinned and looked at her. Then without a word, they began kissing. After a minute they stopped, and he looked at her without letting go of her.

"I thought you didn't like me kissing you at school," he said.

She shrugged. "School's out," she said and then lowered her voice before continuing. "I think the gigs up. Most of the people around here are on to us." She kissed him again and then said, "Let's go find the girls and tell them our news. Did you see Kylie when you came in?"

"I called Penny to come and get her," he said. "I told them we wanted to talk to them. Both of their radars are up. I had to send them to get pizza to distract them."

"All right then," she said. "Let's go home."

"Let's," he answered. He helped her gather up her things and Jan took one last look around the room and smiled at the thought of all kinds of new beginnings.

A few minutes later, the two of them walked into the kitchen of Mark's house, where

Weddings and Funerals

they found Penny and Kylie eating pizza and giggling.

"Thanks for waiting for us," Mark said.

"Sorry," Penny said. "We were hungry. What did you want to talk to us about?"

"Yeah," Kylie said. "What?"

"Well," Mark began. "We have a couple of pieces of news. Jan, why don't you tell them the first one."

She looked at him. "Which news is first?"

He shrugged. "Your choice."

"I may have to think about it," she said.

"Jan!" Penny said. "Please!"

"All right," Jan laughed. "I will tell you. One week from tomorrow, the four of us are flying to Fort Lauderdale to spend a week at Penny's Aunt Barb's house."

"Is that the house with the pool and the beach, and where you got the shells to make the necklaces?" Kylie asked with delight.

"It certainly is," Jan answered. "Isn't that exciting? It's going to be a lot of fun."

"Yes, it is exciting," Penny said. "What is the other news?"

Again, Mark and Jan exchanged looks. He took a moment and then started to speak. "We had some news that we wanted to share with you, but then we decided that we don't need to just tell you but ask you how you feel about this. So now is the time to be honest about your feelings."

"Feelings about what?" Kylie wanted to know.

Mark looked at his daughter and smiled. "When I first looked at this house a couple of months ago, Jan was with me. I wanted to buy the house, but first I asked her if she and Penny would move in with me."

"Did she say yes?" Kylie asked.

"Well," Mark began, "she said that she didn't want to do that while you were still in her class, because she didn't want to run the risk of causing you problems with the other kids. She said she wanted me to ask her again when school was out."

"School was out today, so did you ask her again?" Penny said.

Mark grinned. "Yes, I did."

"What did she say?" Kylie was about to pop with excitement.

"She said yes," he told her, "but we want to know how you the two of you feel about this."

Kylie gave him a look that she couldn't believe he was even asking her the question.

"Are you kidding?" she asked. "Do you know how long I have wanted to be a part of a real family, with a mom and a dad and a sister? I wanted that even when my mom was still alive." She was quiet for a moment and then she continued. "It didn't work out the way I thought it would, but I think this may be even better." She looked up at Jan and then asked another question.

"Do I have to keep calling you Miss Burke now that school is out?"

"No," Jan answered. "What do you want to call me?"

The child thought for a moment. "I think I would like to call you Jan."

Jan smiled at her. "That would be fine."

"Ok," Mark said. "Kylie gives her stamp of approval." He looked over at Penny.

"Honey, you have been through a lot of changes in the last year. We want to be sure that you are all right with all of this and with moving again."

Penny wiped a tear from her eye. "I couldn't have said it better than Kylie did. I want a family too. I love all you guys so much."

Mark smiled. "We love you too."

"Yes, we do," Jan echoed.

"I have question too," Penny said.

"What is that?" Mark asked.

Penny looked a little sheepish. "Can I have the room in the basement?"

Now Mark and Jan laughed together. "We've already talked about that," Jan told her. "It's all yours."

"Daddy, when are they moving in?" Kylie wanted to know.

Mark sighed and looked at Jan. "We haven't really discussed that yet."

"I have given my notice on the townhouse," Jan said. "I have to be out by July 1st."

Kylie looked horrified. "That long?" she asked. "Why can't you start living here right now?"

Mark and Jan looked at each other, not sure how to handle the situation. Finally, he said, "I guess you two could go and get enough clothes and things for the weekend. We do have an extra bed upstairs that Penny could sleep in until we could move her bed here. Can we get by until after we get back from Florida?"

She smiled knowing that his motivation was not entirely because he wanted to please his daughter. He wanted to start their life together too. She had no argument, because she felt the same way.

"I think we can do that," she said.

"Yay," Kylie answered.

"Let me have some of that pizza," Mark told her. He reached for a piece, and so did Jan.

"Oh no," Kylie suddenly said.

"What?" Jan asked.

"Weren't we supposed to go to Jim and Casey's tonight for Casey's birthday party?"

Mark and Jan both froze with their pizza in midair. They looked at each other and Jan said, "Put the pizza down. Let's go family, and let's not tell Casey that we forgot and ordered pizza. We'll never hear the end of it."

Thirty minutes later, the four of them entered the Craven's house where quite a few people were already there.

"I was beginning to wonder about you guys," Casey said.

Before Mark or Jan could speak up, Kylie piped up and said, "Sorry, we were busy talking about our family trip to Florida."

"Oh, you are a family now?" Casey asked.

"Yes," Kylie said. "Jan and Penny just moved in with us."

Chapter Ten

By the end of the next week, Mark and Jan were exhausted and ready for a vacation. Their initial plan was to save the major part of the move until they returned from Florida, but after they started cleaning and moving small items, one thing led to another, and in between Jan's two days of required professional work and Mark's three funerals, the move was complete. Jim took some time from his administrative duties to help move the furniture. Jan gave Penny her old bed and the other furniture from the townhouse was placed in the basement. Penny was beside herself. "It's like I have my own little apartment," she laughed. Jan couldn't remember Penny showing this much enthusiasm since she had known the child.

Jan had also made time to take the two girls shopping for summer clothes for the trip. She also took the liberty of going through Mark's clothes to see if he needed anything new. She wasn't sure how he would feel about that, but he seemed very appreciative. It was then that she realized that if Mark had any shortcomings, it was in the domestic area. He was neat and didn't seem to mind cleaning, but when it came to the kitchen and laundry room, he was close to helpless. She wondered just exactly how he and Kylie always seemed to look so fresh and clean. Curiosity got the better of her, so she asked him. He then confessed to her that he managed that through a good dry cleaner, Pearl, and his mother. When his luck ran out on those two, he hired a woman to come in a couple of mornings a week and do his laundry, and some of the heavier cleaning. Jan was always in school when this occurred, so she had never noticed. Then just a week before school was out the woman's husband got a new job in

Columbus, so Mark was once again at a loss. Jan looked at him, laughed and teased him about how she now knew the real reason that he wanted her to move in. Secretly she didn't mind, cooking for him and doing his laundry. It gave her a sense of joy, and anything she did for him, she felt that got back threefold, because she felt so loved by him.

Another thing that Jan noticed that week was that Penny was spending more time than usual texting on her phone, especially during the mornings and afternoon, and not so much at night. When she finally questioned her about it, the girl lit up like a Christmas tree.

"I have been talking to this guy," she said. "He works at Pizza Hut most nights, so that's why I text him more during the day."

Jan thought for a moment and then decided it was time to be a parent. "Does he go to school?" she asked.

"Yes," Jan answered. "He's in my class. His name is Charlie Miller. He plays football. I'm sure Jim knows him."

After taking an inward sigh of relief that this was a local high school boy and not some unknown from cyber space, Jan thought back to last fall and remembered that name from the football team.

"I know we were all going out to eat with the Cravens on Friday night, but Charlie asked me to go to the movies. Do you care if I go?"

Jan thought for a moment before she answered. "I guess not. What time would you be going?"

"He has to work until five-thirty, so he is just going to make it here by six-thirty, so we can make the movie that starts at seven.," she explained.

"We'll be gone by then," Jan told her, "but we would like to meet him when you come back."

"Sure," Jan said. "I want you to meet him. He's really a nice guy. We won't be out late. He has an eleven-thirty curfew too. I think his parents are...not exactly strict, but...kind of aware and on top of things. Do you know what I mean?"

"I do," Jan answered, "and I like the sound of that."

On Friday night, Mark and Jan loaded her car with their luggage, and then headed toward the restaurant in Mark's truck, leaving Penny waiting on her date.

There weren't any tables big enough for all of them available, so they allowed the three children the privilege of sitting by themselves at a booth across from them.

After they all placed their orders, Casey told Jim about Penny's date, and that he was a football player.

"What's his name?" Jim asked.

"Charlie Miller," she told him.

Jim smiled. "No kidding?" he said.

"Is that a good thing?" Marked wanted to know.

"Charlie is a great kid," he said. "One of my all-time favorites. He comes from a really good family."

"Well, Penny told me that his parents were a little strict. He has an eleven-thirty curfew, the same as hers. I think he works a lot too."

Jim nodded. "I think it is a necessity. His father was a construction worker. A few years ago, he was involved in an accident at work and broke his back. He was off work for a long time. His mother works at a bank somewhere. Now I think his father, sells cars at a big dealership in Lexington. They have several kids, and Charlie is the oldest, I believe. His parents make about enough to get by, but he needs to work for anything he wants. As sad as that is, that kind of adversity builds character."

"It certainly does," Mark agreed. Then he thought for a moment. "I remember him from last fall. He played cornerback, didn't he?"

"He did," Jim answered, "and he played some safety, but he's not a bad field goal kicker. Jerrod Terrell graduated, so I think Mr. Miller just may get promoted."

"Jim?" Casey said in a voice that sounded cautious.

"Yes, dear?"

"You are no longer the coach, honey. You are the principal now."

Jan watched this little scene play out, and soon realized by the look on Mark's face, he knew something that she didn't.

Weddings and Funerals

Jim was quiet for a minute and then he said, "We have one more guy to interview next week. He's not very experienced, so I'm not sure about him."

"And if you don't hire him, what happens?" Casey asked, but all four of them knew the answer.

Jim looked directly at his wife. "Then I will coach one more year. That's it. I swear. These seniors are my boys. I really want to coach them one more year."

"Honey, I know how much your boys mean to you," Casey said quietly, "but we are having a baby in December. That's all that worries me."

"I understand why you are concerned," he said, "but trust me, I will be there for you. The season will be over long before the baby arrives."

"What if you make the state playoffs again?" she wanted to know.

Jim shook his head. "It's not going to happen. We don't have the muscle for that this year. I do have three seniors that have a possibility of getting scholarships, though. I am putting out feelers to some of my scouting contacts. The boys don't know about that. I never want them to know. It puts too much pressure on them."

"Is Charlie one of those three?" Jan asked.

"He is number one on my list," Jim said. "He deserves a break."

A few hours later, the group had returned to Marks and Jan's house. They had just finished playing a few rounds of cards when they heard the front door opening. All four of them looked up. Penny came in first. She was smiling, and Jan could tell immediately that she had a good time. Charlie came in behind her. He was a tall boy with sandy brown hair that looked as if it had been recently been cut into one of those youthful styles where the hair was short everywhere but on top. Like so many young men, he was sporting a beard that resembled a five o'clock shadow.

Penny introduced him to Mark, Jan, and Casey and then said, "I guess you know this guy," referring to Jim.

Charlie smiled. "I sure do. How's it going coach?"

Jim grinned at his player. "Hey Charlie. Are you staying off the Dew?"

Charlie laughed, and his face turned slightly red. "Pretty much," he said.

Jim laughed and looked at the others. "Our boy here has one bad habit. He loves Mountain Dew. I used to threaten to search his bag. I always told him if I caught him drinking that crap that he had to run extra laps." Jim then looked at Penny with an ornery grin. "Mountain Dew probably goes really well with popcorn doesn't it, Penny?"

Now her face turned red. "I don't know. We had popcorn, but I don't remember…" She looked at Casey and said, "Your husband is evil, isn't he?"

"Most definitely," she answered.

Charlie decided to change the subject. "Coach have you found your replacement yet?"

Jim looked at him. "No, we haven't."

"Couldn't you just coach one more year?" Charlie asked.

Jim looked at the boy and then finally glanced at his wife, before answering. "I would say that is a good possibility, but you need to keep that to yourself. Got it?"

"Got it," he said. Then he looked at Mark. "Haven't we met before?"

"I was just thinking the same thing," Mark said, "but I see so many people, especially at the funeral home."

"Oh yeah," Charlie said. "I remember you from my great grandparents' funeral. They were the ones that died from the gas leak."

"That's right," Mark answered. "I remember you being there. You were one of the pallbearers."

"Yeah, I was," Charlie told him. "The two of them dying together like that was hard for my family, but they were so old, and not well, and then I guess they both had awful colds. Then the gas leak just finished them. At least they went together, and neither was left without the other one."

Something rang a bell with Jan. *"They both had awful colds."* Something about that statement bothered her, but she didn't know what exactly. Then her attention was drawn away when Charlie announced that he needed to get home. He shook Mark and Jim's hand and then Penny said she would walk him out.

"I hope this isn't a long drawn out goodnight," Jim said. "I am ready to go home, and it would probably be tacky to go out before she comes back."

"I'll get the kids," Casey said. She was returning with her kids in tow when Penny reentered the room. Jim picked up a sleepy looking Ty and started toward the door. As he passed Penny, he stopped and said, "Charlie's my boy. Treat him right."

Penny smiled and said, "I will, Jim. He's a nice guy."

"Yes, he is. Good night all. Have a great trip," Jim said as he walked out the door. Casey echoed the same wish and followed him leading Lisa by the hand.

Mark locked the door behind him and turned and looked at his three girls. "We have an early flight tomorrow. I think we all need to head off to bed."

"I agree," Jan said.

After the two girls said good night, Jan turned to Mark and said, "Jim has no intention of giving up the coaching position, does he?"

Mark looked at her, laughed and said, "Nope."

"And Casey has known that all along, hasn't she?"

"Yep."

Thirty minutes later, they were all asleep and the car parked down the street in the dark, drove off into the night."

By two o'clock the next afternoon, Mark found himself in the situation that he had looked forward to for the last week. The five of them had enjoyed a great lunch of chicken wraps and homemade potato chips. The group had then taken a long walk on the beach, where Kylie was thrilled with her first ocean experience. Now Penny and Kylie were splashing around in the pool, Barb and Jan were having a conversation in the covered part of the patio, and he was sitting in a comfortable recliner in the sun, drifting in and out of sleep. "It doesn't get much better than this," he thought. Eventually, the conversation between the two women began to capture his attention.

"I have been thinking for a while that it seems like in the last few months that a lot of people in our area having been dying in their sleep, and it always seems that the cause is declared natural causes," Jan was telling Barb. "Then it's just like everybody says, 'Oh that's too bad.' And then it's forgotten until the next one."

"How many people are your talking about?" Barb asked her.

Without looking up, Mark could tell that Jan was thinking. "Let's see," she began. "Marsha Collins, Aaron Fischer, Joe and Sue, Charlie's grandparents, and now Doug Lawrence. I guess that makes seven since last September."

Feeling that the sun was becoming a little too warm, Mark rose from his recliner and joined the two women at the table."

She looked at him and smiled. "Nap over?" she asked.

"It's getting a little warm for laying in the sun," he told them. Then he poured himself a glass of lemonade from the pitcher on the table.

As she looked him, his thoughts became clear to her. "You heard what I was saying, and you are about to tell me that I have an overactive imagination, aren't you?"

"Yep," he said. "However, from your point of view, I understand why you might think the situation strange. I would like to give you another perspective to consider, though. The first person on your list died when?"

"Marsha Collins died around the first of September," Jan told him.

Mark thought for a moment and took a swig of his lemonade. "That was about nine months ago. In my business, I deal with ten to twelve deaths a month, on average. That means I have probably dealt with around one hundred deaths since Marsh Collins died. People die in all sorts of ways; some that you probably wouldn't even imagine. There are hundreds of common diseases, syndromes, and conditions that people die of, and then there are all kinds of outside forces that can cause people to die. When you look at it that way, your number of seven seems a lot smaller, doesn't it?"

Jan nodded. "I see what you are saying," she said. "The thing that is bothering me is something else."

"What?" he asked.

"Last night, Charlie said that his grandparents both had very bad colds before they died," she told him. "I know that is not strange, but this bell went off in my head, and I couldn't figure out why. Then on the plane this morning, it came to me."

Mark leaned back in his chair. Jan couldn't tell by the look on his face if he was going to take her serious or not. "What came to you?" he wanted to know.

"Aaron Fischer and Doug Lawrence also had bad colds just before they died," she said.

"That's four out of one hundred," he said. "Interesting, but purely coincidence. Lots of people get colds."

At this point Barb spoke up and added to the conversation. "I just thought of something that adds to your coincidence," she said.

Mark and Jan both looked at her. "When Penny was here last spring, and we were going through some of her parents' things, she mentioned something to me. I didn't think much of it at the time, but after listening to this conversation, I'm going to share this with you."

"What?" Jan asked.

"She told me that her father and mother both had terrible colds when they left Bellville."

Jan looked at Mark to see if he was going to respond. He thought for a moment and then said, "Six people out of at least one hundred people that died in the last nine months had colds. Interesting, but not alarming. What are you thinking, Jan? There can't be a connection. People get colds all the time. People die all the time. It happens. You know I am sure that I have buried other people that died in their sleep that didn't have colds. You could spend a lot of time studying this and come up with nothing. Let it go."

"All right," she said, smiling. "You are right," she said. "I'll let it go. This is our vacation, but if someone were to tell me that Marsha Collins had a cold before she died, that would freak me out."

"Marsha Collins didn't have a cold before she died," Penny said, as she walked up to the table and took a drink from the glass she had left on the table earlier. "I remember the last night she coached us."

"Hmm," Mark said, with a twinkle in his eye.

"She was in a bad mood that night," she told them. "I think she had a problem with some sort of pills. Chrissy and I saw her take quite a few that night. Then she chewed poor Lizzie out in front of everybody. It was her parents that complained to the board, and they told them about how we saw her taking pills. Lizzie's mom told Chrissy's mom that Marsha claimed to the superintendent that she had an infected tooth and couldn't get an appointment with the dentist. Apparently, he didn't buy it, because he forced her to resign, and then Jan was hired, and everybody was happy." She shot Jan a smile and then turned to Kylie. "Come on, I'll show you how to dive off the board."

As the girls walked away, Mark looked at Jan and grinned. "What does that do to your theory?"

She narrowed her eyes at him. "I'm not sure," she said. "I'll have to study on that and get back to you."

"You do that," he said. "In the meantime, I am going to join the girls in the pool." He ruffled her hair, as he stood and followed the girls into the pool.

Barb and Jan watched him dive into the pool and begin encouraging Kylie who was standing nervously on the diving board.

Turning to Jan, Barb smiled and said, "I think he's a keeper."

"I think you are right," Jan told her. "At first I kept waiting to see if some undesirable flaw in him was going to present itself, but it hasn't, so now I am just enjoying life with him."

"Is there a wedding in your future?" Barb asked her. "Have you put the past behind you?"

Jan looked back over toward the pool before she spoke. "I have put Derek completely behind me, with no regrets, but the trauma of the wedding and the aftermath of the events that followed it still haunt me sometimes. Mark knows that, and he is very understanding. I think that if and when we get married, it will be something very quiet and simple."

"There is nothing wrong with that," Barb said. "big weddings can be overrated and a waste of time and money."

Jan laughed. "Agreed," she said. "What about you, Barb? You seem to be doing very well. Are you still getting out of the house some?"

Barb smiled, and her eyes almost seemed to twinkle. "Yes, I am, and I have some big news."

"What is that?" Jan wanted to know.

"I have decided to buy a car and I am preparing to take the test to get a new driver's license."

"Barb, that's wonderful," Jan said with surprise. "I had no idea that you were making that much progress."

"I am still not completely sure," she said, "but my therapist has encouraged me to go and ahead and purchase the car and get the license, but she told me that there is no time scale. I could take the next step forward when I am ready. Jan, can I share something with you in complete confidence?"

"Of course," Jan answered.

"I have a very important goal in mind," Barb told her. She paused and seemed to be very close to tears. "I want to be at Penny's graduation. I feel very strongly that I need to be there for Joe and Sue, and mostly for Penny."

Jan was so touched by Barb's words that tears came to her own eyes. "I think that's a wonderful goal, Barb. I won't say anything, but I will be pulling for you."

The vacation turned out to be everything Mark and Jan hoped for. They swam in the pool every day and walked on the beach at morning and at night. On Tuesday they took the girls parasailing. Barb declined to go with them, saying that she had an appointment. Jan guessed that the appointment was with her therapist. The girls were thrilled with the experience. The two of them went up side by side and then watched from the boat as Mark and Jan went up together. The group returned sun and windburned, but happy.

Barb surprised them on Thursday with a private airboat tour of the Everglades. She surprised them even more by joining them. The trip was thrilling. They were able to see lots of beautiful wildlife, including quite a few alligators. On the way home, they stopped at a local seafood restaurant. The owners were friends of Barbs and they provided them with a semi-private room and lots of special service.

On Friday morning, Mark and Jan got up early so they could walk out on the beach and watch the sunrise. After finding a comfortable spot in the sand they sat side by side, quietly staring at the horizon which was slowly beginning to lighten.

"A penny for your thoughts," Mark said.

"Oh, lots of things," she told him. "I was thinking about the past the present, and the future. Then I was thinking about how happy I am for Jim and Casey. They were so excited when they called to tell us that the baby is a boy."

He laughed. "That's a lot of thoughts in a short amount of time."

She shrugged and giggled. "One thought leads to another."

"I guess women's minds work differently than men's."

"I imagine they do," she said.

They were quiet for a few more moments, and then she spoke again. "Mark?'

"Yes?"

"Would you like to have a son someday?"

He didn't answer immediately. Then he looked at her and said, "Was that an offer?"

She giggled. "Maybe in a sense. I guess what I want to know is if you want to have more children someday."

Looking down at her, he put his arm around her and kissed her on the head. "I guess we have never really talked about it in so many words, but yes, Jan, I very much want to have more children. What about you? Do you want to have children?"

She moved a little closer to him and looked up at him. "Yes," she said. "I want that very much."

He leaned down and began to kiss her. The two of them sat on the sand kissing for a while. Eventually they looked up and noticed that the sun had risen completely.

"Could that be a sign?" he asked her.

"It could be," she said. "As far as having children, aren't we getting the cart a little ahead of the horse?"

He smiled and laughed a little. "I think maybe we are. I am getting hungry. Are you ready to go in and have some breakfast?"

"Let's go," she said. As they walked back to the house, hand in hand, Jan realized something. She was ready; ready to marry this man, and ready to have his children. However, a question was beginning to form in her mind. Was he ready?

On Friday night, Mark and Jan decided that a date night was in order. At Barb's suggestion, they chose to go on a sunset dinner cruise. The thought occurred to Jan that for someone who rarely left her home, Barb certainly was knowledgeable about fun things to do in the area.

The cruise was an excellent choice. After watching a gorgeous sunset, they enjoyed a delicious dinner, followed by dancing under the stars on the top deck of the cruise ship. It was late when they returned to the house and the other three had already gone to bed. They quietly entered their room where they made their most passionate love yet. Later Jan lay curled up in

Mark's arms listening to the even sound of his breathing as he slept.

She thought about their conversation the morning before. It was clear that he was interested in having a larger family, but when she mentioned getting the cart before the horse; referring to marriage, he agreed, but didn't seem to want to continue the discussion. It seemed clear to her that he loved her. He constantly told her that he did, and he seemed very happy with their situation. She thought about it for a little bit longer, yawned and then decided that once again she was over analyzing a situation. They had just moved in together and maybe he was being wise enough to realize that they everyone in this situation needed time to adjust. She yawned again and then drifted off to sleep; not knowing anything until morning.

Saturday was their last day in Florida. They decided to spend the day at the pool and on the beach. Barb planned to cook them a farewell dinner. She took requests for menu ideas. Mark and Jan voted for shrimp, Penny asked for crab legs, and Kylie wanted pizza. Barb thought over and decided that she could manage all three requests. Jan offered to go to the market for her, and Barb agreed, but then decided to go with her.

It was a fun outing. They first went to a small market to get the staples and then Barb directed Jan to drive to a seafood shop close to the water. It was one of those fishy smelling places that sold seafood right off the boats.

When they returned, Kylie was excited because she had finally found a conch shell after searching all week. It wasn't very large, and one end was partly broken off, but it was a treasure nevertheless.

They had lunch on the patio, and then Barb went to work in the kitchen cleaning shrimp, while the other four spent time playing in the pool.

A while later, Jan left the pool, dressed, and went to help Barb with dinner. Mark went to the pool recliner for his daily nap. Kylie wandered off to her room. Jan assumed that she was going to read for a while.

Penny found her own recliner and went to work on her phone. Jan guessed that she was texting Charlie. Smiling at the sight, she expressed to Barb how nice it was to see Penny so happy.

Barb agreed and then brought up another subject that had been dancing around the outskirts of Jan's mind and apparently around Mark's because he had broached the subject with her the night before.

"If this goes much further, should you have *'the talk'* with Penny?" Barb asked her.

Jan smiled at her. "Mark and I were discussing that last night," she said. "I think I am going to take care of that shortly after we get home."

"That's probably a good idea," Barb told her, "but Penny is a pretty level-headed girl. I don't see her doing anything foolish."

Jan laughed. "I agree, but she is very infatuated with him. She wouldn't be the first young girl to do something *'foolish'* in the name of love. I just want to keep the lines of communication open and help her make good decisions. The good thing is that he works quite a few evenings a week and he plays football. That takes up a good bit of his time. Then his parents are on the strict side. His curfew is 11:30 and he is only allowed to go out on dates two nights a week. The high school football coach is a good friend of ours and he says that Charlie is a really good kid."

"I am happy that she is able to have some remnant of a teenage life," Barb said. "Since school's out she isn't seeing the counselor, is she?"

"No," Jan answered. "I offered to set up an appointment with an outside counselor, but she said that she would be all right for the summer. I do think that sometimes she goes to her room and cries. I think that's all right. She needs to express her grief. Overall, I think she is doing well. Her new romance and our move into Mark's house have been happy distractions for her."

"I would agree," Barb told her. "I think it has been good for all of you. The four of you seem to fit well as a family. Penny and Kylie have really bonded, haven't they?"

"Yes," Jan answered with a smile, "they have both found the sister they always wanted."

Later that evening, the five of them sat down to their dinner of shrimp, crab legs and pizza. It was an enjoyable meal with lots of chatter and laughter. Kylie was teasing Penny about Charlie and being *"in love"*. Penny was telling Kylie that her day would come.

Later that evening, they took one last walk on the beach. The girls ran ahead and were jumping in and out of the edge of the waves. Mark and Jan walked more slowly holding hands. Jan looked at the sinking sun with all the beautiful late evening colors surrounding it and realized that her heart was full. Their vacation was ending, but their new life was beginning. She smiled as she thought how disappointing it would be if they were going home and she and Penny had to return to the townhouse. That was not the case though. They had many things to do when they returned. Jan needed to give the townhouse its finally cleaning. She and Mark planned to sit down and organize their finances. They also planned to have a discussion with the girls about rules, expectations, and chores. It was time to think about next year's flag team too. Tryouts had been held the first of May to fill the spots left by last year's seniors. Quite a few girls had signed up for the tryouts, so to be fair, Jan had organized a selection committee. She was planning a camp for the girls in July, so she had a lot to do to get it organized. Her list of things to do was long and the weeks ahead promised to be busy, but she looked forward to every minute of it.

She looked up at Mark, who was smiling and watching the girls. This morning they had both woken up early again. They talked about going out and watching the sunrise again, but in the end, they decided that they would rather stay in bed and make love leisurely. Afterwards they both fell back asleep and were the last ones up. Remembering the warmth of their lovemaking, she squeezed his hand without thinking about it. He looked down at her and smiled, as if he were reading her mind. Life was good.

Chapter Eleven

This time as the wheels of the plane touched down in Lexington, Jan couldn't help but think about how much her life had changed since the last time she had returned from Florida. As they walked through the terminal toward the baggage claim, Jan was holding Kylie's hand. Mark and Penny were following right behind her, and there was a warm wonderful feeling of family that seemed to surround them.

An hour later, they were home, where the girls immediately dispersed to their rooms. Mark sat at the table going through the mail, that one of the funeral home workers had collected and left on the porch that morning. Jan sat across from him, making a shopping list.

It was quiet for a few minutes, until both Penny and Kylie appeared in the kitchen at almost the same time. Penny wanted to know if it was all right if Charlie came over for a few minutes before he went to work. Mark and Jan gave each other a short look, and then Jan consented, but requested that they stay upstairs. They were welcome to sit alone in the family room, but the rule was going to remain that no boys would be allowed downstairs. Penny happily agreed with total acceptance of this rule. Kylie's request much simpler. She wanted to use a phone to call Sue Ann and Lisa. Mark gave her his phone and she quickly disappeared again.

Jan went to the grocery and the drug store, and when she returned, Charlie was just leaving, and Mark was getting ready to go to the funeral home to check on some things. She smiled to herself, thinking that this was her new norm.

Later that night, as they were getting ready to go to bed, Mark asked Jan if she was planning on talking to Penny soon.

"I found an opportunity to do that earlier when we were working on laundry in the basement," Jan told him.

"How did that go?" he asked.

"Good," she answered. "She assured me that they have already discussed sex. They both agree that their futures are too important to risk ruining them by doing something stupid."

"Really?" Mark asked.

"That's what she told me," Jan said, "but she promised me that if anything changed, she would come to me."

Mark thought for a moment and then said, "I guess we can't get too hypocritical when we are living together."

"I thought about that," she told him, "but we are adults. Hopefully we can deal with our situations better than star struck teenagers, and if we would slip up and got pregnant, we are in a position to be responsible about it."

Mark finished brushing his teeth, spit in the sink, and wiped his mouth with a towel. "Are you trying to tell me something?" he wanted to know.

"Yes," she said, and tried not laugh as she thought she saw about half the blood drain out of his face.

She giggled. "Calm down. What I am trying to tell you is that there is a difference in the two situations. That's all."

He stared at her for a moment before he spoke. "Jan, I swear, sometimes, you are just evil," he told her as he headed into the bedroom.

She followed him, and then decided to just ask the question that was pressing her mind. "Mark?" she said as she slid into bed next to him.

"What?" he asked.

She took a moment to form her question, and as she did, he seemed to sense the fact that this was important, so he sat up and gave her his full attention.

"If I had been trying to tell you that I was pregnant, would you have been upset?" she asked him.

He stared at her for a moment as if he were trying to contemplate either the question or his answer. After a minute, he spoke. "I would have been a little stunned, but once I got over the shock, I think I might have been excited. Now I could ask you the same question. Would you be upset?"

"Not totally," she said. "I want very much to have your children, like we talked about, but I would prefer to be married first."

"But you are not ready to be married, though, are you?" he asked.

She stared at him, somewhat confused. "Why do you say that?" she wanted to know.

Now he was somewhat confused. "When we were sitting on the beach, on the morning we watched the sunrise, you talked about getting the cart before the horse. I took that to mean that you weren't ready yet. After all you've been through, I thought you needed some space, so I let it go."

"Let it go?"

He looked at her and smiled. "I was giving some serious thought to proposing to you that morning, but then after our conversation, I thought maybe it was too soon."

She sighed. "Mark, I think we have a communication problem."

He raised his eyebrows, as she continued. "The reason I said that about the cart was that I was just trying to express the fact that I wanted to be married first. I'm sorry. Maybe I should have been a little clearer about that. When you didn't respond, I wondered if maybe you weren't ready."

"So, you are saying that you are ready to get married?" Her only response was to smile and slowly nod. Then after a minute she asked, "And you?"

He nodded back at her. "I would marry you tomorrow."

She laughed. "Well, I don't think we can manage that, but there is one thing I am struggling with."

"You don't want a wedding, do you?" he asked.

She shook her head. "Certainly not a big one," she said. "My first choice would be total elopement. Just run away and do it, but I realize that would cause problems."

"Such as?"

"The girls? They would be upset. And what about your parents? They would be heartbroken. Oh, can you imagine trying to tell Casey that we got married behind her back?"

He laughed out loud. "Yeah she would have a hissy that would wake the dead." He was quiet for a moment and then asked, "Would you be open to something small with maybe just the girls, Mom and Dad, and Jim and Casey?"

"I think that we could work something like that out," she told him. "We can start planning that as soon as we get engaged."

He frowned as if he were confused, then realization dawned on him. "All right then," he said now smiling. "That's what we will do. I love you, Jan."

"I love you too," she said, just as he was leaning forward to kiss her.

The next few days found Mark and Jan very busy, and the subject of marriage did not come up again. Jan wasn't overly concerned because she that both funeral homes were busy and with two of the morticians on vacation, so Mark found himself working back and forth between the two places. Jan had her first flag team practices. Kylie happily followed along and the girls accepted her as their mascot. She easily learned the routines with the older girls. By Friday afternoon, things had calmed down. Surprisingly, all four of them were having breakfast at the same time. They were eating waffles and talking about everything that had happened during the week and what each of them planned to do with their weekend.

Suddenly, Kylie got a strange look on her face and said, "Oh no. I completely forgot."

"Forgot what, honey?" Jan asked.

Kylie looked at her father sheepishly. "Remember when you let me us your phone to call my friends the day we got back from Florida?" Mark nodded.

"While I was talking to Lisa, Grandma called."

"What did she say?"

"She said that she and Grandpa were coming to visit," Kylie said in a quiet voice.

"Oh really," Mark said, "and when are they coming?"

"Is today Friday?" she asked.

"Yes," Mark answered.

"Then they are coming tonight," she said, in a quiet voice. "She said to tell you to call if it was a problem. I promised I would tell you, but I forgot. I am sorry."

Mark looked up and saw that Jan and Penny were trying not to laugh. He picked up his phone and went into the living room. Kylie looked at the other two. "Do you think I'm in trouble?"

Jan smiled at her. "I don't think so, honey. It was an honest mistake; careless but honest."

Mark returned a few minutes later. "They are coming, and they will be here by five. She said that she wondered if Kylie forgot. Then she told me not to make a fuss, because they had reserved a room in a bed and breakfast. I told her that they didn't need to do that, but she said not to worry about it. She also said that they have a big surprise for us."

"That's interesting," Jan said. "I wonder what that is about."

"I don't know," Jim said, "but we'll find out tonight. We are all going out to dinner at Morelli's."

Jan raised her eyebrows. "Dad's favorite and his pick," Mark said.

"Well, that's nice," Jan said, "It should be fun. If they are going to be here in a couple hours, I need to get my Walmart shopping done. Kylie, do you want to go with me?"

"Sure," she said. "Let me get my shoes."

"Kylie," Mark stopped her in her tracks. "I know it was a mistake, but next time, write it down. Got it?"

"Got it," she grinned and was off to her room.

Twenty minutes later, they were gone, and Mark headed down to the basement. He found Penny sitting on the couch, watching TV. "I need to talk to you," he said. "I need your help."

Dinner at Morelli's was fun. At the last minute, Charlie was called off work because of overstaffing, so he was invited to join them. As soon as the seven of them, were led to their seats they noticed that the Cravens were seated in the same room. When the host realized that the two parties knew each, he kindly offered to pull some tables together and soon they were a party eleven.

When everyone was nearly finished with their dinners, Martin Owens tapped on a glass with his spoon to gain everyone's attention.

"I guess it's time to make our big announcement," he said. After getting a nod of approval from his wife, he continued. "The first news is that we sold our house in Knoxville."

The first reaction to his news was silence. Then Mark finally spoke. "Really?"

"Yes, really." Linda Owens answered.

"Where exactly do you plan to live?" Mark asked.

"Right here," Martin told him, "in Bellville."

"Whoa," Mark said. "You are moving here?"

"It's not a problem, is it?" Linda asked.

"Not at all," Mark said. "I think that's awesome."

"You have a whole family now," she continued. "We don't want to miss out on any of that. We had so much fun with the girls when they spent the weekend with us, that we decided that we needed to be in Bellville to be close to Mark and his family, so we listed the house and it sold two weeks ago. The closing is next week, so we decided that we better get up here and find a place to live." As she finished talking she looked at Jan, seemingly searching for approval.

Jan smiled at her with a glint of tears in her eyes. "That is wonderful news, Linda…My mother has been gone for several years, and it will be so nice to have Mark's mother living…" Then she got a little choked up, so she did not see Mark give Penny a very subtle signal.

"I have an announcement," she said. "I baked a cake this afternoon, and you are all invited back to the house to have some."

Everyone agreed that was a good idea, and soon they were all headed back to the house. Penny took Charlie, Kylie and Lisa into the kitchen to help her serve cake. It was a strawberry cream cheese cake with chocolate frosting decorated with little silver sequins. Penny and Charlie cut the cake and placed the pieces on plates and then handed them to one of the girls and told them who to serve them to.

When they returned the final time, Lisa said. "That's all, we don't need anymore."

Penny handed a plate to Kylie. "This is Jan's," she told her.

"Jan doesn't want any," Kylie said. "I'll take it."

"No," Penny said. "This is *Jan's cake.* Take it to her. I'll bring yours."

Kylie sighed in frustration. "She said that she is full and doesn't want any."

Penny and Charly exchanged a look. "Girls, that piece of cake is for *Jan*," Charlie said.

Suddenly Lisa's face lit up and she said, "Kylie just give her the cake. Come on." Then she walked out of the kitchen and Kylie followed her, although she was still perplexed. Penny rolled her eyes at Charlie and the two of them followed the girls.

In the living room, the adults were all chatting, and eating cake. The two girls walked over near Jan and Kylie handed the plate to her.

"Honey, I told you that I didn't want any cake," Jan said.

Kylie sighed. "It's *your* cake."

Jan looked confused. "Why is it *my* cake?"

"I don't know," the child answered, "but Charlie and Penny and Lisa all said that it is *your* cake, and that I should give it to you. So, please just take it."

Jan looked down at the plate that Kylie was holding. She took the cake, and suddenly realized that the room had become very quiet.

"Am I missing something?" she asked.

"Just eat your cake," Penny said, "I've never made one like this before. I want to know what you think." Then enjoying her little joke, she looked around the room. Charlie had turned almost clear around because he was trying not to laugh. Jim was trying to hide a laugh. Ty was oblivious to the whole situation and happily eating his cake. Casey still had not gotten it, so she looked confused. Martin Owens also seemed baffled, but Linda, who was sitting close to Jan, had completely caught on. She was smiling and was almost glowing. Mark looked up at Penny and the two of them exchanged a grin.

Jan finally shrugged and picked up the fork and cut into the cake. Just as she was about to lift the fork off her plate, she froze. At that exact same moment, Kylie gasped because she saw what Jan was looking at.

Smiling, Jan said, "I guess you were right, Kylie. This is *my* cake." She then set the fork down and picked the diamond ring out of the cake. Then taking the napkin that Kylie had handed her with the plate, she wiped the cake off it. Then she looked over at Mark. She set the cake down on the coffee table and they both stood at the same time. In a short amount of time, they were in each other's arms.

After a minute he took the ring from her and slid it on her finger.

"Aren't you going to ask her?" Casey asked.

Still keeping his arm around her, Jim looked at Casey and said. "We actually became unofficially engaged a few days ago. This just makes it official, doesn't it honey?"

"It does," she said through her tears, gave him a kiss on the cheek.

"Mark!" Casey was not going to let go of this.

He looked at Jan and grinned. "Jan, will you marry me, please?"

"Yes, Mark, I will marry you. Thank you for asking."

"You have to kiss now," Lisa suddenly piped up.

Mark looked at her and pretended to be annoyed. "Do I have to?" he asked in a phony whining voice.

Lisa gave him a look that she had obviously learned form her mother. "Yes, you do."

"All right," he said. "If I have to.

He leaned down and gave Jan a kiss that he hoped curled her toes. Then he looked at Lisa and asked, "Happy now?"

"Yes," she told him.

"So, did everyone know about this?"

"Penny and I worked this out this morning," he said. "She told Charlie, but they were the only ones.

Jan looked around. "You mean Jim and Casey just happened to be in the restaurant?"

"Oh," Mark said, "I forgot. That was a setup. He knew and the whole thing was set up ahead with the restaurant."

Casey narrowed her eyes at her husband. "You knew?"

"Yes, honey. I knew, but if I had told you, then you would have giggled the whole night and ruined the whole thing. Right?"

Casey sighed. "Yes, I probably would have. Anyway, I'm excited. So, have you made any plans yet?"

Mark and Jan looked at each other. "Not totally, but it will be something simple, and none of you will miss it. I promise," Jan told them all.

She looked around again and asked, "What about your Mom and Dad? Were they in on this?"

"No," Mark answered. "That was pure coincidence. I had this planned for tonight anyway and then us finding out that they were coming at the last minute, thanks to my ditzy daughter, worked out perfectly."

Kylie frowned and looked at Penny. "What does ditzy mean?" she asked.

"I'll explain it to you later," Penny said quietly.

"Well, let us see the ring," Casey said. Jan then spent the next few minutes, showing off her ring and receiving hugs. When Linda hugged her, she spoke quietly and said, "If there is anything at all I could do to help with the planning of the wedding, please let me know. If you go shopping for a dress, I would be happy to...I mean since ...your mother..." Jan felt her awkwardness and decided to rescue her. "That would be nice, Linda. Thank you. I will let you know, and I would be happy to help you get settled when you find a new home."

"Perfect," Linda answered with a smile. "I will let you know too."

Jan's heart was full. One short year ago, she was very much alone, worrying about how to avoid Casey's wedding. Now she had family and friends and was about to plan her own wedding.

Finally, she was able to look forward to her future with happiness and anticipation.

    Martin and Linda stayed in Bellville for nearly a week. On the third day of their home search, they found a small home in a new subdivision on the far side of town. The home was newly built and was ready for immediate possession. They left planning to return with a moving van in two weeks. After saying good-bye to his parents, Mark and Jan found a quiet moment to sit down and discuss marriage plans. After much discussion, they decided on a small wedding in their backyard on the last weekend of July. When the final plans were made, instead of feeling anxious like she thought that she would, Jan felt a mixture of relief and excitement that the plans were set.

    The next day Jan found some time to call Barb to tell her the news. She couldn't have been more excited.

    "Oh Jan," she began. "I couldn't be happier for you. You two are so perfect together. Have you made any plans yet?"

"Well," Jan told her, "as a matter of fact, we have. The wedding is going to be here in our back yard. It is going to be a very small simple ceremony." As soon as she spoke Jan felt bad. This was going to be a conflict for Barb. She was going to wish she could be there, but Jan didn't think there was any way that Barb could manage trip all the way here at this point in time.

"What is the date of the wedding?" Barb asked. Jan gave her the date and then waited for her response.

"Jan, I have some great news to tell you."

"What is that?" she asked.

"I bought the car, and I passed my driver's test."

"Oh, Barb that is wonderful news," Jan exclaimed.

"But that's not all," she continued. "I have been driving around in my car, and it's been very enjoyable."

"Oh, my goodness," Jan was stunned. "How exciting!"

"Then this morning, I did something that I never thought I would do again."

"What was that?" she asked.

"I drove to the drugstore," Barb said. "I sat in the parking lot for about twenty minutes trying to find my nerve, which I finally did."

Jan took a breath. "Did you go in?"

"I did," Barb told her, and Jan thought that she was close to tears. "I went in and shopped for about ten or fifteen minutes. It wasn't nearly as bad as I thought it would be. I haven't been this excited in a long time. I am going to take little trips every day and I am actually looking forward to it. Now you have called and told me this wonderful news." She paused a moment and then continued. "I just wish…Jan, I think there is a chance that I might be able to make it to your wedding. That is if you would like to have me."

Jan caught her breath. "Oh course. We would love to have you. I never dreamed that it would be possible. I guess you would fly?"

"Yes, I would. I think that the best thing for me to do would be to come in a private jet. Crowds are still one of the most frightening things to me and airports are full of crowds and commercial airliners can be well."

"I understand," Jan said, "Traveling is tough enough, but doing it alone can be stressful for anyone. We have plenty of room here. Penny's room is in the basement and there is an extra room down there. You could stay down there with her. You probably aren't ready for a hotel yet?"

"That sounds wonderful," Barb told her, "but don't say anything to the girls just yet. I need to be sure that I can work all of this out."

"I won't tell anyone except Mark," Jan said. "He will be so excited."

After they finished talking, Jan hung the phone just as Mark walked in. "You are not going to believe this," she told him with a smile.

On Wednesday night of the first week of July, Mark and Jan sat down to dinner with the two girls. Because of flag practices and funerals, it was the first time in several days that the four of them had been able to have dinner together. Jan noticed that Kylie was more quiet than usual, and she wasn't eating her taco, which was usually one of her favorites."

"Do you feel all right?" she asked her. "You're not coming down with something are you?"

"No, I'm not sick. I have been thinking about something," she said.

Mark looked at his daughter. "Are you worried about something?"

Kylie nodded.

"Would you like to talk to us about it?" he offered.

The child thought for a moment before she replied. "When you and Jan are married, she will be my stepmother, right?"

"Right," Mark told her.

"And since my real mother is gone, it will be almost like she is my real mother, don't you think?"

Mark decided to answer this question carefully. "I would imagine so," he said. "Does that bother you?"

"No," she answered. "I love Jan. It's just that…" she stopped as if she were having difficulty verbalizing her thoughts and feelings.

"What honey?" Mark asked her. "Just say whatever you are feeling.

"Mark?" Penny interjected. "I think I know what she is trying to say."

He nodded at her and Penny turned to Kylie. "Are you feeling guilty about loving Jan, almost like you are afraid of hurting your mother's feelings, even though she is gone?"

Kylie's eyes watered up a little, and she nodded.

"I know exactly what you are talking about," Penny told her. I have had those same feelings, so I have talked to Miss Carson about it and she said that I should not feel guilty about enjoying my life. What she told me to do was talk to my parents and tell them what is going on in my life. At first, I thought it seemed silly, but I tried it and it did make me feel better. It made me feel closer to them and then I realized that they would want me to be happy. So, when I tell them about good things going on, I get the feeling that they are glad that things are going well for me."

Kylie was completely absorbed in what Penny was telling her. "Do you mean you just start talking to them, out loud?"

Penny laughed. "Not exactly, but I do it more inside of my head; you know, like at night before I go to sleep. That works for me, but maybe we can think of something that works for you."

"I have an idea," Jan said. "You like to write Kylie. Maybe you could write your mother a letter."

Kylie seemed to turn this over in her mind, before responding. "I could that," she said. Then after another moment of thought, she turned to her father. "Mommy's grave is near where we used to live in Louisville, isn't it?"

Mark nodded. "You remember the funeral, don't you?"

"Yes," she answered. "I do. It isn't far is it?"

"It's about an hour away," he told her. "Did you want to go there?"

"Yes," she told him. "I want to write the letter and take it there, at least the first one. Could we all go? It would be like showing her my new family that I am going to write about." She looked at Jan and then at Penny. Both of them smiled at her and assured her that they would be happy to make the trip with her and her father.

When dinner was over, Kylie went off to her room, in a much happier mood. Jan received a phone call, and she went in the other room to take the call. It was Penny's turn to clean up, so she began to clear the table. Mark grabbed a few dishes and followed her into the kitchen. He set the dishes down on the counter, put his arm around her, and gave her a kiss on the head. "You're something. Do you know that?"

She smiled. "She and I are dealing with some of the same issues. We have talked about it before."

"Well you handled that very well. Thank you."

"Do you know what I have been thinking about?" she asked him.

"What?" he asked her.

"I think there are lots of kids who need help sorting out their feelings. Maybe that is what I want to do with my life."

"I think that is an excellent idea," he told her.

"I have been researching colleges that have good psychology schools," she said. "I will need to start applying soon."

He grinned at her. "That's a good idea. Research away before you choose UK." Then he walked off with a laugh.

Penny shook her head, smiled and began to load the dishwasher.

The following night Mark had a visitation at the funeral home. It was late when he returned. Jan was reading in bed, when came in. He walked in and hung his jacket in the closet.

"Hi," she said.

"Hi," he answered. "Where is Kylie?"

Jan got a funny look on her face. "She was in her room reading just a little while ago. Isn't she there now?"

"No," he said. "I looked in because I was going to tell her good night. She's not there or in the bathroom. The door was open when I went by. There was nobody downstairs either."

Jan thought for a moment and then said, "Wait here a minute."

A few short minutes later, she returned with a grin on her face. "I found her. She is down in Penny's room. They are both sound asleep on her bed. I didn't have the heart to bother either one of them."

Mark laughed. "I don't why that didn't occur to me. I think those two are counseling each other." He then told her about his conversation with Penny.

Jan nodded. "I know they have been talking. It really warms my heart. We have a couple of good girls."

"Yes, we do," he added as he stretched out on the bed next to her. "Just one thing worries me tough."

"What's that?" she asked.

"I am afraid that we will have three more girls, and I will be surrounded by a sea of pink and purple and I will spend the next twenty years stepping over barbies and pretend kitchen furniture."

"You want to step over a few hot wheels too?" she asked.

"Yep," he said. "I can only hope."

"Well. Don't worry. Maybe one of those girls will be a tomboy that likes hot wheels."

He thought for a moment and let out a small laugh. "That just might be fun too."

The plan was to visit Kylie's mother's grave on Saturday afternoon. Then they were going to stay in the area and have dinner and watch a firework's show. The four of them left in Mark's truck just after four. As the he backed the truck out of the garage, and into the street, not one of them noticed the car parked down the street. When Mark reached the corner, he stopped and then turned left, and the parked car pulled out and slowly followed, making the same left turn.

It took over an hour to get to the cemetery. Mark had remembered what a large place it was, and when they arrived he was glad that he had the foresight to research online exactly what part of the cemetery Tammy was buried in. It still took some time to walk from the car to the correct area and then locate the grave. The first thing Mark noticed was that the grave was very well kept and there were reasonably fresh-looking flowers on the grave.

Kylie stood quietly for a moment. She had the letter in a plastic bag in her hand. After a moment, Mark asked her if she wanted to be alone. She shook her head no and stepped forward is if she were going to set the letter on the headstone, but she stopped when all of them heard a woman's voice behind them.

"Kylie?"

All four of them turned around and Mark and Kylie both gasped.

Chapter Twelve

It took Mark a moment to regain his composure.

"Nancy?" he finally asked.

"Hello, Mark. I see you have finally seen fit to bring my granddaughter to pay respects to her mother," the woman said in a monotone voice.

Jan tried to piece this situation together. This woman was apparently Tammy's mother. She had never met Tammy, but there was a strong resemblance between the woman she was looking at and Kylie. She had the same petite frame and fair complexion. Then there was something about her eyes that was similar to Kylie's.

"She asked me to bring her here," Mark told her, "and of course I did."

"Who are these people that you brought with you?" the woman asked in the same tone. Jan didn't know why, but she was beginning to feel uncomfortable.

Mark turned and looked back at the three of them. "This is my fiancée, Jan Burke, and her daughter, Penny. This is Kylie's grandmother, Nancy Roush."

Nancy Roush glanced briefly at Jan and Penny before she focused on her granddaughter. "Hello, Kylie. How are you, child?"

Jan looked at Kylie. It didn't appear that the child was the least bit happy to see her grandmother, but she did give a polite response.

"Hello Grandma. I am fine."

"It is good to see you. I am glad to see that you have come here. You must be missing your mother terribly."

Kylie thought a moment before she replied. "Sometimes I do, but not all the time. I wrote her a letter to tell her about all the good things in my life. I wanted her to know how well things are going, because I know she would want me to be happy."

Nancy looked confused by Kylie's statement. She looked at Mark and then at Jan. Then the expression on her face changed. Jan wasn't quite able to read her thoughts, but apparently it was clear to Mark, because suddenly he seemed to get over the initial surprise of this encounter and took over the situation.

"It is getting late, and we do have other plans for the evening," he said. "Jan why don't you and the girls start toward the parking lot. I want to speak to Nancy for a moment."

Nancy's expression didn't change as she replied. "Yes, Mark, I think we do need to have a discussion." She then turned to Kylie. "It was good to see you. Are you going to leave the letter on your mother's headstone?"

Kylie looked down at the letter in her hand. "No, I think I've changed my mind. I'm going to read it to her tonight before I go to bed. It doesn't matter where I read it to her. She'll hear me. Good-bye Grandma."

The child then turned and began walking toward the parking lot. Penny immediately began to follow her. Jan looked at Mark. He was watching his daughter and Jan could have sworn that she saw a look of pride cross his face. He then turned and looked at Jan. He gave her a look of reassurance that was almost a smile, so she started walking behind the girls.

"Jan," he stopped her.

She turned around and looked at him. He reached into his pocket, pulled out the keys and tossed them to her. After catching them, she caught up with the girls. When they reached the truck, she unlocked it and the three of them climbed in. Jan started the engine and set the air conditioning to high. Penny and Kylie immediately began to have a discussion as if she weren't even there.

"You didn't seem very excited to see your grandmother," Penny told her.

"I wasn't," Kylie said. "She's nuts."

Penny giggled, and Jan swallowed down her own laughter as she listened to this conversation. "How do you know?"

"That's what Mommy always said," Kylie answered. "She didn't like me being around her very much. She got one of those orders that said she had to stay away from us. At the funeral Grandma acted crazy."

"How was she acting crazy?" Penny asked.

"Oh man, she was wailing and crying really loud. Then we went to my great aunt's house afterward and she kept on and on. Finally, my aunt came over and told Daddy to just take me and leave. On the way home, Daddy told me that Grandma had some problems in her head. He said not to worry because Mommy had a will that said that if anything happened to her that she wanted him to take care of me, and she left a letter for him in case she died."

"What did the letter say?"

"It said that she trusted him to take care of me, and to please keep Grandma away from me."

"Wow," was Penny's only response.

Listening to Kylie's story brought some serious thoughts to Jan's mind. What struck her was the fact that Tammy had the foresight to have a will with very specific requests. She looked back at the two girls. Jan had no will. What if something happened to her? Penny would be all right because she had Barb, and she was nearly of legal age. Kylie would of course remain with her father, but what if something happened to Mark? She had learned in her life all too well, that you never knew what the future held. If Mark died, (she felt her stomach clench at the thought) what would happen to Kylie? Even if they were married, would she be allowed to be her legal guardian? Did Mark have a will? She realized that the two of them needed to have a serious discussion.

It wasn't long before Mark returned to the truck. He jumped in and adjusted the air vent, before saying, "That sure feels good."

Then he turned and looked at Kylie. After winking at her he said, "You handled yourself very well, honey. Good job."

"She's still messed up in the head, isn't she?" Kylie asked.

He grinned. "Oh, maybe not quite as bad as she was before," he said. "She was pretty flakey before your mother died, but since that happened she has had a real hard time." He thought for a moment but then continued. "I think that I understand that. If something happened to you, I think I would go crazy too."

She smiled at him. "I love you, Dad."

"I love you, too. Now who's hungry?"

"Me," Penny and Kylie said at the same time.

"Me too," Jan added, smiling at him.

"All right. Red Lobster, here we come." He winked at her, fastened his seat belt, and pulled the truck out of the parking lot.

The name Nancy Roush did not come up for discussion again during their meal. Jan put her concerns about the future on hold. After dinner they drove to a small town holding a holiday festival. They just happened to catch a parade going through the town. Jan and Penny carefully watched the flag team following the local high school band. When they had completely passed, Jan asked Penny, "What did you think?"

Penny shrugged. "I don't know. Maybe with six months or so of hard work, they could be almost as good as us."

Jan grinned. "I did like their uniforms though."

"Yeah," Penny said. "Any chance of us getting new ones?"

"Not this year," Jan told her. "My goal is for next year."

"Well, that's not fair."

"Well, neither is life. I am craving funnel cake. Come on. Let's find some to take to the firework's."

A couple of hours later, the four of them were in the bed of the truck, which they had parked at a local park. Mark and Jan were sitting on lawn chairs and Penny and Kylie were sitting on the tailgate with their legs dangling over the edge. They were all sharing an assortment of junk food that they had collected at the festival.

Mark looked down at the two girls. "They are something aren't they?"

"They certainly are," Jan agreed. "Kylie is going to be lost next year when Penny goes away to school."

Mark sighed. "Yes, that is true, but that's a whole year away. I guess we'll deal with it when the time comes."

A few minutes later, when Penny took Kylie to the bathroom, Jan just had to ask him a question.

"What happened at the cemetery? Did that woman get upset with you?"

Mark looked at her smiled. "I thought she was going to. That's why I sent you girls back to the truck. But she didn't. She asked some questions about how Kylie was doing and our plans for the future. I answered them, and she wished me well. I thanked her and wished her the same. Then while I was walking back, for some reason, I turned and looked back. She was standing right next to the headstone with one hand resting on the top of it and her head bowed. It was a very sad picture."

She told him about the conversation between Kylie and Penny. He laughed and said, "That is just about exactly the way it happened."

"Mark," she began, and then stopped because the girls had returned to the truck.

He was looking at her expectantly. "Later," she said quietly, just as the first of the firework's rose into the air.

The next morning, Jan woke early and went downstairs to start the coffee. Just as the pot was full, Mark appeared in the kitchen. He kissed her good-morning and reached into the cabinet to get a mug. As he poured his coffee, he spoke to her.

"Did you have something that you wanted to talk to me about without the girls hearing?"

"Yes," she said as they both sat down at the table. "Listening to Kylie talk about how her mother had the foresight to make arrangements for her in the event of her death got me to thinking. What if, God forbid, something happened to you? Where would that leave Kylie?"

He smiled. "I'm glad that you brought that up. My current will names my parents as her legal guardian in the event of my death. I don't think anyone in Tammy's family would contest that. I have communication with Nancy's sister, Pam. I am going to call her later this morning and let her know about yesterday and to tell her that my situation has changed."

"Are you talking about us getting married?"

"Yes," he said. "Jan, obviously I am going to change my will after we are married, because you will be my benefactor, but I also want to name you as Kylie's guardian. That was my first thought, then something else occurred to me."

"What was that?" she asked.

"How would you feel about adopting Kylie? That seems to be the simplest solution. That way you would always be her legal guardian, no matter what. You could sign for her, at any medical facility, at school, or anywhere. Besides dying, I could be in an accident and be temporarily incapacitated, you know. I think it would be in her best interest for you to legally adopt her. How do you feel about that?"

"Of course, I will adopt her," Jan said. "And it's isn't just about protecting her legally, it's about commitment. I want her to know that I want to be her mother in every sense."

"That will make her very happy, I'm sure," he said as he leaned across the table to kiss her. He was just about to suggest that they go back upstairs together when they were interrupted by Penny's voice.

"Aw jeez, they are at it again." They looked up and saw both girls standing in the doorway. Jan sighed and stood up. "All right. What are your breakfast requests?"

The next couple of weeks flew by. Jan thought planning a small wedding would be simple, but she soon realized that nothing was as simple as it seemed. Linda Owens tuned out to be a Godsend. She had a natural organizational flair and was very detail oriented. They made several shopping trips to find clothes for everyone involved. After some thought, Jan decided that it was important for Linda to understand why Jan did not want a large wedding. So, just before the first shopping trip, she sat down with her and explained why the small wedding was important to her. Linda didn't act shocked or concerned about what Jan was telling her, and she said they she thought big weddings were overrated. She laughed and told her that she and Martin had nearly eloped until her mother found out and insisted that they have a wedding. From that point on, the two of them bonded and enjoyed the experience together. The thought crossed Jan's mind that this was what it felt like to have a mother. During one of their trips to the mall, Jan did express that thought to Linda, and explained about her mother. Linda accepted this story about Jan's life the same as she did the other and told her that she was happy to be here to help.

Barb had made all her arrangements to fly in for the wedding, but the week before the wedding she had been walking on the beach with Myra, and she had tripped over some drift wood and sprained her ankle very badly. Jan could tell that she was broken hearted. She did promise that she was coming for the holidays, no matter what.

Jan woke early on the morning of her wedding. She went downstairs and waited for Linda and Casey to arrive. She was alone, because Mark and Kylie had spent the night at his parent's home, and Penny was still in the basement. For the first time in a long time, Kim was on Jan's mind. She realized that it was probably because it was her wedding day; *again*. Somehow, she knew that Kim wanted to be here to see it through. She felt that her father was with her too. On this day she did miss him more than she had in a while. She had struggled with how to make her entrance, without her father. Casey had told her that Jim would be happy to walk her across the yard, but since he was Mark's best man, that didn't seem practical. They finally decided to keep it simple and each of them walk across the yard from different directions and meet in front of the minister.

She looked out the window where everything was set in the yard. Mother nature had smiled on them and they were able to set everything up the day before. There were about twenty-five rented white chairs, because, they had decided to invite a few of the teachers from school and the people Mark worked with at the funeral homes.

As she was looking out the window, Penny emerged from the basement stairs. She was smiling and came over to give Jan a hug.

"This all feels so right," Penny told her. "Do you know what Mark asked me yesterday?"

"I have an idea," Jan said. "I knew that he was planning to talk to you."

"He told me that you were going to adopt Kylie, and he offered to adopt me," she said tearfully.

Jan smiled. "What did you tell him?"

"I don't know," Penny said. "It is a different situation than with Kylie because I am older. We talked about that. He said that he just wanted me to know that he was willing to make the commitment. Maybe that's enough. I don't know. Mark told me that I could think about it, and he would support whatever I decided."

"I am sure he will, so you go with whatever is in your heart," Jan told her.

At that moment, Casey and Lisa knocked on the door. Linda arrived with Kylie who had spent the night with her, and the pre-wedding activities were in full swing.

If Jan thought that she would experience anxiety due to what had happened six years earlier, she was wrong. This time she actually had fun. Casey and Jan fixed everyone's hair and make-up amid a lot of laughing and giggling.

Just as Jan was about to get dressed in her simple tea length Ivory dress, Linda spoke up and said, "Oh I almost forgot." Then she went over to her bag on the counter. After digging through it for a moment, she pulled out an envelope and handed it to Jan.

She took it and looked at her name written on the front. It was Mark's handwriting. She smiled and opened it. As she read the words, tears came to her eyes. It was simple and to the point.

"I'll meet you in the backyard at 1:30. I'll be there. You can count on it. Thanks for marrying me."

"Must have been something mushy," Penny said as they all stared at her.

"No, not really," she said. Then she read the card out loud.

"Ahhh," they all said, each of them understanding why Mark felt that she needed reassurance.

After that, everything seemed to glide along in a warm and pleasant haze. Jan soon found herself standing next to Mark in front of the minister in their backyard, and she heard each of them saying the promising words to each other. Then they were dancing together on the lawn, eating the delicious catered meal and cutting the cake.

Then suddenly they were saying their good-byes and getting into Mark's truck amid a shower of rice, and bubbles. They could see both girls waving and throwing the last of the rice as they drove off. Kylie was staying with her grandparents for the four days they would be gone, and Penny was staying with Chrissy. For their short honeymoon, they had rented a cabin at Lake Cumberland, which was about two hours away.

A few hours later, Jan lay drowsily wrapped up in Mark's arms, listening to the night sounds of summer coming through the open window.

"Are you still awake?" he asked.

"Uh huh," she answered.

"Did you want to get up in the morning and watch the sunrise?" he asked.

"I don't think so," she told him. "These next few days will probably be my last few chances to sleep in before school starts."

"I see how it is," he laughed. "Now that we are married all the romance has left your soul."

"I have plenty of romance in my soul," she told him. "It just doesn't want to get up before nine tomorrow."

The four days that they spent at the cabin were blissfully spent. They slept late and spent their afternoons on the lake, on rented jet skis, kayaks, or canoes. They grilled their dinner each night and then relaxed in the hot tub on the back porch of the cabin.

They were a little sad to leave, but anxious to get home and see the girls, and start their married life.

They settled very easily into their lives. A week after they returned the two of them visited a lawyer concerning their wills and the adoption of Kylie. He gave them paperwork to fill out and return. He said that the process should not take very long.

They sat down with Kylie and explained the situation to her. Her response was very positive. She told them that she had written another letter to her mother, and she had asked her if it was all right if she called Jan "Mom". She had always called Tammy "Mommy", so she thought it would be a good way to keep them separated in their mind and heart. Mark told her that he thought that was a very good plan and Jan agreed, so from that time on, Jan was "Mom".

August had rolled around and Jan and Casey were in the new school building almost every day unpacking and decorating their rooms. To their disappointment, their rooms were no longer in the same hallway, but they were just around the corner from each other.

One day about two weeks before school started, Jan was in her room organizing the drawers of her new desk, when Casey came bursting into her room, at least as much as she could burst these days with her now bulging belly.

"Jim just called me, and you are not going to believe what has happened?"

"What?" Jan asked, almost afraid to hear the answer.

"You know Ben Richards, right?"

"Umm, trying to place the name."

"One of the high school janitors?"

"Oh yeah. What about him?"

"They just found him dead in the janitor's office. I guess he was just sitting in his chair like he had just dozed off."

Jan felt a cold chill go through right through her. "That makes eight," she said.

"What?"

Jan explained to her about how odd she thought it was that quite a few people had died in their sleep lately. Then she told her how Mark had pointed out another perspective to her.

"What do you think? Jan asked her.

"I do think it's kind of odd," she said, "but I understand Mark's point too."

Jan thought for a moment and then asked, "You don't know by any chance if Ben Richards had a cold, do you?"

"I don't know, why?"

"Because almost all of the other people that died in their sleep had colds; Aaron Fisher, both of Penny's parents, Charlie's grandparents, and Doug Lawrence."

Casey thought for a moment and then she said, "Maybe they didn't have colds, but there is a really serious virus is going around."

"I don't know about that," Jan said. "I would think more people would have it if it was contagious. Besides Marcia Collins didn't have a cold. She had an infected tooth."

"Good point," Casey said thoughtfully.

"I am curious to know if he had a cold," Jan said. "Can you find out if Jim knows anything about that?"

"Yeah, I will see what I can find out."

"Don't make a big deal out of it, please. Mark already thinks my thoughts about this are a little…"

"Out there?"

"Right."

"Ok, I've got your back. By the way Jim did say that Mark came to get his body."

"He did? Ok, but if I ask him questions, he will start giving me that look again."

Casey laughed. "Well, we certainly can't have your new husband giving you looks, can we now?"

Later that night, when Jan and the girls returned from flag practice, the girls each went to their own rooms. Jan found Mark in the family room, stretched out in his recliner, watching a ball game on TV. She leaned over and kissed him before she sat down in the love seat.

"How was practice?" he asked.

"It was good," she answered. "Things are coming along really well."

"Kylie has a dentist appointment on Friday morning," he told her. "Are you going to be able to take her? I have a funeral."

"I was already planning on it," she said. "Not a problem. I heard about the janitor at the high school. That was kind of creepy, wasn't it?"

He switched his attention from the ball game to her. "Are you going to add him to your list?" he asked.

"No," she said. "It's just that people don't very often just sit down at work and die. Do you think he had a heart attack?"

Mark turned back to the TV and waited a few seconds to see if the fly ball was going to caught, before he responded. "It didn't appear as if he struggled for breath or anything. It just looked like he had drifted off to sleep. I guess that's what the other janitor thought had happened. Apparently, he was fond of taking cat naps in the chair. Jim said that the office had called him on the phone several times, and when he didn't answer, they paged him on the intercom. Then eventually the other janitor went looking for him and found him in his chair. He tried to wake him and realized that something was wrong.

"How old was he?" Jan asked.

"I think he was in his fifties," he told her.

"He didn't do drugs, or anything did he?"

Mark shrugged. "I don't think so. Just the penicillin he had in his shirt pocket."

"He was taking penicillin?" she wanted to know. "Then he was sick?"

Weddings and Funerals

"I don't know, Jan. I don't analyze them. I just bury them."

"Is there going to be an autopsy?" she asked.

"No," he told her. "The family didn't want one. He is being shipped out for cremation tomorrow." Then before she could speak again he yelled, "Yes!" toward the television, and Jan decided that she had pushed the subject far enough.

The next morning Jan and Linda took Kylie school shopping. They had a great time, and Jan found a few things for herself as well. The three of them enjoyed a late lunch at Perkins. Then Jan dropped the other two of them off at Linda's, where they were going to fix dinner for all of them. She had a grade level meeting at three and arrived there just in time. When the meeting was over, she was surprised to find Casey still working in her room.

"Hi," she said. "You are here late."

"I haven't been here very long," she said. "I had a doctor's appointment this morning and then I had to take Lisa to the eye doctor and then run the kids to meet Rich. He is taking his weekend now, because it's his mother's birthday tomorrow and they are having a party for her. He called last night and dropped a bombshell on me."

"What's that?" Jan asked.

"His company is offering him a job in Germany. He leaves in two months," she said. "He said that it will be an excellent opportunity to make some great money."

"Permanently?" she asked.

"It would seem so," Casey told her. "He tried to get me to tell the kids, but I told him no way. That was his choice and he would have to tell them."

"Do you think they will be upset?"

"I don't know," Casey said, "but I don't think he understands that this decision could cost him his relationship with his children, or maybe he doesn't care. Anyway, he is a fool, because Jim is waiting in the wings, happy to be a father to my children."

Jan shook her head. "Good for Jim," she said, "but it's sad."

Casey looked at her then and said, "Oh, I almost forgot, before all that went down, Jim and I were talking about Ben Richards and he did tell me that he saw him early yesterday morning and he had a terrible cough."

"I am not surprised, because Mark told me that he had a bottle of penicillin in his pocket," Jan said.

"Does that mean that you are adding Ben Richards to your list?"

Jan sighed. "I am afraid so."

A week later, Jan had to attend her first professional work day of the school year. She rose early and had coffee with Mark. They discussed plans for the day. He was going to mow the yard while it was still cool. Then he was going to the funeral home to take care of some paperwork and prepare for the visitation that evening. He promised to check in with Penny and make sure she knew that she was responsible for Kylie until Jan got home. When she was ready to leave, he wrapped his arms around her and kissed her generously. They both smiled and promised to pick up where they left off later that night after the girls had gone to bed.

Jan arrived at school, and went to her room, to drop off her bag and purse, before heading the welcome breakfast in the cafeteria. Just as she was about to head in that direction, Casey stopped on her way. "Are you ready?" she asked.

"I was just leaving," Jan told her.

"I wanted to warn you," Casey said. "Shelly is in a mood and a half. Steer clear."

"She has been giving me dirty looks since she realized that Mark and I were dating," Jan answered. "It has been especially bad in the last few weeks."

Casey laughed. "Because you had the audacity to marry Mark?"

"I guess." Jan answered.

"Well, this morning in the mail room, she was crying and wailing about something. I didn't hang around long enough to find out."

"Oh jeez," Jan said.

At this point they had entered the cafeteria and were soon in line to get some bagels and fruit. When their plates were filled, the two of them scanned the tables and found a seat near Cindy, which was quite some distance from Shelly, who was apparently telling her troubles to the other fifth grade teachers. He eyes were red, and she was holding a well-worn tissue.

Jan forgot about Shelly and was soon enjoying the attention of being congratulated on her marriage. A few minutes later, Blake Walters began the first district staff meeting of the year. He went through the usual routine of introducing new staff and announcing changes, including Jim's new position as high school principal. Then he asked that they have a moment of silence in remembrance of Doug Lawrence and Ben Richards. When that was finished, he went on to discuss some other housekeeping issues and then he dismissed them to building level meetings.

There was a slight break between the two meetings. Casey headed straight to join the line for the restroom. Jan went back to her room to text Penny and see if everything was going well. When she returned to the cafeteria, Casey was apparently still in the bathroom, so Jan saved her a seat. She slid into it just before the meeting started.

"I found out what Shelly is upset about," she told Jan.

"Really?" Jan laughed. "By the look on your face it must be good."

"It sure is," Casey said, just as the principal began her welcome to the elementary staff. "Gary Baker is missing."

Chapter Thirteen

Jan stared at Casey and then her attention was drawn back to the principal, who had already moved on to the first item on the agenda, which was lengthy, so she had to put her questions to Casey aside. An hour and twenty minutes later, the meeting finally broke up. Jan stood and stretched. She was mentally exhausted from listening to so much discussion. It was a new school year in a new building, and everyone had opinions about procedures and schedules of everything from lunch to who used the bathroom when. Jan was not particularly passionate about any of it. At this point she just wanted someone to hand her a paper telling her where to be and when.

Casey motioned at her to follow. The two of them worked their way through the malingering staff in the hallway, greeting a few of them along the way. When they finally reached Jan's room, Casey shut the door and then turned around quickly.

"All right," Jan said. "Tell me what you heard."

"Well," Casey began, "I was in the bathroom when I heard Shelly in the stall next to me on her phone. I don't know who she was talking to, but she was telling them that no one in the family has seen or heard from Gary in over a week. His car is not at his apartment and his cell phone has gone dead. I guess that they have reported it to the police, but they said they can't get involved yet, since his car is gone, there is no evidence of foul play, and, he apparently he left of his own free will."

"He is probably off on a drinking binge," Jan told her. "As soon as he sobers up, he'll come home, looking for money to support his next big drunken party. What a prince."

"You may be right," Casey said, "but I have a strange feeling about this."

Jan shrugged. "Who knows? Don't put it past Shelly to overdramatize this for attention, either."

Casey thought for a moment and then said, "You may be right about that. She probably wasn't talking to anybody but putting on a show for everyone to hear. I mean, who sits in a bathroom stall talking on their phone loud enough for everyone to hear?"

"Exactly," Jan answered. "I'm hungry. Let's go eat."

One week later, school began, and Jan found herself so totally busy that she could have sworn that she was meeting herself coming and going. It was a good busy, though, and she had never been happier.

Football season was soon in full swing. Jan received a lot of compliments for the new routines that she had taught her team. Only a select few people knew that the *"new"* routines that Jan had taught her team were actually recycled versions of dances that Jan had learned when she was on her high school flag team. She had worked with Penny and Chrissy during the spring and early summer to work the old routines into updated versions. The two girls had been elected as co-captains of the team and were showing good leadership to the younger girls.

Time passed quickly and suddenly it was only a week before homecoming. As Jan took Penny shopping for a homecoming dress, she couldn't help but think about the fact that it had been a year since Penny had first come to stay with her. During the past year the girl had been through quite a lot of changes; some good and some not so good, but she had emerged through all of it as a much stronger happier girl. Jan was sure that she still had some down moments, but she chose to deal with it alone.

On homecoming night, Jan and her girls stood on the side lines and cheered as Chrissy was crowned homecoming queen.

The next night she and Mark did the parent thing of taking way too many photos of Charlie and Penny as they were dressed to go to the dance. Jim and Casey's kids were staying with them because the two of them were chaperoning the dance, and the three younger kids were jumping around more excited than the older kids. Eventually the two teenagers managed to escape the photo session, and then the younger ones headed down to the basement to watch TV, and just like that, the house was quiet.

"Do you know what" Jan asked.

"What?"

"I feel kind of old, tonight."

He laughed. "You certainly don't look old," he told her. After a minute he asked, "Do you remember your high school dances?" Then he wondered if he should have asked, considering that her high school years weren't that memorable.

She smiled as if she were thinking back. "Yes, I remember that my senior year I decided that I was going to find a way to enjoy myself. Whenever there was a dance or something, Dad would give me money to go buy a dress. I would go to the mall and buy a dress and shoes. Then I would take it straight to a girlfriend's house and leave it. Then I would arrange for a double date and to have him pick me up at my friend's house. The friends' parents were always understanding of my situation, because they would take lots of pictures and then they saw that my dad got copies. The night of my senior prom, my dad snuck away from my mother and came to see me going into the school and took some pictures of his own. It meant the world to me. My mother found out later and threw a hissy about me going to the prom and how expensive it was, and how ridiculous it was that he supported that, but I didn't care. That's when I stopped hoping that she would get better someday and start being my mother."

Mark walked over and put his arms around her. "All the more reason for you to see that Penny has a special senior year, right? It's like a do over?"

She looked up at him and nodded. "Something like that. I hope that they have a good time. Sometimes the anticipation of these things is better than the actual event."

"Stop worrying, '*mom*'. She will have a great time as long as she is with Charlie. Jim was right. He is a good kid."

"Yes, he is. I think they have both been good for each other," she said.

"I forgot to tell you," he told her. "Last Sunday when you and Kylie went to the grocery and I was helping them with their chemistry, he started asking me all kinds of questions about where you would go to school to be a mortician."

"Really? That's interesting."

"Yes, he said it is something he is considering," Mark said. "I told him that he could come over anytime and I would show him around."

Jan thought for a moment and then she said, "You've never showed me the whole funeral home."

Mark gave her funny look. "No, I haven't, but you have an aversion to funeral homes. I didn't think it was anything you were interested in seeing."

She wrinkled her nose. "That is true, but since we are married, and the business is part of our livelihood, maybe I should show a little more interest."

He laughed out loud. "I tell you what, you just let me know when you are ready, and I will give you the grand tour."

"All right, but just let me know a good time when you have no…"

"Guests?"

"Yes."

"You don't have to worry. I wouldn't take you or anyone in the back with 'guests' in there. It would be disrespectful," he told her.

"Speaking of guests, we have some downstairs that need fed. Let's get our bonfire going."

He pulled her closer and kissed her gently at first and then more passionately. He pulled away and winked at her. "Later?" he asked.

"It's a date," she told him and the two of them walked toward the kitchen arm in arm.

As the weeks moved on, late autumn was not particularly kind to Kentucky. There were a few nice days here and there, but quite often Mother Nature reminded them that winter was not far off. The Friday of the last home football game was one of those few nice days. It was senior night, along with parent appreciation night. Mark and Jan proudly walked in the line with Penny. If she felt any emotion over her parents, she didn't mention it. After they were introduced, Penny gave each of them a hug and a kiss. Jan noticed some tears in her eyes, and she suspected that it was a combination of missing her dad and being grateful that that the two of them were there for her.

After the game, Mark, Jan, Penny, and Kylie met Charlie and his parents at a local restaurant. They were a nice couple who seemed to be very proud of their son. During the course of the meal, the subject of Charlie's interest in mortuary science came up. Jan knew that Mark was a little concerned that his parents might have reservations about their son's increasing interest in the field. He didn't want them to think that he was pushing him in that direction, but that did not turn out to be the case. Steve and Ellen Miller were completely supportive of their son. Mark offered to help Charlie by giving him a part time job working at the funeral home, by setting up for funerals, transporting flowers and chairs to and from the cemetery, and delivering the flowers back to people's homes. He laughed and told them that there were always vehicles that needed washed, and that there was no limit to the amount of odd jobs that needed to be done.

Charlie was very excited to hear that, because he had just learned that the Pizza Hut that he worked at was going to close soon for extensive remodeling, so he was soon going to be out of work. It was the second major disappointment that he had had in the last two weeks. A scout from a small college in eastern Kentucky had come to watch him play but Charlie had not had a particularly good night and the man had passed on any interest in signing him. At that point, Charlie had no plan as to where he wanted to go to school.

Mark had an idea, but he chose his words carefully, before explaining his thoughts.

"Charlie, since you are undecided about your future, why don't you consider staying home next year? You could probably take your basic 101 college courses online from any school. Then you could continue to work for me, and maybe after a year of being around the business, you might have a better idea of whether you want to pursue a career in mortuary science." He looked first at

Steve and Ellen to see their reaction to his suggestion. Ellen was smiling broadly, and Mark quickly realized that she wasn't ready for her son to leave home. Steve Miller was looking at his son as if her were thinking about the idea and wondering what Charlie's response would be.

It was quiet at the table for a moment. Everyone seemed to be waiting for Charlie to speak. The boy seemed to be trying to decide how to put his words together. Eventually he did manage to verbalize his thoughts.

"That's interesting that you mentioned that, Mark. I have been thinking about the same thing. Dad and I were just discussing that yesterday, now your job offer makes that seem even more practical, doesn't it Dad?"

Steve smiled. "Yes, it does. I appreciate your interest in my son, Mark. Thank you."

Mark smiled back. "Charlie is a good kid. We enjoy having him around, don't we Jan?"

"Yes, we do," she answered.

"But next year Penny will be gone away to school and we won't see as much of Charlie," Kylie said sadly.

Charlie looked at Penny and seemed to give her a slight nod. She got a funny look on her face and seemed to shake her head slightly.

Charlie sighed and then spoke. "Penny doesn't want to leave home either. I got the idea of staying home from her. She wants to do her first year online too."

"Charlie!" Penny seemed slightly agitated with him.

"They will understand," he said.

"Understand what?" Jan asked.

Penny was quiet for a moment before she spoke. "I have been through a lot of change in the last year, and I don't want this to come out wrong and have everyone think I am disrespectful of my parents...but for the first time in my life I am happy at home and I just don't want to give that up yet. I...want to stay home for a while longer."

Mark and Jan looked at each other as if to say, "Why didn't we see that coming?"

Then Mark leaned across the table toward Penny. "Of course you can stay home, sweetheart. Our home will always be your home."

"Yay," Kylie interjected. "Penny is staying home."

"Yay," Charlie echoed as he leaned over and kissed his girlfriend on the head. "Penny is staying home."

"The last football game of the season was the following Friday night. It was an away game with their county rivals. The weather was predicted to be cold, windy, and rainy. Jan and the band director discussed the possibility of cancelling the trip for the band and the flag team. It would have been a no brainer, if it weren't the last game of the season. They finally decided to let the students vote on whether they wanted to perform in the bad weather. It was nearly a unanimous vote. They wanted to perform one last time that season. Jan was disappointed. She had hope to avoid the trip in bad weather, but she went along with the decision.

The weather turned out to be worse than predicted. When the rain became icy during the fourth quarter, Jan and the band director loaded the students back on the buses and the group headed home early. They did not hear one complaint. Inside the warm bus, Jan just could not get warmed up. She stayed chilled all the way home.

Once she was at home, she took a long hot shower trying to warm up. Mark was not home from the game yet, so she took some Tylenol and went to bed.

She woke the next morning with a pounding headache and a very sore throat. During the afternoon, a nasty cough joined her other symptoms. Mark felt her forehead and then insisted on taking her to Urgent Care. She felt too miserable to argue, so she went upstairs to change her clothes. Penny was at Chrissy's helping her get ready for the party she was having that night, so Mark called his mother, who came over to stay with Kylie.

The doctor told her that she was suffering from a cold/virus that had been circulating around the area. He wrote her a prescription and told her to take it easy for a few days.

Mark took Jan home and then went to get her prescription filled. She told him that her regular drug store was probably closed by that hour and that he should go to the other one that had her insurance information on file.

Linda Owens immediately went into her mother mode by setting her up on the couch with pillows and blankets and began to fix her a light dinner. Jan lay back and tried to control her anxious thoughts. Mark had read her mind in the doctor's office. On the way home, he had tried to alleviate her worries.

"Jan, lots of people have had this virus. Only on one or two have died. Please don't stress over this."

Thirty minutes later, as Jan was dozing on and off, she heard Mark in the kitchen talking to his mother. He appeared next to her five minutes later, with a prescription bottle in his hand. He opened the bottle and shook out two pills into his hand. Then he picked the glass of juice that Linda had fixed her and handed it to her along with the pills.

Jan started to take them and then had a thought. "What kind of medicine is that?" she asked.

"It's an antibiotic of some kind," Mark told her. "Does it matter?"

"Yes," Jan said. "Let me see the bottle."

Mark sighed with frustration, thinking that her request had something to do with her death paranoia, but he handed her the bottle.

Jan looked at it and said, "Damn it."

Mark was confused. "What?" he asked.

"This is penicillin," she said. "I'm allergic to it. I can't take this. I told the nurse that." She dropped the bottle down on the coffee table in frustration. "Now what am I going to do? Urgent Care is closed. I was the last patient. I can't get to another doctor until Monday morning."

"Maybe I can help," Linda offered. She had walked in the room just in time to hear Jan's remarks.

Mark looked at his mother and let out a slight groan.

"What?" Jan asked.

Linda Owens gave her son a look that Jan could not quite interpret. "Jan, honey, I haven't taken prescription medications in years. Nature provides us with everything we need to take care of ourselves. I can cure your cold in three, maybe four days."

Mark rolled his eyes at his mother. "An antibiotic could do the same thing."

"We don't have any way of getting her one now, do we?"

"What are you two talking about?" Jan wanted to know.

"I am going to fix you an old-fashioned poultice," Linda told her. "If you keep one constantly on your chest for the next couple of days, I guarantee you will be better, or at least well on your way to recovery."

"I guess it can't hurt," Jan said. "I can try it until Monday and if I'm not getting better than I will go to the doctor."

"That's all I ask," Linda told her.

Jan looked at Mark and she could have sworn that he was trying not to laugh. "All right, if that's what you want," he said. At that moment Kylie came downstairs from her room,

"What's going on," she asked.

"Jan is sick with a bad cold. Grandma is going to take care of her and we are going to go stay with Grampa. Go pack a bag with a few days' worth of clothes."

"That's probably a good idea," Linda said. "I'll help you, honey. Come on." She then herded Kylie off toward the stairs.

When they were alone, Jan looked at Mark. She went into another round of coughing, took a drink of juice and then said, "I guess you don't want to catch this."

He laughed. "I've already been exposed to it. That's not the reason." Jan couldn't help but notice that he had a kind of devious twinkle in his eye.

"Then what?" she wanted to know.

Mark leaned over and kissed her on the forehead. "You'll find out," he said, almost with a laugh, and then added, "I may have forgotten to mention to you that my mother is a witch doctor." Then he laughed and then walked toward the stairs.

A little while later, Mark left with Kylie and Linda fixed Jan some sort of soup that was basically beef broth. She gave her some more

Tylenol to take and right after Jan dozed, off she left.

An hour later, she returned with a bag from home and a bag of groceries. She instructed Jan to take a shower and put on some clean pajamas. When Jan came back downstairs, Linda had set up a vaporizer in the room, which was going full blast. The most interesting thing was that she had several onions cut in half placed around the room. She could smell the onions, but that was not the most offensive odor that was finding its way into her nose. There was something else that smelled suspiciously of garlic.

"I know this isn't exactly pleasant, but I just need you to trust me," Linda said.

"All right," Jan decided that at this point she had no choice. Shortly after that Linda laid a folded towel with the offensive smelling mixture inside of it on her chest. She then then covered her up and turned out the lights. Jan settled in for what she anticipated to be a long restless night, but to her pleasant surprise, she soon drifted off into a deep peaceful sleep.

She woke the next morning, feeling somewhat better. She was still coughing, but it was a more productive cough. Her fever was gone, and a little of her appetite had returned. Linda changed the poultice on her chest every few hours. Jan didn't argue, because as the day wore on, Jan slowly began to feel better.

By evening, Jan was feeling much better. Linda changed the onions which interestingly had turned an ugly dark color. Linda explained that the onions had absorbed the bacteria from the air. She told Jan that she would need to sleep with the poultice one more night and stay home one more day, and by tomorrow evening, she should be almost as good as new.

To Jan's continued amazement, Linda was right. By Monday night, Jan did feel remarkably better. With his mother's all clear, Mark returned with Kylie, and Penny came out of hiding in the basement. Linda returned home and life in the Owens' home was normal once again.

November rolled around and Jim and Casey quietly celebrated their first anniversary, since Casey was quite encumbered with her pregnancy at this point. Mark and Jan took them to dinner to celebrate.

Weddings and Funerals

They returned to the Owens' house where Charlie and Penny were babysitting for the three children. The found the five of them playing Monopoly. The got a good laugh out of the fact that Ty was cleaning up.

A week later, Jan and Casey were in Jan's room after school, discussing Thanksgiving plans when Cindy burst into the room and closed the door. Both Jan and Casey looked up expectantly.

Cindy took a breath. "They found Gary Baker," she told them.

"Where is he?" Casey asked.

Cindy paused a moment and then said, "He's dead."

Jan's eyes flew open wide, and a cold chill went clear through her. "What happened to him?"

"He was found dead in their family's hunting cabin near Livingston.," Cindy told them.

"That's why Shelly wasn't here today," Casey said.

"Right," Cindy answered. "I guess she emailed her lesson plans to Claire and the told her the whole thing. Supposedly, he left a suicide note, but the family isn't buying it. They are demanding a full-scale autopsy."

"Wow," Casey said.

"They are probably going to find that he died of alcohol poisoning," Jan said.

"But what about the suicide note?" Casey asked. "If he wrote it, it wasn't alcohol poisoning. If someone faked it, it still wasn't alcohol poisoning."

"I guess," Jan answered. "The whole thing gives me chills."

"I guess the autopsy will answer a lot of questions," Cindy said.

Gary Baker's death was the talk of the school for the next couple of weeks. The rumors that were circulating grew more ridiculous by the day. Shelly did not return to school before Thanksgiving and the particular rumor concerning her was that she had asked for a leave of absence until the end of the school year. Jim confirmed that story to be true. Jan and Casey thought that was a long time to recover from the death of a cousin, but then Jim revealed in confidence that

Shelly had been having a lot of emotional issues at school, and in general, and Gary's death had pushed her over the edge. She had been sent by family members to another state for psychological treatment.

    The weekend before Thanksgiving, Jan, Penny and Kylie were sitting at the kitchen table, working on a menu for Thanksgiving. There was going to be the four of them, Charlie (his family always celebrated the Sunday before), Mark's parent, Jim and Casey and the kids, and Jim's parents. Casey's doctor did not want her going far from home, because her first two children had delivered early and quickly, and she was showing signs of following the same pattern. Jim's parents were happy to come to Bellville for the holiday. Jan wanted Casey to rest, so she was ordered to not show up until dinnertime on Thursday. She assured her that between herself, Linda and the girls, that everything would be under control.

    While they were working, the doorbell unexpectantly rang. Jan left the girls to see who their visitor was. In the kitchen, the girls heard Jan speak in a loud surprised voice.

"Oh, my goodness. I wasn't expecting you until next month!"

The two of them looked at each other and then jumped up and ran into the living room. Both of them stood and stared in shock until Penny finally ran forward, squealing, "Aunt Barb, what are you doing here?"

The two of them shared a long hug and then Barb explained. "I was planning to come as a surprise for Christmas. Mark and Jan knew that, but with Thanksgiving coming, I decided 'Why wait?' I got a private jet, flew here, rented a car, and here I am."

Penny continued to stare. "But Aunt Barb, you don't ever leave…I mean…how?"

Barb laughed. "I have been keeping a secret from you dear. Jan knows about it. I got a new counselor and she has really helped me. My goal was to be able to come here for your graduation, but things have gone a lot better than I expected, so here I am."

"I'm so glad," Penny said, hugging her aunt again, this time with tears in her eyes.

Then Barb turned to Kylie and opened her arms. "How are you sweetheart? It's good to see you again."

Kylie went running into her arms. "Aunt Barb," she said. "We were just planning Thanksgiving. Would you like to help us?"

"Try and stop me," Barb laughed.

"Come on in the kitchen," Jan said. "Mark will be home before long. He will bring your bags in."

"There is an extra bedroom in the basement," Penny said, "Would you like to stay down there with me?"

"That sounds just fine," Barb said. "We can stay up late and you can tell me all about Charlie."

Penny smiled. "He is helping Mark with a funeral. He'll be here after it's over, because we were going to the movies tonight, but it looks like it's going to be family night."

"Can you make pizza for us Aunt Barb?" Kylie asked.

"Honey, we can order pizza," Jan said. "We can't ask Barb to cook five minutes after she got here."

"Don't be silly," Barb said. "Of course, I can make pizza. As a matter of fact, I think that Kylie is perfectly capable of making pizza if I just give her a little help. What do you say?"

If Jan and Penny thought their quiet Thanksgiving the year before was special, this one was even more so. The house was full and noisy, but it was a wonderful noisy. Jan's heart was full. Everyone seemed to enjoy themselves. Jan found it interesting and pleasing to see that Linda and Barb seemed to bond almost immediately. When dinner was over, she ran upstairs to use their bathroom. When she came out, Mark was standing in the bedroom.

"Hi," she said.

"Hi," he said.

He didn't move. "All yours," she told him.

"I didn't come up here to use the bathroom," he said.

"Oh," she said. "Then what did you come up here for? We have a house full of guests."

"Our guests are fine. I came up here to tell you how much I love you." Then he pulled her close and kissed her lovingly."

When they finished, she looked up at him and said, "I should have come up here sooner."

He smiled at her, but Jan could tell the wheels in his mind were turning. Pulling her closer and holding her a little tighter, he spoke softly.

"The house is full."

"Very full," she answered.

"I like the feeling of the house being full of happy noise."

"Me too."

He smiled and said, "Maybe it's time for us to think about filling it up a little more."

She smiled back at him. "Maybe it is."

Later that night, the house was quiet. The Cravens and Martin and Linda Owens had returned home. Charlie had stayed for a while and played cards with the rest of the family. He left around ten, and the rest of them turned in shortly after. The car parked down the street from the house waited for a few minutes, and then quietly crept away into the night.

The next afternoon, the five of them were enjoying a feast of leftovers. They were discussing their plans for the weekend. Mark had no funerals to deal with. The holiday parade was that evening, so they were debating about going to the festival of lights at the zoo, or to the one at Coney Island that was a drive through on Saturday night. Since the forecast was to be bitterly cold, they decided to go with Coney Island light show. Just as Barb and Jan were clearing the table and loading the dishwasher, the doorbell rang.

Mark went to answer it. When he opened the door there was a man standing there that Mark had never seen before. He was a middle-aged man wearing brown khakis pants and a dark grey sweater.

"Could I help you?" Mark asked.

"Yes," the man answered. "I am looking for Jan Owens."

"May I ask what this is in reference to?"

The man reached into his pocket and pulled out a police ID. "I am detective Larry Coleman. I am with the Bellville City Police Department. I would like to speak with her concerning Gary Baker."

Chapter Fourteen

Jan sat very nervously at the kitchen table, as she watched Larry Coleman pull a small notepad and pen from his shirt pocket. He looked at her very concerned face and smiled at her.

"Mrs. Owens," he began, "this is just routine questioning. I am basically on a fact-finding mission."

"May I ask if there is something suspicious about Gary Baker's death?" Mark wanted to know.

Larry Coleman looked across the table at Mark. "Not at this point," he said. "It appears to me to be a classic suicide, but the family is making a lot of noise and they have some distant relationship to the mayor., so I have been instructed to conduct an investigation, just to quiet things down; like I don't have enough to do. When the autopsy report comes back in the next few days, this will fade away in to the sunset." He sighed and took a breath before he continued.

"Now Mrs. Owens, I understand that you and Mr. Baker had a romantic relationship?"

Jan frowned. "I would hardly call it a relationship. I went out with him exactly three times last January. I didn't enjoy myself very much. On our last date, he became intoxicated within the first thirty minutes, and then hooked up with an old girlfriend. I walked out of the club and went to a diner across the street. I called Mark and he came and got me. We started dating shortly after that and we were married in July."

"Did you have any contact at all with him after that night?"

Jan shook her head. "I didn't see him or speak with him after that night."

"Did he ever give you any indication that he was depressed?" the detective asked.

Jan shrugged. "We never had any conversations that were much more than superficial. On all three of our dates, he did drink quite a lot and then he became the life of the party."

Mark and Jan watched him write in his notebook for a moment.

When he finished, he spoke as he put his pen and notebook back in his pocket. "I guess that's all I really need to ask you." He stood and walked toward the living room. In the living room, he stopped and started to speak, but something caught his eye. He was looking at a framed picture on a table near the doorway. It was a picture of the four of them taken in Barb's backyard last summer.

"That's a nice picture," he said. "Was it taken somewhere in the south?"

Barb, who had just come back upstairs, walked up to them. "Yes," she said, picking up the picture to show him. "That picture was taken at my home in Florida."

"Ahh," he said. "I recognized the oleanders. They don't grow around here."

"No, they don't." She smiled and then continued. "They are such beautiful flowers, but unfortunately they are also deadly poisonous. Have you spent a lot of time in the south?"

"I have done a fair amount of time traveling through the southern part of the country," he told her. "I am hoping to retire somewhere in the south very soon. Where is your home?"

"My home is near Ft. Lauderdale," she answered.

He smiled. "Really? That is an area on my short list. Well, I won't bother you people any longer. My apologies for interrupting your holiday weekend. Enjoy the rest of it."

After he left, the three of them were quiet for a moment. Finally, Jan spoke. "Should I be concerned about this?"

"No," Mark answered. "The guy was just following orders from the mayor's office to keep some annoying people quiet. I wasn't going to say anything, but he questioned Jim and Blake Walters too. I think what he is trying to do is paint a picture to show the family that he was capable of suicide. That's why the only thing he wrote down from your interview was that Gary drank a lot."

"That makes sense," Barb added. "The man had an unhappy life that came to an unhappy ending."

Jan thought a moment and then said, "You're right, and it's getting late. Penny and I need to get ready to go to the parade."

Mark put his arm around and said, "Yep, let's get our weekend started."

The following Monday morning James Michael Craven made his entrance into the world, after only three short hours of labor. Casey stayed in the hospital only one night and was home with her family the next afternoon.

Weddings and Funerals

Jan visited her on Wednesday after school. As she sat holding little Jamie, feelings inside of her were beginning to swell. She was ready, and she knew that Mark was too. After their conversation on Thanksgiving, she had made an appointment with her doctor and if all was well, they were going to begin trying to get pregnant. Just the thought of having Mark's baby nearly brought tears to her eyes.

She looked over at Casey, who had seemed to have magically morphed back into her old self. Not only was she bouncing all over just like she did before she was pregnant, but she had almost regained her tiny figure back. Jan smiled and hope that pregnancy was as easy for her as it was for Casey.

"So, tell me what all is going on at school," Casey said.

"Not much," Jan answered. "Just the usual Christmas craziness." She laughed. "Cindy caught Nellie Burns selling her mom's Christmas cookies in the bathroom yesterday morning."

Casey laughed. "That girl. She kept me on my toes all last year. How much was she charging for them?"

"A dollar for the big ones, and fifty cents for the small ones," Jan told her.

"Remember last year when she brought her mom's purple lipstick to school and started a club?" Casey asked.

"Yeah, what was it? If you wanted to be in the club, you had to wear the lipstick all day?"

"That was it. I'll never forget seeing all my girls come parading out of the bathroom with purple lips."

They both laughed, and Casey said, "I wouldn't trade my job for anything in the world."

"Has there been any more news about Gary?" Casey wanted to know.

"The story going around is that the police have declared it a suicide," she told her.

"That's what Jim said," Casey answered.

"There is another crazy story going around," Jan said, "but I don't put a lot of stock in it."

"What's that?"

"Supposedly, they found a strange substance in the body, and it was sent off to a more advanced lab somewhere to see if it could be identified," Jan told her.

"*If* that's true, the plot thickens," Casey answered.

"It sure does," Jan agreed. "They went ahead and had him cremated, and the family had a private funeral last weekend."

"Did Mark or George have it?"

Jan shook her head. "He was cremated somewhere in Lexington and the funeral was at a church somewhere near Louisville. I guess they want the gossip to die down."

"I can't blame them for that," Casey said. "Was Shelly there?"

"I have no idea," Jan said. "She has not communicated with anyone at school." She looked at her watch. "I need to go. Linda and Martin are having us all over for dinner." She stood and regretfully handed Casey back her baby.

"That's nice. Barb and Linda have become quite good friends, haven't they?"

Jan smiled. "They certainly have. I think it's really nice. Apparently, Martin and Linda are already talking about making a trip to visit Barb later this winter."

"How long is Barb going to stay?"

"She is planning to stay through the holidays, then I think that she will head back before winter sets in. She is asking if both Penny and Kylie can fly down for spring break."

"Are you going to let Kylie go?"

"Probably," Jan answered. "Penny is pretty responsible." She leaned and gave the baby a quick kiss. "I really have to go. Bye little Jamie. I'll see you soon."

On Christmas Eve, Jan stood admiring their Christmas tree which was glowing with its multicolored lights in the darkened family room. The sight of it warmed her heart. She heard Mark's footsteps on the stairs, so she turned around to see him coming through the door. He was smiling, and he came right to her, gave her a kiss and after putting his arm around her shoulder, he too began admiring the tree.

Weddings and Funerals

"Are the girls all settled in downstairs?" he wanted to know.

"Yes," she answered. "Barb and Penny promised to keep Kylie occupied until she went to sleep, so I guess we can go ahead and setup."

"I think maybe they are working on some Santa surprises of their own," he said, "with a little help from Barb."

"I know," she told him. "I am glad we are carrying through with the Santa plan. Kylie is on to us I'm sure, but it's fun and I say we keep it as a family tradition. What do you say?"

"Excellent idea, Mrs. Clause. Now let's get moving."

The next morning, Barb followed Penny and Kylie who were bounding up the stairs. Mark and Jan were waiting in the kitchen with coffee for Barb. They handed it to her and the three of them followed the girls into the family room.

Kylie stopped short when she saw the piano in the corner of the room. She turned and looked at them.

"For me?" she asked.

"Yes," Mark answered. "You wanted piano lessons. How can you have piano lessons without a piano?"

Kylie's face was almost as bright as the tree. She walked over and hit a few of the keys. "How soon can I start lessons?"

"How about later this morning?" Mark asked.

"On Christmas day? Who is my teacher going to be?"

Penny giggled. "Mark the Spark."

Kylie mouth opened wide. "Daddy you know how to play the piano?"

"Yes," he said. "Grandma insisted that I learn, and now I am glad she did." He walked over to the piano, leaned over the bench and played a chorus of Jingle Bells.

They all applauded. He placed his hand over his waist and took a bow. "If you do well, next year we will move to the drums."

"Oh no!" Jan and Penny both chorused at once.

Mark laughed and winked at his daughter. She giggled and went to hug him and then Jan.

"Where were you hiding it?" Kylie wanted to know.

"At the funeral home," Mark told her. "Yesterday Charlie and I loaded it onto his truck. Then late last night he came back over here, and he helped me bring it into the house."

"Hey," Penny said randomly, and she walked over to the other side of the tree, where she picked up the guitar that was leaning against the wall. "Is this for me?"

Jan smiled. "Yes, it is."

Penny looked at Mark. "Please tell me that you know how to play the guitar."

He grinned. "I do, and by the way, Charlie is getting a guitar about now, so I will teach him to play too if he wants."

"Cool," Kylie said, excitedly. "We can start a band."

Jan gave Mark a look that said, "What have you done?"

"Will you teach me to play the piano too?" Penny asked.

"And me the guitar?" Kylie echoed.

"I will be happy to teach any of you to play anything you want," he told them. "All I ask is that you take it seriously."

"What else can you play?" Penny asked.

"Yes," Jan said, "What else can you play, Mark the Spark?"

He grinned at her. "I am a man of many talents, as you should well know by now. I can play a little trumpet, and some baritone. I tried to play the saxophone, but I didn't care for it. Too many buttons."

Barb laughed. "My goodness, Jan, it is getting a little deep in here isn't it?"

"It certainly is" she answered. "Let's open some other gifts. The music man can serenade us later."

An hour later, all the gifts were opened, the wrapping mess was cleaned up and Jan and Barb were in the kitchen making more coffee and waiting for the breakfast casserole to bake. The pies sat waiting on the counter to take to Mark's parents' house later. They both laughed as the sound of Winter Wonderland on the piano came drifting into the kitchen.

"He is very musically inclined, isn't he?" Barb asked.

"Yes, he is," Jan answered. "I realized that the night I watched him play the drums. He hadn't played in years and he walked right up on that stage, picked up the drumsticks and never missed a beat. Truthfully, I thought he was better than the regular drummer." She let out a small laugh. "I have to admit that he is man of many talents."

"I told you he was a keeper," Barb said.

"He certainly is," Jan said with a smile.

Another week passed, and New Year's Eve was upon them. Mark and Jan stayed at home. Kylie's birthday was the 5th of January and she asked if she could have a slumber party on New Year's. The two of them agreed. The weather had turned cold, and Jim and Casey were staying home with the baby, so it seemed like a good plan to let Kylie have her fun. It was decided that the girls would spend the night in the basement with Penny's agreement. Barb wisely decided to spend the night in the upstairs guest room. Charlie and, who were turning into quite the homebodies, decided to stay in and avoid the cold too. Barb turned in fairly early as usual and the other four enjoyed a night of cards.

About one-thirty Mark and Jan lay in bed talking about the coming year. They were excited their future that looked bright. They had the two girls that meant the world to them, and by this time next year, they hoped to have one more child to love.

Barb had a private jet scheduled to take her back to Florida on the sixth of January. On the morning of Saturday, the fifth, Jan returned from the grocery store. They were planning a good-bye dinner for Barb that night and her bags were full of staples for the dinner. As she walked in, she found Mark in the kitchen rooting around in the cabinets looking for something.

"You are making a mess," she complained, seeing the various items that he had drug out of the cabinets and strung all around the counter.

"Here it is," he said and then went into a horrendous coughing fit. She watched him and then he realized that he was rather flushed looking.

"Honey," she said. "You are getting sick." She felt his forehead. He didn't feel warm, but his skin did feel clammy."

"Let me take you to Urgent Care."

"*No*."

She tried not to giggle. "I could call your Mom."

He gave her a stern look. "Don't you dare! I don't need my mother performing her black magic on me and I don't need to go to the doctor." He held up a green prescription bottle. "I have these."

"What is that?" she asked, taking the bottle and then realized that it was the penicillin that was prescribed for her last fall.

"All right," she said, "But take some Tylenol with it and go lay down for a while."

"Can't", he said as he swallowed one of the pills with some water from a bottle he had open on the counter. Then he grabbed his jacket off the back of the chair.

"What do you mean, *can't*?"

"I have to go pick up a body in Lexington." he told her.

She sighed. "Isn't there anybody else that can go?"

"Nope," he said. "Everybody else is busy. George has a big funeral going on right now, across town, and everybody that isn't there is either sick or on vacation."

"What about Charlie? Can't you send him?"

"No, he hasn't driven the hearse enough to drive it in the city. I am taking him with me and I think I will let him drive, just for the practice. I've got to go," he said. "I promise to rest as soon as I get back." Then he put on his coat, blew her a kiss and he was gone.

Jan sighed in frustration and began to clean up the mess he had made. She considered the possibility of going back to the store and getting some onions and putting them in their room, but she figured he would take one whiff, get mad and throw them away.

Almost four hours later, Mark returned. Jan took one look at him and was immediately concerned. His face was now extremely pale, and his eyes had a glazed look to them. Charlie followed him in and Jan could tell by the look on his face that he was worried too. He started to speak, but Jan made a motion toward Kylie, so he wouldn't frighten her. She followed Mark as he walked into the living room, becoming more frightened by the minute, because he wasn't walking steadily, and he seemed to be in a trance. Everyone in the kitchen came running after her, when she screamed as Mark collapsed at the bottom of the stairs.

"Mrs. Owens, I am going to be very honest with you," Dr. Snider said. "Your husband is very ill."

Jan tried very hard to keep the trembling in her hands from spreading to the rest of her body, at least long enough to digest the information that the doctor was giving her.

"Are you telling me that what Mark has is worse than a cold?"

The doctor paused as if he were choosing his words carefully. "He does have a cold, but that is not what is making him so ill. We are still running tests, but I believe his body is reacting to something that he may have ingested or come in contact with. I need your help in letting me know what he did during the day today."

Jan thought back and described his day as far as she knew. She told him about his cold symptoms and the penicillin.

"It couldn't go bad in that short amount of time, could it?" she asked.

The doctor shook his head as if he were dismissing that idea. "Did he eat anything after that?" he wanted to know.

Jan texted Penny and asked her to find out from Charlie if Mark ate anything. Since he was at the house with her, it didn't take long for the answer to come back. He didn't eat or drink anything while they were gone.

The doctor told her that he would be back to give her a report in a couple of hours. As he walked away, Jan stopped him. "Doctor Snider, please tell me. Is my husband going to die?"

The man stared at her for a moment before he responded. "He is very ill, but I promise you that I am going to do everything in my power to see that he survives."

Before he left the room, he turned and added one more statement. "If you are a praying person, and even you are not, this would be a good time." Then he was gone.

Jan left the conference room and fell into Jim's arms and began to cry hysterically. Martin and Linda froze because they interpreted her actions to mean the worst. Jim realized this and tried to get Jan's attention. Eventually, she understood what he was saying and calmed herself enough to repeat to them what the doctor was saying. Each of them digested the information differently. Martin went and stared out the window into the dark night. Linda sat by Jan and the two of them held hands without speaking. Jim sent a long text to Casey and then sat quietly.

A thought occurred to Jan and she handed him her phone. "Please text Barb and update her. My hands are shaking too hard."

Jim took care of that and then continued to sit quietly. Jan alternated between praying feverishly and being haunted by Mark's words a few short months back, when he was discussing the possibility of her adopting Kylie; *Besides dying, I could be in an accident and be temporarily incapacitated, you know.*

All of the sudden, she felt the need to use the restroom. She excused herself and left the waiting room to go down the hall. When she walked out of the restroom, there was an elderly gentleman man standing in the hallway. He was bent over and appeared to be looking for something. Jan noticed a ring on the floor about ten feet from where he was looking. Without giving it a thought, she bent over and picked up the ring. She stepped over near him, held up the ring and said, "Excuse me. Is this what you are looking for?"

The man smiled and leaned over slightly to see the ring. He took it out of her hand

"Thank you, so much, young lady," he said and then winked at her and walked on down the hall. As he walked away, she got a sudden whiff of the Old Spice soap that Mark used, and she felt immediately better. In some instinctive way, she knew that it was a sign. She looked up in the direction the man had walked just in time to see the elevator door close. A peacefulness came upon her and she knew that she had found the strength to continue.

Mark held his own through the night. His stomach was pumped out in hopes that if he ingested something poisonous that some remnants might remain.

By Tuesday morning, Mark was beginning to turn the corner and improve slightly. He began to regain consciousness that afternoon. The doctor began encouraging her to sit by his bed in ICU and speak to him. That evening he looked at her and smiled. "Am I going to die?" he asked.

"Don't you dare!" she said and kissed him on the head.

"Don't worry about me," he told her. "I'm tough." Then he looked at her more clearly. "but you look like hell." Then he laughed and drifted off again.

She went to the waiting room and happily reported the news to Linda, who frowned. "Jan go look in the mirror," she said.

For some reason, Jan didn't argue, but went straight to the restroom. When she got in there, she looked in the mirror and gasped. She didn't even recognize herself. There were big dark bags under her eyes, and her hair was hanging dull and listless. The door opened, and Linda stepped in. "Martin is going to stay here tonight. Let me take you home to my house, please. You can take a nice hot shower and get some sleep. In the morning you can stop and see the girls, they need reassurance. Then you can come back and see Mark without scaring him."

Jan knew that she was right, so she only nodded and followed her out. A short time later, she was standing under a deliciously hot shower. The pulsating water soothed her muscles that were aching from sitting in the stiff chairs for hours on end.

A few minutes later, she fell into a soft bed and knew nothing until morning. When she woke from her deep sleep, she sat up quickly because she wasn't sure where she was. Then it all came back to her, and she jumped out of bed and dressed in the jogging suit that Linda had loaned her. She went to the kitchen and found her mother-in-law making French toast. She absolutely insisted that Jan eat before they left. Having no choice in the matter, she sat down and quickly discovered that she was hungry.

They then went back to her house where she spent a few minutes with the girls, reassuring them that she had spoken with Mark and that he was getting better.

An hour later, they were back at the hospital. Mark was asleep when she arrived. The nurse said that he had been awake earlier and was asking for her. She said that his vitals were improving, so Jan decided to let him sleep. After about twenty minutes, he opened his eyes and smiled at her.

"That's better," he said.

"How do you feel?" she asked him.

"Weak," he told her. "Very weak. What the hell happened to me?"

"The doctors aren't sure," she said. "They think that you either ate something or came in contact with something that may have poisoned you."

"That's crazy."

"I know," she told him. "They took a bunch of stuff out of your stomach and are having it analyzed."

He turned and looked at her with a serious look. "I think I came close to dying, Jan, but I just couldn't leave you and the girls. I fought it every inch of the way. I love you so much."

She took his hand and squeezed it. "I love you too."

He then drifted back off to sleep, and a few minutes later, the nurse opened the door and beckoned her out of the room. "The doctor wants to talk to you," she said and motioned Jan toward a conference room. She tried not to let anxiety take over her again as she went to the little room. Doctor Snider was waiting for her.

"Good morning, Mrs. Owens. As you can tell, your husband is doing much better. I believe we are just about out of the woods. He is weak, but his vitals and labs are improving greatly."

Jan sighed with relief, as the doctor continued. "We have determined that your husband did ingest some poison, so by law we had to report this matter to the authorities. I understand you are familiar with a Detective Coleman?"

Jan nodded. "Yes, I am."

"He will be here later this morning and he would like to speak with you."

"All right," Jan answered as all kinds of new questions ran through her mind. How was Mark poisoned and most importantly, why?

An hour later, Larry Coleman arrived at the hospital and met with Jan in the same conference room where she had met with Doctor Snider.

After their initial greetings, the detective came right to the point. "Did the doctor explain to you that your husband ingested poison?"

"Yes, he did."

"We still don't know the specific type of poison that was found in your husband's stomach, but there is an interesting fact about the substance."

For reasons that she wasn't sure of, Jan began to get nervous. "What is that?"

The detective stared a moment before he spoke. "The same substance was found in Gary Baker's stomach."

Jan's blood ran cold. "What is it?" she asked him.

"We don't know yet," he told her. "We sent what we found in Baker's stomach to a high-level lab, and we haven't received a report back yet. What we do know is what was found in your husband's stomach was the exact same substance that your husband ingested."

"I thought that Gary's death was ruled a suicide."

"It was," he answered, "but that could change, considering what we have learned here. Maybe his family wasn't so far off. It was strange. Right after his death, they were hell bent on the proving that he couldn't have committed suicide, but for some strange reason the loud voices in the family were shut down and as soon as the body was released they had it cremated as quickly as possible. I don't know why, but they are an unusual group." He was quiet for a moment before he continued. "Doctor Snider told me Mark took some penicillin just before he became ill. Is that correct?"

Jan nodded. "They were prescribed for me last fall by mistake. I am allergic to penicillin, so I didn't take any of them. Mark put them in the cabinet and when he started feeling bad last Saturday, he dug them out and took one."

"Just one?"

"Yes, I was standing there when he found them in the cabinet. I watched him take it. Then he left. He didn't take the bottle with him, because I remember putting it back in the cabinet. He came back four hours later and then collapsed immediately. I called 911 and he was taken straight to the hospital."

"So, the bottle is still in the cabinet?" She nodded. "I would like to have that bottle of pills so can we can analyze them."

"That's not a problem," she said. "I am sure they are still there. I do have one question though."

"What is that?"

"Are thinking that I had something to do with this? You are looking at me in a very strange way."

"No," he said, "I am not thinking that you had anything to do with this, but I am looking at you very seriously, for a reason that apparently has not occurred to you yet."

"I don't understand what you are getting at," she said.

He leaned toward her before he spoke. "Mrs. Owens, if those pills have a poison in them, as I suspect they will, that means Mark was not the intended victim."

Jan still didn't see where he was going with this. She was confused.

"Then who was?"

"The medicine was prescribed for you. Someone wanted you to take those pills."

Chapter Fifteen

Later that evening, Larry Coleman knocked on the door of the Owens home. While he waited for the door to be opened, he thought about the strangeness of this situation. At the end of his career, this kind of situation normally gave him a migraine, but for some unknown reason, he felt a strong compulsion to dig deeper into this mystery. He had received a phone call from the mayor earlier that afternoon that he found perplexing. The news of Mark Owens' poisoning had somehow reached his office, and he was trying to make a very strong suggestion that it had surely been accidental. Larry found the suggestion disturbing, so he didn't mention the pills that he was about to take possession of. The mayor had eyes and ears everywhere, so he would learn about it sooner or later, but by then the pills would have been shipped off to the same lab that was working to identify the substance found in Gary Baker and Mark Owens stomachs. If both of those substances matched up with any substance in the pills, he felt certain that the FBI would become involved. At that point the mayor would be helpless in his efforts to keep his town's image neat and clean.

His thoughts were interrupted when Jan Owens opened the door. She greeted him warmly, and he asked about how her husband was doing this evening.

She smiled as she responded. "He is feeling much better this evening. He was allowed to have some soft food, which he growled about, of course, because he has regained his appetite. He is going to be given regular food tomorrow, and if he tolerates that he will most likely be home Friday morning."

"Well that certainly is good news," he said to her.

"I have the pills in the kitchen," she said. "Please come in."

He followed her into the kitchen, where he noticed two things; there was fresh coffee brewing, and the Owens' friend from Florida was there removing cups from the cupboard.

Jan looked at him at then spoke. "I guess when you were here before, I didn't introduce you to our friend, Barb Summers. Barb this is Detective Coleman."

"Would you both please call me Larry?" he asked. "My title can seem a little formal, and sometimes puts people on edge."

"Fine, and please call me Barb."

"And you may call me Jan."

Barb laughed. "Now that we are all on a first name basis, Larry, would you like some coffee?"

Weighing the options of going home to an empty house or spending a few minutes in this warm kitchen with two pleasant ladies, he decided to accept.

Jan picked up the bottle of pills off the counter and handed them to him. He studied the label for a moment and then opened the cap and looked at the pills. They were capsules. He found that interesting. Capsules would be much easier to contaminate than tablets. He made no comment but closed the lid and dropped the bottle into his pocket.

Barb Summers poured coffee for the three of them and then seated herself at the table with the other two.

"You have a home in southern Florida, but you are here during the worst weather month of the year?" he asked her with a smile.

She returned his smile. "I was just here for the holidays," she told him. "I was planning to return last Sunday, but when Mark became ill I decided to extend my stay. As soon as he is home and their lives get back to normal, I will make my return travel plans and get out of their hair."

"You are not in our hair," Jan said adamantly. "We love having you here, especially the girls."

Barb turned back to him. "Penny is my niece."

"I see," Larry said. "Penny is the older one?" Both women nodded. "She is your daughter?" he asked Jan.

"No," Penny told him. "You see Penny lost her parents in an…accident last year, and I share guardianship of her with Barb, so that she can finish school here. Kylie is Mark's daughter. She lost her mother about two years ago, and after Mark and I were married last summer, I adopted her. We are I guess what you would call a blended family."

~~Mark~~ LARRY studied on that situation for a moment, and as was his habit from years of detective work, he filed the information away for later reference.

"Jan is there anyone in your past or present who might want to do you harm?" he asked her.

"Not that I know of," she said. Then she looked at Barb and a silent message passed between the two of them. She turned back to him and took a deep breath before she spoke.

"There are others," she told him.

"Excuse me?" he asked.

"In the past year there has been what I feel are a large number of people who have died in their sleep while suffering from colds. I have talked to Mark about it, but because of the nature of his profession, he doesn't concern himself about the nature of people's death. I find it unusual though."

Larry stared at her and thought about what she was saying. "Tell me more," he said.

Jan took a breath and plunged in telling him about everyone on her list. When she finished, he pulled out his notebook ad said, "All right, let me get these names down. Tell me again slowly."

When he had the information down, he looked it over carefully, trying to make a connection. Then he looked up at Jan. "Quite a few of these people are connected to the school system, aren't they?"

"Yes," Jan said. "Except for the old couple." She thought for a moment. Then something occurred to her. "The people on this list are connected to the school because this is my list. There may be others that I am unaware of."

"That is a very good point," he said. He looked from one to the other of them. "I am going to send these pills to the lab on the morning. Just so you are aware, if there is any poison found in these pills, I am certain that the FBI will become involved. In the meantime, I need to implore you to keep this to yourselves. If this gets out it will set off a panic, which could compromise the investigation." What he was really thinking was that he did not want the mayor to get wind of this twist in the situation.

"You have our word," Jan said, and Barb nodded in agreement. Larry studied the woman while trying not to stare. It was interesting that she seemed to display a radiant beauty and a somewhat hidden sadness at the same time.

The three of them talked for a few more minutes and shared a second cup of coffee. He asked Barb a few questions about life in southern Florida. He told her that he was officially retiring on the first of June, and that he was planning to take an extended vacation in her area. She smiled and told him that she would be happy to show him around. Jan watched this exchange in amazement. Barb's recovery seemed to be advancing by leaps and bounds.

Just before he left, the three of them decided that they would not tell Mark about the latest in the investigation until he had been released from the hospital. Jan found it interesting that Larry made a remark about hospitals often having "eyes and ears."

Mark was released from the hospital on Friday morning. Mark and Jan had both insisted that the girls return to school on Thursday and told them that it would not be necessary for them to stay home on Friday. They could have a welcome home dinner for him that night. When he and Jan entered the kitchen, they found Barb waiting with a lunch of tuna salad sandwiches, Mark's favorite.

After they finished the lunch, Jan and Barb talked to him about their conversation with Larry Coleman. Jan waited for Mark to tell her how ridiculous she was being, but he didn't. He seemed thoughtful for a moment and then said that he thought that they just needed to sit tight until the results came back, but in the meantime, they needed to be cautious, especially with the kids. Barb offered to stay longer to help keep an eye on the girls. Mark and Jan both gratefully accepted her offer. She told them that she had been watching the weather and there was a major winter system moving in on Sunday and she could use that as an excuse for staying; telling the girls that she was nervous about flying in bad weather.

Shortly after the lunch dishes were cleared, Barb discreetly disappeared to the basement, and Mark and Jan found themselves alone. Mark looked at her smiled, while he stifled a yawn.

Jan smiled at him. "Why don't you think about going upstairs and taking a nap?" she asked him.

"I am going to do more than think about it," he said. "I am going to do it, right after I take a long hot shower."

"Good idea," she told him.

"Are you going to pick up Kylie?" he asked.

"Yes," she answered. "I am going to stop by my room and pick up papers from my sub. I am sure that I will need to spend the entire weekend catching up on grading papers."

"Wake me up before you leave."

"How about I wake you when Penny gets home?"

"No practice today?" Penny and Chrissy had kept the team practicing in Jan's absence.

"No," she told him. "There is only one game this weekend. It is tomorrow night and it is an away game."

"Then we should hope for a nice quiet weekend?"

She laughed. "We can always hope."

A couple of hours later, she went up to wake him shortly before Penny was due to arrive at home. When she walked into the room, she found him already awake. He was looking in the mirror and saw her walk in. He turned and stared at her, with an expression that she had never seen before.

Jan immediately panicked. "What's wrong? Are you feeling bad again?"

"No," he said. "Well, not physically ill. I just realized something."

"What?"

"I came very close to losing you," he said in a choked voice. "What if you had taken those pills?" he asked in a choked voice.

She walked over to him and put her arms his waist. He wrapped his arms around her and pulled her close. "I know exactly how you feel," she told him. "I thought I had lost you."

They stood quietly for a moment holding each other until he spoke. "All right, we are both still here and we are both all right, for whatever reason. I plan to thank the good lord every day for that."

"You are right," she said with a smile. "I'll go get Kylie, and we'll spend the weekend counting our blessings. Let's place the other situation in God's hands for now."

The weekend did turn out to be peaceful. Then on Sunday evening the winter storm system moved in and stalled over central Kentucky. School was cancelled for the entire week. Mark and Jan enjoyed the family time at home for a few days, and then things began to wear a little thin. On Thursday afternoon, they banished both girls to their rooms to enjoy some peace and quiet.

That lasted for about two hours. Around four o'clock Charlie showed up and he and Penny went to the family room. Mark and Jan were curled up together on the couch in the living room watching a basketball game. Jan was about half asleep when suddenly Charlie, Penny and Kylie were in front of them all requesting an audience.

"All right," Mark said, as he turned the volume down, but left the picture on. "Who's first?"

"I am," Charlie said. "Do you want the funeral cars washed this weekend, since we don't have anything scheduled and there is more snow coming the first of the week?"

"No," Mark told him. "You can hold off on that. Next."

"Can I go with Charlie to the away game Saturday night?" Penny asked.

"Where is it?" he wanted to know.

"Mt. Sterling," Charlie told him.

"The roads should be good by then," he said. "Jan?"

"Sure," she said. "Next." they both eyed Kylie who looked like she was about to pop with anticipation.

"Can I move my room to the basement?" she asked.

Jan laughed out loud. Kylie then had a look of total disappointment. "I am sorry honey. I just didn't see that coming. I thought you were going to ask to go to a friend's house to spend the night."

"Where exactly do you plan to put your room in the basement?" Mark asked her.

"In the room on the other side of the bathroom," Kylie told him.

"Where Aunt Barb is staying?" Jan asked.

Kylie nodded. "She said that she would trade with me."

"You understand that you would be getting a smaller room?" he asked her.

She nodded. "Yes, but Charlie said that if we knocked out the wall between that room and the storage room next to it, that would make a huge closet and the old closet would make a cool place to put a dresser and a TV."

"Oh, he did, did he? Thanks a lot Charlie," Mark said giving the boy a pretend stern look.

Jan narrowed her eyes. "Just exactly when was Charlie in the basement? I thought that was a no boy zone."

Charlie and Penny's face both turned slightly red. "I asked him to come down," Kylie said. "You said that Penny couldn't have boys in the basement. You didn't say anything about that to me."

Jan could tell that Mark was trying not to laugh as he started to speak to his daughter. "All right, you caught me on a technicality this time, but let me make this perfectly clear. From now on neither one of you are to entertain boys of any age in the basement. Got it?"

"Got it," she said. "Do I get to move downstairs?"

"We will think about it."

"For how long?"

"For however long it takes," he told her, "and the more we are questioned about it, the longer it will take."

The next two weeks passed slowly. Mark regained his strength and was back to normal. The weather remained snowy and school was hit and miss with many days starting with delays. The off days gave them an opportunity to move Kylie to the basement. They decided that as long as Penny was staying home for a while that Kylie would be fine in the basement.

Larry Coleman had stopped by the house to update them a couple of times. He didn't have much news to give them, but he did have questions for Mark about some of the people on the list that Jan had given him. He wanted to know if Mark had noticed anything unusual about their bodies. Jan was impressed with the fact that the man certainly did his homework. It also didn't escape her notice that he always seemed to show up around dinner time. She mentioned that thought to Mark, and he laughed and told her that George had told him that Larry's wife died of cancer about five years ago.

About three weeks after Mark had come home from the hospital, Larry called one afternoon and said he would like to come over later, because he had some news to share with them. Jan could tell by his voice that something was up.

He didn't show up until about seven that evening. After the girls were semt to their rooms to do homework, he sat with the three of them at the kitchen table looking very serious.

"We finally got the complete report back," he told them. After a pause he continued. "The contents of Gary's Baker's stomach, your stomach, and the pills showed the exact thing. There was a particular kind of poison in them."

"What kind?" Mark asked.

"Nerium," Larry told them. Barb gasped, and he looked at her and nodded.

"What is that?" Jan asked.

"Oleanders," Barb said softly.

Then Jan gasped, and Mark went pale. "Inside of the capsules were ground up dried Oleander leaves. Traces of the same thing were discovered in your stomach as well as Gary Baker's," Larry said.

"But how did they get there?" Jan asked.

"That's a good question," Larry told her, "And a very serious one. I anticipated something of this nature and I have been doing some research, and I learned something interesting." He paused for affect and then continued. "Everyone on your list received medicine from the same drug store a few days before they died."

"Do you think that someone in the drugstore planted the dried Oleander flowers in the pills?" Barb asked.

He stared at her and nodded. "They were all capsules, not tablets."

"Easier to add the ground leaves to?" she asked He nodded.

"Is the owner of the store aware of this?" Mark asked.

"Yes, and obviously he is very upset and nervous," he told them. "The FBI is involved now, and he is offering his full cooperation because he wants to get to the bottom of this to be sure it is clear that he has no involvement."

"I get the feeling that there is a plan brewing here," Mark said.

"Yes," Larry said, "but we need some help. Very late tonight cameras are being installed in the drug store. Tomorrow I need a decoy to go into the store with a prescription." He turned and looked at Jan. "Someone who has been targeted before."

"Oh, I don't know about that," Mark began.

"All she has to do is walk in and hand in a script," Larry told him. "There will be two agents meandering in the store the entire time she is in there. As soon as her script is filled, she leaves the store and turns the meds over to us."

"I can do that," Jan said. "This has to be stopped."

"I agree," Barb said.

Mark stared at his wife for a moment. "All right," he said.

Jan was quiet for a moment and then she said, "Now I remember. It was Shelly."

The other three stared at her in confusion. "I was trying to remember who I heard talking about Oleanders. It was Shelly. Last year when I got back to school, after Penny and I spent Christmas in Florida, Shelly was telling me about taking her Aunt Edith to Georgia and back for Christmas. She said that it was annoying that she always brought back Oleander plants to decorate with."

"Shelly?" Barb asked.

"Shelly Patterson was a teacher at my school. Gary Baker was her cousin. After his death, she had a nervous breakdown and the family sent her off to get treatment somewhere out of state. She was not fond of me because she wanted to date Mark, but he was smarter than that."

"That's very interesting," Larry said, and then made a note in his now nearly full notebook.

The next day was Saturday and Jan entered the drug store around four-fifteen in the afternoon. She walked directly to the drop off counter of the pharmacy and left the prescription. She told the clerk that she would shop in the store until it was ready. The clerk told her that it would be ready in about twenty minutes. As Larry had instructed her, she wandered around browsing through the store picking up a few items and placing them in the basket that she had picked up. Ten minutes later, as they had planned, Mark called her on her cell phone. She informed him that she was at the drug store and asked him if he needed anything. He mentioned a few items and she went to get them and asked him some questions about his preference of the items, just to make it appear natural.

About ten minutes after she finished talking to him, her name was called over the intercom, and she worked her way back to the pharmacy. She unloaded the items in her cart and watched the clerk ring them up along with her prescription. While she waited she happened to glance back at the prep area and she had a flashback of seeing that woman stare at her more than a year ago. The same woman was there again and this time her stare seemed to include a strange smile. Jan remembered how uncomfortable it had made her feel then, and now it gave her downright chills. The clerk announced her total and she slid her card into the machine. Two minutes later, she walked out of the store, unable to look at the strange woman again. She got into her car and drove directly home where Mark and Larry were waiting for her.

When she entered the house, Mark immediately asked her if she was all right, because she was very pale. She sat at the kitchen table and told them of her experience concerning the woman and she had forgotten that it had happened before. The two men exchanged a look and Larry dug the bottle of pills out of the bag and placed them in his pocket. He was taking the pills to the police station, where an FBI technician was waiting. Now that poison had been identified, it would not take long to confirm whether Jan's pills had been tampered with.

"I'll call you as soon as I know anything," he told them before he left.

Then Mark and Jan were alone. Both girls were spending the night with friends and Barb had gone with Martin and Linda to see a play in Louisville.

The two stared at each other and then he motioned her to the living room. They sat on the couch and cuddled up together. Without even asking, he picked up his phone and ordered pizza.

Two hours later, Mark's phone signaled a text message. He picked it up. It was from Larry.

"The test came out positive for dried oleander. We have video confirmation of how it was done. The pharmacy is about to close. We are preparing to move in and pick up a suspect. I will probably be over tomorrow to update you."

After a restless night, Mark and Jan sat in the kitchen with Barb waiting for word. They were expecting a phone call, so they all jumped when they heard a knock at the door about 10:30. Mark went to answer it and then led Larry into the kitchen.

He looked rough. "I'm sorry that I didn't call, but I've only had a few hours of sleep, and I forgot to plug my phone in. I've got quite a story to tell you."

He sat down and without asking, Barb poured him a cup of coffee. "Thank you," he said taking a healthy swig of it before he began to talk.

"We have an arrest and a complete confession," he told them. "Do any of you know a woman named Nora Patterson?"

They all shook their heads. "Is she related to Shelly?" Jan asked.

"Yes," he told her. "She is Shelly and Gary's grandmother and she is the pharmacy tech that was staring at you. We have that on video. She is the matriarch of a very large family and she ruled them with an iron will. Nora was like a mother bear who would do anything to protect her cubs, even kill."

"She confessed to killing people?" Barba asked.

"Once we detained her and explained what we knew and what we saw on the video, she led us right to her home and took us to her basement. It was unbelievable. She had a whole laboratory set up. She had containers of dried oleanders on a shelf."

"Where was she getting them?" Jan asked him. "From Edith?"

Larry nodded. "Edith is her daughter. Nora would encourage her to go with Shelly to Georgia every chance she got, because she knew Edith would return with Oleanders. Shelly didn't like taking her, but no one argued with Grandma. Then once a week or so, she would go to her daughter's house and have tea. When Edith left the room, Nora would slip some flowers in her purse, to grind up later.

"So, no one else knew what was going on?" Mark asked.

"No," Larry answered.

"How was she managing it at the drug store?" Barb wanted to know.

"She was stealing empty green bottles every chance she got. Then in her basement, she would fill them with the poisoned capsules. She would keep a few in her white coat pocket, and then if someone came in that she had a vendetta against she would switch the bottles, before she put the labels on them. We watched her do that on the camera. She was very quick. It wouldn't have been almost unnoticeable if we weren't watching closely."

"Did she confess in general or did she confess to each person's death?" Jan asked.

"She went right down the list," he said, and then pulled out his notebook. He began to read directly from it to them.

"Marcia Collins — she was the flag team coach. Lizzie Sanders was her great granddaughter. Marcia humiliated her and degraded her in public.

Aaron Fisher — his only crime was being married to Carol Fisher who accused her grandson of stealing and got him suspended.

Joe and Sue Taylor — she was a disgusting alcoholic. She only intended to kill her. It wasn't her fault that Sue shared her penicillin with Joe on the boat.

John and Nellie Miller — they were old and sick and needed to go.

Doug Lawrence — he fired Gary for no reason. He was not drunk.

Ben Richards – he dated her daughter years ago and dumped her."

"The next one on the list would be Gary?" Jan asked.

"Yes," he answered. "This is where it gets interesting. Apparently, he stumbled on to her little secret. He tried to blackmail her into giving him money. That was his fatal mistake. She didn't come right out and say she killed him, but she laughed and said that he had to go so he obliged her by committing suicide."

"Then there was Mark?"

Larry let out a small laugh. "She said that she felt bad about him. Like we figured, you were the target, Jan."

"Because of Mark?"

"No, because of Gary. When you started dating him, she thought he was going to turn around and go down the path of the straight and narrow, but you didn't give him a chance. He told her a big story about how bad you treated him and how he liked you, but you broke his heart, so you had to go." He paused and then finished his thought. "She hired a private investigator from

Weddings and Funerals

Lexington to watch your house and follow you, but apparently she creeped him out, because he quit the job."

"What about Shelly? Did she really have a nervous breakdown" Jan wanted to know.

"I can't be sure about that. Gary and Shelly were very close," he said. "Nora thought that it was possible that he may have tipped her off. That why she was so upset when he disappeared, and so distraught when he died. She said that she considered taking care of her too, but she thought it would look too suspicious, so she shipped her off to a sanitarium, so if she talked people would dismiss her as the crazy one."

"Wow," Mark said. "The woman was some kind of crazy."

"That's an understatement," Larry said, and then he seemed to shudder.

"This is going to devastate a lot of families when it gets out," Jan said in a sad voice, "including ours."

Larry sighed. "It's not going to get out. There is one more piece to the story. Nora Patterson was found dead in her cell early this morning. About two hours ago the mayor had a meeting with the FBI agents and a phone conference with some elected official. I personally don't know what went down, but right now some agents are cleaning out the Oleanders from her basement and her family is being told that she was detained for questioning about stealing medications from the drugstore, and that she died of an apparent heart attack this morning."

It was quiet for a moment and then Barb spoke up. "Maybe it's for the best. I really don't want Penny to know that her parents were murdered."

Jan looked at her and nodded. "I agree," he added.

"Nora didn't die of a heart attack, did she?" Barb asked.

Larry looked at her and smiled. "No, Barb, she didn't. Like I said, she was very smooth. I am sure that she managed to slip a capsule or two down while we were in the basement. She was so cooperative that we hadn't searched her yet. I hate to say this, but I'm glad she did. Nora Patterson was one demented woman. I've dealt with a lot of things in my career, but this takes the cake. When this is wrapped up which will be very shortly. I am putting in for a leave of absence which will carry me to the first of June when my retirement kicks in. I may get to south Florida before you do, Barb"

She smiled at him. "Then you better start packing. I just decided to leave next weekend." She paused a moment and then continued. "You are welcome to share my plane."

"Share your plane?"

"I bought a package of small jet charters. I have a thing about crowds, and I knew I would be back in the spring for Penny's graduation and the holidays, so it seemed the best direction to go. Please feel free to join me."

Larry stared at her for a moment and Mark and Jan were looking at each other as if to say, "Do you believe what you just heard?"

Then Larry began to smile and said, "I just may take you up on that."

The next Memorial Day Weekend, Mark and Jan watched Penny walk across the stage and receive her diploma. Jan turned to look at Barb.

Her eyes were glistening, but she was not crying. Jan knew that part of her thoughts must have been of her sister and brother-in-law. It must have been a bitter sweet feeling.

One week later, they had a cookout in the backyard for Penny and Charlie. There was quite a crowd attending with all of their families and friends. Mark found a quiet moment and spoke to Jan. "Are we going to make our announcement with all of our friends and family here?"

Jan thought for a moment and said, "No, this is the kids' day. Let's wait. We can tell the girls in the morning."

He leaned over and gave a quick kiss. "Sounds like a plan," he told her.

Epilogue

One Year Later

Kylie ran up to water's edge and tried to jump over the wave ahead of Sue Ann. Spying a good shell in the water, she leaned over to pick it up and didn't see the big wave coming. Sue Ann squealed with delight as she watched Kylie fall into the water. Mark and Jan were walking behind them and had seen what happened and they began to laugh along with the girls. Seven-month old Robby laughed because he could hear his parents laughing. He was enjoying his perch on top of his Dad's shoulders. Jan looked up at her husband and son and smiled.

Life had been good over the last year. The unpleasant business with Nora Patterson had died very quickly. As far as Jan knew none of the victims' families ever learned the truth about how they died. It was never clear whether Nora's family ever knew or suspected the truth, but after her death and private funeral, several members of her family quietly moved away from town. Casey learned from Jim that Shelly resigned. The rumor was that she had moved to Tennessee and had obtained a position at a private school. Jan was relieved that the ugly truth had not surfaced, and Penny did not have to deal with the truth. It would have brought up and all the pain of her parents' deaths all over again. As it was, she had done very well with her first year of college. She had worked hard at her online classes. At the suggestion of Mark, Barb, and herself, Penny had found a part-time job at a local clothes store. She didn't need the money, but it gave her another focus in life besides school and Charlie. Jan put her hands up over her eyes to block out the sun and she could barely see the of two of them way up the beach, walking hand in hand. After a year of working with Mark, Charlie was still interested in becoming a mortician. His plans were to stay home one more year and then attend a school in Pennsylvania.

Jan's wish had come true and her pregnancy had been almost as easy as Casey's. After eight hours of labor Robert Martin Owens made his entrance into the world. He had been a good baby and was a delight to his entire family. Barb had very generously sent a plane to fly all of them down for a family vacation. When Penny had begged for Charlie to come with them, they decided that Kylie needed to have a friend with her also. Jim and Casey were taking their family to Disney World the same week, so Kylie did not have to agonize over which friend she would choose.

Casey was pregnant again, so she had decided not to go to back to work the next school year. Tom Spicer's company had transferred him to Columbus, so Jan was going to be without Cindy or Casey at school the next year. After several long discussions, she and Mark decided that she would work one more year and then they would plan to have another baby and Jan would then plan to be a stay at home mother.

As for Barb, something about the death of her sister had spurred the woman back into the land of the living. Jan had all the admiration in the world for her. The woman had lived in a dark hole for years, but she climbed out of that hole right before her eyes. Larry Coleman had flown back to Florida with her that weekend over a year ago. In Jan's conversations with her following that she seemed happy and mentioned Larry a few times. They were not able to go down as a family last summer, but Penny and Kylie flew down for a week and came back happily reporting that Barb and Larry were dating. Then the two of them showed up just before Christmas, announcing that they were married. From what Jan could tell they were a very happy couple.

Mark took Robby off of his shoulders and shifted him to his hip. He put his other arm around his wife. Jan put her arm around his waist. The sun broke out from behind a cloud at that moment and warmed her face. It was a sign that life ahead of them was good.

Made in the
USA
Middletown, DE